DOMINANCE:

South Africa

DOMINANCE: SOUTH AFRICA

For more information, to inquire about rights to this or other works, or to purchase copies for special educational, business, or sales promotional uses please write to:

The Zharmae Publishing Press, L.L.C.
1827 West Shannon Avenue
Spokane, Washington 99205
www.zharmae.com

FIRST EDITION

Printed in the United States of America

Jabari & Jaser, the J&J logo, Zharmae Publishing, logo, and the TZPP logo are trademarks of The Zharmae Publishing Press, L.L.C.

ISBN: 978-1-937365-24-0 (pbk.)

10 9 8 7 6 5 4 3 2 1

DOMINANCE:
South Africa

John Whitaker

JABARI JASER

Spokane, Washington

Dedication

President Nelson Mandela—a great leader who taught his people that hatred and racism were prisons.

Acknowledgments

I would like to thank the many people who helped with the writing and editing of *Dominance*—my wonderful wife, Lynda, who read and reread numerous passages, inspired me to write a better story, and always believed in my "gift" for writing, as well as in my alter-ego, David Reasons, the hero of *Dominance*; my sister, Jeanette Wilmot, who gave me constructive criticism, my cousin Paul Haylock who read versions of *Dominance* and gave me good critical advice; Louise Venter of the Tourist Information Office of the Mangaung Metro Municipality in Bloemfontein, who provided an abundance of knowledge about that city; Wayne Cooper, who introduced me to a new Canadian from South Africa who gave me tremendous advice about the customs, geography, and traditions of the country; the many friends in writers' groups who encouraged me and criticized my work; Warren Kinsella, whose book *Web of Hate* helped me understand the thinking of terrorists; and Noah Baker, editor at Jabari & Jaser, who helped to turn the raw product of my imagination into this action-adventure novel.

DOMINANCE:
South Africa

Prologue

David Reasons huddled in a cold, abandoned warehouse on Gdansk harbor's H Wharf. Rust had eaten through the walls in places, allowing the cold, offshore wind to invade his hiding place. Through the dust and cobweb-covered windows over the door he could barely make out the outline of the *Vartok*, a Russian spy ship masquerading as an ancient Alpinist Class fishing trawler. He had been observing the berthed vessel for the past ten hours.

David was dressed in a tight-fitting wool toque, a blue checked lumberjack shirt under a dirty navy pea jacket, and grimy, worn jeans. His hands and feet were numb from cold and inactivity. It was his first foreign mission in a country known for its repression of all things democratic, and he felt a deep, visceral terror of the unfamiliar forces arraigned against him.

A shaft of light followed by three noisy seamen exited the *Vartok*'s crew deck hatch. David's immediate instinct was to follow them, but their behavior made him pause. *If these three were being sent ashore to assassinate someone, they would hardly act like drunken sailors.* As soon as they had left the dock area, David heard the rear hatch open again. This time it was not backlit by the companionway lighting. A darkly dressed figure slipped into the fog at the front of the warehouse and strode briskly toward the section where David lay hidden.

Hearing a brief rasping sound as the overhead door was partly opened, David flattened himself against the top of the corroded shipping container of corrugated steel that had been his lair for the past two days.

Since commencing surveillance, he had been using a door on the opposite side of the warehouse from which the *Vartok* was berthed. This entrance opened onto a small, littered, glassed-in office. A passage, sheltered on both sides by shoulder-high bales of cardboard, led from the office to where David was presently hidden. If anyone approached him, he had hoped to use this passageway to quickly make an exit to the relative safety of the street, but the stealthy stranger's advance on his position had been too quick to allow this.

The seaman stood completely still and peered into the gloom. He was aware that something or someone was on the wharf. Even over the noise of their onboard gear, the ship's sophisticated listening equipment was able to pick up the little, irregular sounds made by David and other smaller creatures.

David spotted quick movement against the relative brightness of the open door. He followed the sound of the sailor's progress to the far end of the warehouse. His gut wrenched as the dark figure held a right arm in front of him.

From the sounds coming from the far side of the warehouse, it was obvious that a thorough search was in progress. David pressed himself even closer against the top of the container.

A few minutes later, he saw the ship's hatch open once more, and heard a gruff, impatient voice call out in Polish, "Have you found any rats in the shed yet?"

"I haven't finished looking," an annoyed reply called from somewhere to David's right and just behind him.

As he neared the container, the man stopped and started down the escape passageway to the abandoned office. When he spotted the door to the office left partly open, the hunter called out to his companion, "Looks like more than rats were here." The searcher joined his companion at the head of the gangway, passing within a foot of David's overhead position, and the two went back through the crew hatch. David nearly missed a third man, dressed in black, who moved slowly past the other two without a word and slunk into the fog.

David's joints ached from the cold. Fear permeated his being when he realized how close the search had come to ending his mission and perhaps his life. He put a new tape in his receiver and slid down the side of the container, quietly making his way out of the warehouse. As he headed toward the street, he reflected on the events that had brought him to Gdansk. It was his first mission for the Defense Intelligence Agency (DIA). He had come to Poland as Gregory Henson, assistant cultural attaché, his stated purpose to replace his predecessor who was about to retire from State. In actuality, he was there at the request of the spiritual leader of Solidarity, the underground resistance to the government dictatorship, to stop an expected attempt to assassinate Lech Walesa, recently announced winner of the 1983 Nobel Peace Prize.

The election of President Reagan and his hard-lined, hunker down attitude toward the communist regime in Poland made the CIA very reluctant to infiltrate the country with their own agents. When the request went over to the DIA, their brass was equally hesitant about getting involved, but Jankowski's request for help eventually did find a taker. Grant Weldman, recently retired from Military Intelligence, sat at the bottom of the DIA totem pole. One day his boss, himself Polish, returned from a staff meeting and mentioned the Polish underground request for help protecting Walesa. Grant thought he had an answer to the problem: a friend from his Vietnam days, who he was surreptitiously training to carry out intelligence missions and who would jump at the chance to be involved in a real operation.

David Reasons...

David had tired of all the improvised training missions on which Grant had been sending him and readily agreed to help. For the next two months, Grant produced all the paperwork necessary to set him up as a bona fide diplomat by the name of Gregory Henson and get him into Warsaw. He took a course in Polish at the Berlitz School in New York City and boned up on Polish politics and the Solidarity movement to prepare for his mission.

When he reached the edge of the warehouse, he shook away his reminiscences and picked out the furtive figure he had seen leaving the ship slide into the fog across the street. *This must be the man sent to assassinate Walesa.* The man turned into a rundown restaurant.

Approaching the restaurant himself, David noted a phone booth about twenty feet from the street corner. He checked the phone for a dial tone, then made his way across the street to the restaurant. Pushing open the restaurant's heavy aluminum door with cracked safety glass panels, he was reminded of an old movie theater foyer, except without a kiosk. David stopped just inside the entrance and scanned the shoulder-high plywood booths that effectively blocked his view of their occupants. He was forced to pass all the tables to find his quarry.

The man dressed in all black was sitting with a reasonably well-dressed, gray-haired man who seemed vaguely familiar. Both looked out of place in this dive. They were talking over large mugs of draft beer at the last table beside the noisy open kitchen. The conversation ceased as David went by, and he thought he saw a flicker of recognition from the gray-haired man. He also noticed the three noisy sailors in a booth near the door as he left.

David slipped quickly out into the street and called the number of his Polish contact. After giving his location, which was within five blocks of Lech Walesa's house on Pilotow Street, David described the suspected stranger and his companion and hung up. He was on his way back to the car he had parked about ten blocks from the wharf when he heard heavy footfalls behind him.

He turned to see one of the sailors raise a weapon to attack him. Reacting quickly, he moved his head only the necessary two inches to avoid the two-foot section of a boat hook handle from delivering a striking blow to his skull, but it glanced off his right shoulder, immobilizing that arm. With his left, David delivered a flat-handed jab into his assailant's solar plexus. The man went down, his breath rushing out of him. Without any more thought, David took off running. The other two sailors charged out of the restaurant and gave chase, leaving their companion to catch his breath.

David made for the lighted Robotnicza Street, south of the docks. It was foolish to think he could handle two healthy men with only his left arm. The rush of combat still coursed strongly through him, but now flight seemed to be the appropriate outlet.

Having spent two days going to and from his warehouse hideout, David was familiar with the dock area. He thought his best chance of giving the seamen the slip was to get back into the fog near the waterfront. It would be dark soon. He veered east through the alley at full speed, then doubled back to Jaracza Street. His pursuers kept pace. He headed for the cover that a row of rusted, harbor marker buoys would provide.

Flying across the street, he realized that wooden clubs were not the only weapons his enemy possessed. Two rounds hissed past his head, one making a loud ping off a buoy across the street. *Why hadn't the sailor shot him in the phone booth? Did they want to capture him, or was it simply luck that the first sailor was armed with only a club?*

David needed only minutes before he could go aground and let his pursuers become the quarry under cover of darkness. Their rough approach left no doubt in his mind that he would have little trouble with them once the night befriended him.

Reaching the row of buoys, David ran at full speed. Their random spacing did not permit accurate shooting lines. Soon the sound of his pursuers' footfalls began to diminish. The constant physical training for mock missions meant his conditioning was better than the sailors'.

At the end of the buoys, he cut back across Jaracza Street and headed toward Jana Z. Kolna Street, only one block away. He had arrived at a well-lit neighborhood where some people might be concerned about two men chasing a third through the night. He slowed to a brisk walk, letting the enemy gain on him. If it were not for the tape in his pocket, he would not have minded getting stopped by the police or a Polish Navy shore patrol.

At the corner of Kolna he heard a crash, and turned to see one of his pursuers collapse into a shop window. The other stopped to check on his companion.

As David turned back in the direction he was walking, he saw the street light glint dimly off the barrel of a silenced rifle protruding from a second story window at the opposite corner of the street. Crossing Waly Piastowski, he heard a voice call out, "Come inside. Quickly!" His Polish contact let him in, checked up and down the street, and quietly closed the door behind them.

It took David a moment to catch his breath. "You got my message?"

"Yes, I convinced Lech not to attend any meetings tonight. He will receive his prize in Stockholm on the fifteenth, thanks to your help."

David's right arm was definitely stiffening, and it was with great difficulty that he removed the tape from his pocket. "This tape may be useful. There's another in the warehouse beside the *Vartok* on top of a shipping container."

"What happened to your arm?"

"One of the men chasing me took a hack at it with a boat hook. My shoulder may be broken."

"Christ, we better get you to the hospital. Great job, Gregory!"

* * *

Following David's return to the States, the Polish and Russian secret police both opened files on Gregory Henson. The tape from the recording device recovered from the top of the shipping container, plus the one that was given to his polish contact, eventually found their way to the CIA. The man David had described was indeed an infiltrator, an employee of the secret police. After analyzing the tapes, the CIA concluded that it was the KGB who had instigated the assassination attempt. They also broke two Soviet codes.

David Reasons had solidified a new name for himself. *Henson.*

1

Lufthansa flight 732 and a breathtaking sunrise were both approaching Johannesburg International Airport when David Reasons got up and headed to the forward washroom. "Last-minute pit stop," he told his seatmate as he squeezed out and yanked his carry-on from the overhead. "Sometimes those line-ups at Customs take forever."

During the flight, David learned that his seatmate worked at GM Diesel and was on a mission to sell some Coyote reconnaissance vehicles to the South African Defense Forces as replacements for their aging Rattles. In addition to the regular chitchat about family, women, and politics, they had discussed the changes in international trade introduced by the new government of Nelson Mandela.

In the washroom David removed the fine, black, carefully combed hair, neatly trimmed moustache, and creased, Cartier pinstripe suit and donned an unkempt wig of indeterminate reddish color, a similarly scruffy moustache, and a beige and brown hound's tooth sport jacket atop dark brown polyester pants. He had made this kind of transformation many times; it took less than five minutes.

On his way back to his seat, he stumbled as he passed the last row in business class. He dropped a couple of papers on the seat beside a man with fine, black, carefully combed hair, neatly trimmed moustache, and a creased, Cartier pinstripe. Bill Saunders, another friend from their Vietnam days, was security chief at the American consulate in Frankfurt. He just glanced over as David excused himself and scooped up a duplicate set of papers, scanning the faces around him as he turned to go back to his seat. Passengers, tired and packing winter clothing into their carry-ons in preparation for their imminent arrival in the heat of summer, took no interest in him. An enemy agent would. David wondered if there was one on this flight. He had spotted a blond-haired man in faded jeans with holes at the knees and backside eyeing passengers at Gate 27 as they queued up for boarding in Frankfurt. *Did this man have an accomplice on the aircraft? Was he a member of Dominance?*

"What have we here?" his seatmate exclaimed as he got up to let David back to his seat. "What's with the disguise?"

"The lady I'm meeting knows me as a slovenly professor, not a salesman." David belted in just as the pilot made the landing announcements in perfectly accented English.

"Ah hah. Good-looking guy like you—probably a girl in every port you don't want finding out about the others."

Ten minutes later, the A320 greased onto the smooth, newly refurbished runway, precisely five hundred yards past the threshold. Within another five minutes they had stopped and the exit door was opened.

As his seatmate got up to leave, David said, "I've enjoyed talking to you. Good luck with the Defense people."

"Good luck with your research, or whatever visiting professors do," was the reply as his seatmate moved toward the exit.

"Oh, that's just a cover for Irena's benefit. By Wednesday I'll be Jim Kildare, peddling steel mill equipment."

"Maybe we can get together on the fifteenth after my meetings. I'm staying at the Hilton Plaza in Pretoria." The line began to move faster.

"I'll call you."

David made sure that a large number of other passengers were off the aircraft before he started to move. He had no weapon and no idea of who or what to expect. He also wanted to make sure anyone checking the deplaning passengers would have many identities in their mind before their real quarry appeared. Experience told him that Dominance agents were usually vigilant. His hands were damp, and his jaw clenched like a vice as he started up the aisle.

Sweat trickled down David's brow as he felt the fear of the impending danger wash over him. He was getting older and wondered if his reflexes would be fast enough to engage an alert enemy. It could be that both the South African police and Dominance agents awaited his arrival. He was certain Bill felt a similar danger.

Except for Bill as a red herring, David was on his own. He had boarded the flight as James Kildare, VP of Sales for Bethlehem Steel, to sell some used mill equipment to Iscor, South Africa's largest steel company. He was leaving as Hans Geldhart, a professor and writer at Penn State University, currently visiting the country to research a book about the post-apartheid constitution. He knew that the name Henson, the alias by which Dominance knew him, would set off alarms. The agent in Frankfurt had no doubt reported the Kildare alias. Geldhart had to work.

Terminal 1 for International Arrivals was spacious and efficiently laid out but left no escape route for passengers wishing to avoid an enemy. Gate 6, where Flight 732 had just disgorged its passengers, was located at the far west end of the building. Passengers leaving the flight had only one direction in which to go: the Arrivals area.

Everything seemed peaceful. One other flight had arrived shortly before 732, so there were a few passengers in the area. Excited neophyte travelers babbled incessantly, and seasoned frequent fliers strode purposefully out the gate. A handsome and neatly dressed JAL flight crew was carrying out a debriefing in a corner in Gate 5 just across the corridor.

Henry Jackman and Marion Aflect had stationed themselves at the exit to Gate 6, where they could study all passengers as they entered the terminal. They were looking for only one man and knew his alias and physical description. They sipped cups of coffee and chatted quietly. An untrained observer would notice only two things: Marion was the most attractive woman in the terminal, and the two seemed very much engrossed with each other.

As David spotted them, he slowed like a downfield tackler covering a kick. He knew from experience that a rush past them would give him away. The slower pace would allow greater lateral movement—vital if he had to disable them—and would be far less likely to attract attention. The flow of sweat increased. Just as he suspected, the enemy knew he was coming. His knuckles whitened as he clenched the handle of his bag. When he came within about ten feet of them he inhaled deeply, hoping that would steady him.

Henry and Marion ran their eyes over him but showed no interest. They swung their attention to Bill. As planned, he increased his pace as he came out of the gate, passed David, and headed down the brightly lit corridor toward Customs.

The Lufthansa flight staff in Frankfurt was more concerned with getting Bill on the aircraft before the cabin door closed than the fact that he looked like a passenger who had previously boarded. David was sure the agent watching for Gregory Henson would be sharp enough to see through his disguise and have gone to report his boarding before Bill's last-minute appearance.

David silently wished Bill good luck as he followed the three down the fifty feet of corridor to Customs and Immigration.

Bill was in a hurry. He wanted to get away—away from a danger he had not experienced since he left Defense Intelligence ten years earlier. Having two enemy agents follow him through an airport in what he knew was a violent country made him realize how far removed he was from the comfort of his current position. If David hadn't talked him into the mission, he would have been seated at his desk, organizing security for consular functions or preparing classified reports on the suitability of prospective immigrants to the United States.

Even though he carried only a light bag, Bill was out of shape and seemed to struggle with the pace. As they followed him, Henry and Marion showed that fluid, easy stride of well-trained athletes. They spoke softly to each other, Henry pointing toward Bill and shaking his head, Marion nodding while looking around at the other passengers. David stayed well behind them.

Bill's first stop was the men's room in the Arrivals area. Henry tailed him. David wondered if it might be a good time to cut down the odds but immediately dismissed the idea. The commotion would give him away and would not help Bill much.

Bill removed his disguise as Gregory Henson, in a vacant cubicle. As he sat on the can behind the locked door, he wondered how in hell he would give his tail the slip. Hearing a flush next door gave him an idea. He flushed his toilet, hoping the noise would cover his move to the adjacent cubicle. No chance. When he emerged two minutes later, fear gripped him. Henry was holding the door open for him. If he had not been so afraid, it would have seemed a comical gesture.

Henry was quite sure he was following the wrong man but thought this one might lead them to the one they knew as Henson. He grabbed Bill roughly by the shoulders, patted him down, and yanked at his hair. Bill stifled a scream.

"Son-of-a-bitch, you aren't Henson!" Henry swore, slamming Bill painfully into the Arborite counter. Henry cuffed him and dragged him out the door. "I don't know who this guy is, Marion, but maybe we can take him to HQ and sweat him."

"We better phone the boss. We're not official."

David watched nervously from a sportswear kiosk near the end of the passageway from the gates. Its window displayed a life-sized poster of Michael Jordan—a tribute to that athlete's ability to sell, even from ten thousand miles away. David agonized over whether he should risk attracting the attention of the airport police by taking out the two and rescuing Bill. That might help Bill, but would jeopardize his mission. He waited.

Marion strode over toward David. His heart jumped. *Could Bill have given him away so quickly?* She flipped open her cell.

"Marion here. I think we lost Henson...Don't get mad, we have a guy posing as him...Do you want us to bring him in? This guy may lead us to Henson...Okay, we'll check with car rentals...I'll get the airport police to bring him in...We'll try to find out who he is first...Yes, sir!"

David could see she was talking on the phone, but she moved too far away for him to pick up the end of the conversation.

When Marion returned, Bill was getting something out of his bag.

"Henry, he might have a gun!" she shouted. Henry placed his Berretta deep into Bill's kidney.

"It's just my passport," Bill stammered. Passengers were beginning to stare at the trio.

"I checked him for a weapon. Oh, shit, it's diplomatic," Henry complained, re-holstering his Beretta.

"Gene told me we better find Henson before he leaves the terminal. Remember, the airport police don't know what we're up to. Looks like Henson got this diplomat to impersonate him."

"Isn't that against the law?"

"No. If we were at war with the States, we could've gotten him for espionage."

"You're right. Isn't this your lucky day?" Henry undid the handcuffs. "Get out of my sight before I change my mind."

Bill walked away, heading toward Customs and Immigration. He could scarcely hold back a grin as he put some distance between himself and his captors. The enemy had neither David's name nor his Geldhart alias. A second secretary from the US embassy in Pretoria waited for him after he cleared.

David had not heard the conversation, but relief flooded through him as he saw the two agents spin away from Bill. He followed his friend into Immigration and watched as Henry and Marion headed to car rentals.

The Customs and Immigration area was bright and open with short queues at four officers' desks. *Would the Customs agent stop me? Would they have my name?* His level of tension had not eased as he stepped up to the uniformed redhead at the Immigration counter. She asked him the usual questions, taking some time over his passport. This caused David's already tight jaw to clamp even more firmly. She consulted a file under the counter but eventually returned his documents to him with a friendly "Enjoy your stay in South Africa, Professor Geldhart."

As David headed to car rentals, he realized the power of Dominance. They could even get Immigration to look for Henson.

David was very relieved to find that the Fiat 1500 was ready at Dolphin Rentals. Just a show of passport and credit card and he was on his way out of the terminal—away from immediate danger. As he turned toward the exit where the Dolphin cars were parked, he noticed the young clerk who had helped him pick up the phone.

* * *

Henry and Marion waited quietly in a lounge just off the car rental and taxi area. They were sipping Perriers and chatting when Marion's cell phone rang. "Yes, okay...What was his name and what did he look like?...Geldhart, you say...What's the license number?" She shut the phone. "It doesn't sound like Henson. He wasn't using Geldhart as an alias when he boarded, but we better check it out before whoever it is gets away."

As they approached, the clerk pointed toward the exit through which David had passed three minutes earlier. "Area 27B," he called as they rushed for the door, "and where's my money?"

There was no response from the rushing couple.

* * *

David shoved his papers at the smiling overall-clad young blonde who was ready to check him out on with the Fiat. "I have to be in Pretoria by nine. Just give me the keys."

"But, sir, we need to check it over."

"I'll take responsibility for damages. Give me the keys now, please...Now!" Something in David's voice—a ruthless unwavering demand—made the girl stifle her huffy response and hand him the keys.

David started the car, dropped it in gear, and sped out of the Dolphin rental area. The two agents he had seen earlier raced toward him.

Marion shouted to Henry, "It must be Henson." She stepped out in front of the car and drew her weapon before she realized he was not going to stop. She jumped aside as the Fiat tore by, the side mirror slamming her left hand. She fired twice after the car whipped past, but the pain and unbalancing foiled her aim and the rounds went harmlessly into the trunk. Henry's Berretta took out the Fiat's side mirror and the windshield of a Hertz Mercedes as David squealed out of the garage, into the blazing sun, and out of the maze of airport roadways onto the highway to Klerksdorp.

Henry went over to where Marion was holding her left hand. It had started to swell and discolor. "We better get you to a doctor."

"To hell with that! We better get after Henson or Eugene's going to kill us."

"How are we going to chase him? We don't even know which road he'll take, and our car is over at Terminal 1."

"My hand feels like it's broken. Why didn't you hit him, Henry?"

"He was moving too fast. Let's check in with the boss first."

"We should get on the range, too. We better not miss the next time we see him."

* * *

David had chosen Klerksdorp very carefully as the first destination en route to Bloemfontein. It was a city of over half a million, where he could get by with his English and a few poorly accented words in Afrikaans. The enemy would have a great number of hotels, motels, and guesthouses to search. There would also be a number of shops where he could buy new clothes, makeup, and wigs.

He was in the open now. The enemy knew his car and appearance. He must not be picked up before he could change his identity. No amount of talking and deception could save him.

The quickest way to get from Johannesburg to Bloemfontein was the Johannesburg to Cape Town highway that cleft the country from north to south all the way from the Zimbabwe border to the Cape. He hoped that

17

was the route an enemy would watch. The Klerksdorp–Kimberley–Bloemfontein route would get less attention.

He checked his rearview mirror several times as he traveled through the spectacular landscape. There was no sign of a tail, but then again, with professional pursuit, there never was.

2

Six months before David Reasons's arrival in Johannesburg, Dieter Volmar, the head of Renaissance Developments, received a call from South Africa. Dieter was seated on his custom-built brocade swivel chair in his office on the fifth floor of the Volmar building on Luisenstrasse in Baden–Baden, Germany. Two matching side chairs faced the seven-foot blond oak desk, leaving considerable open space on the hand-woven Turkish carpet that covered the 40-foot by 30-foot room. Three beige leather love seats surrounded a polished brown feldspar coffee table adorning the other end of the carpet.

Dieter stood six foot six inches tall and was heavily built. He was dressed impeccably well in a Gieves and Hawkes three-piece dark gray silk suit, a maroon and gray tie with the Renaissance company logo discretely displayed in the center over a brilliant white Irish linen shirt. Two-carat diamond-studded cufflinks glinted below the jacket sleeves, and handmade tasseled loafers by Bally completed his wealthy appearance.

In addition to Renaissance and a large fortune, Dieter had inherited something else from his father. He had control of the organization Heinz Volmar had been quietly building over the past twenty years—an organization of highly specialized white-collar terrorists called Dominance.

A phone rang, located in a dull-looking steel cabinet masked by a brocade curtain behind Dieter's desk. He drew the curtain, unlocked and opened a drawer in the cabinet, and removed a strange-looking device. It was about twice the size of a regular telephone handset and had a multitude of wires running to it. The surface had an ordinary keypad and three lit knobs. The center knob was flashing, announcing an incoming call. To answer, Dieter dialed a combination of numbers into the keys, and the other two knobs lit up in compliance.

"Two here."

"Forty-seven calling. I have an operation planned that may interest you. Details with the courier this morning." Eugene den Kamp's voice had a hollow ring to it—the result of double encryptions sent on low frequency carriers, unused since the last war. Heinz's Renaissance engineers had developed the system in total secrecy. They were told it was necessary that their master's communications be impervious to electronic espionage. It was also inaudible to the inquisitive ears of various nations' security agencies. The German Bundesnachrichtendienst, French Sureté, and American NSA did not monitor those frequencies.

"Does it involve our group?"

"A member I plan to hire. He executed a black major at our army training base and escaped unscathed."

"Trustworthy?"

"Impeccably so."

"Good, you may look forward to my early approval." The leader of Dominance was pleased that his new recruit, den Kamp, was getting right down to business. There was nothing like a simple operation to instill confidence. South Africa would be a major player in the revolution to come.

Dieter was following in his father's lead. After his empire had been firmly established, Heinz had run a few small operations to test the determination and loyalty of his recruits. Just before Heinz's death, the Canadian province of Quebec was holding a referendum to determine if the people of that province wanted to remain part of Canada. Heinz and Twenty-nine, his Canadian lieutenant, felt that in the long run it would be easier to dominate Canada if it was fragmented. The two of them worked out a scheme to secretly pay scrutineers, who counted referendum ballots, to spoil a large number of those that indicated the voters favored remaining in the country. It very nearly worked. Had they hired about five times as many ballot spoilers, they might have reversed the result. The margin of victory of the federalist forces was only about fifty thousand.

One of the first men Heinz tried to recruit was the deputy head of KGB operations. The general was mildly interested, partly because of timing—he had just been passed over for promotion to head of the KGB—and partly because of the amount of money Heinz promised would flow once they were successful. After two weeks of thinking it over, the general declined. Heinz always thought it was the old Soviet lack of trust in anything Germanic. They remained in contact, however, and it was through him that Heinz learned the name and reputation of Gregory Henson.

* * *

In spite of the efforts by President Mandela's government with its Reconstruction and Development Program to reconcile the hostility between black and white South Africans, racism failed to completely wither in many parts of his country. Mandela and Bishop Desmond Tutu had been the driving force in the healing process with the Truth and Reconciliation Commission in the early nineties, but in a country that had actively promoted vicious racism for decades, the inculcation of new attitudes needed more than legislation and confession. It needed time—for a generation of hatred and hurt to dissipate—and trust. The white population would retain the privileges they had enjoyed for years, and the new government would improve the standard of living for the black population.

The agents of Dominance did all they could to slow that process.

* * *

Louis Terbose was an excellent marksman. He had risen to the rank of lieutenant at the South African Defense Force Infantry School and now taught marksmanship there. The school was nestled in a fertile valley in the Schwartzburg and Outeniqua mountains halfway between Cape Town and Port Elizabeth. The area was famous for raising ostriches.

Terbose was a long-time member of the Broederbond, a secret Masonic-type organization. The Brotherhood was very pervasive in the power structure under apartheid and continued to wield considerable influence after democratic rule was established. Many Brothers, including Eugene den Kamp, held high office and used their influence to protect the privileges of the white man.

Terbose's boss was a major—a black major. He was responsible for all recruit training and kept reminding Terbose that development of inductees would be better served by spending more time on military and physical discipline and less on the rifle and pistol ranges. Terbose disagreed and made his feelings known to his boss several times in private, in front of the recruits, in his boss's office, and over beers in the officers' mess hall.

The mess was supposed to be the center of social life for the base's officers. With the officer corps now racially integrated, dinners, dances, and after work wind-downs were intended to foster a spirit of tolerance and acceptance among the ten black and nineteen white officers. The army was even more politically unjust than the police, so except for Friday evenings, attendance was poor. Even when an excellent Marabi band was hired for a dance, perhaps six black and only two white couples would attend.

A picture window in the main lounge, in front of plush chairs around a mahogany coffee table, presented the commanding officer and his guests the best view of the valley. Sturdy leather seats arranged around smaller tables covered the remainder of the area.

One Friday night in the fall of 1994, about fifteen officers, including the deputy mayor of Oudtshoorn, were enjoying after-dinner drinks in the main lounge. The officers talked of nothing more than the upcoming Pan–African rugby matches, their latest sexual conquests, and what they had planned for the weekend. The mayor and his wife were discussing the impressive showing of both races, while their host, the commanding officer of the base, was at the bar getting them drinks.

Terbose's boss, Major Auland, had cornered the CO at the bar while he was waiting for his drink order. "But, sir, the men will probably never use a rifle in battle. Why does Terbose persist in keeping them hour after hour on the range? I've told him countless times they need drills and conditioning. Those are the qualities that will help them become real soldiers."

"Lieutenant Terbose is the top marksman in the army," the CO told him, "and has record scores to prove it. He lives and breathes rifles. I wouldn't be surprised if he slept with his."

"Do you agree with his emphasis on shooting to the detriment of their other training?" At this point the lieutenant himself sauntered up.

A black major should have known that the CO and Terbose were both members of the Brotherhood. Both were long-term infantry and white, but he had failed to make the connection. He was newly promoted and recently arrived from the Cape Town garrison where antiracist sentiment seemed to be gaining ground more quickly than it was at the school.

"I heard the major's question, sir. Don't you agree that marksmanship is extremely important for infantry soldiers?"

"Yes, Lieutenant Terbose. Marksmanship is important, but are you overdoing it?"

"Certainly not, sir. I only keep them on the range until their scores reach the agreed target for the day. That is protocol."

"Who sets the agreed scores?" asked the CO.

"I do, of course."

"How can I run new recruit training if Mr. Terbose doesn't even tell me what he's up to?" asked the major.

"It's my business how well they do on the range. I've been doing this for years."

"But you report to me," said Auland. "You'll do what I say."

"Now, gentlemen," the CO intervened, "I think we should settle this in my office on Monday morning. We have guests in the mess."

"I think we should settle it NOW!" Terbose responded.

"You may run the range," said the major, "but I run the new recruit training. I order you to decrease the time on the range by one half."

"To hell with you."

"What did you say?"

"To hell with you. No black son-of-a-bitch is going to tell me how to run my section."

"Calm down, gentlemen." The CO knew that a fight between his officers would not hasten his promotion to general.

"Not until you tell this big black prick to let me run the range, sir."

"Enough of this. Auland, leave the mess now," the CO ordered.

"Why should I leave? Terbose is the one being abusive."

"Leave now, major."

"No, sir, I'm staying."

At this point, the deputy mayor, attracted by the shouts from the bar, walked by. "Is there a problem, gentlemen?"

"I'll remove him, sir." Terbose grabbed his boss by the collar.

The major was a big, strong man. He easily shrugged off Terbose's hand. Louis got in one good shot to his major's cheekbone and jumped back. "Take that, you bastard."

"You'll pay for that, Terbose!" he shouted as he moved in, swinging a left.

Terbose was able to block the major's hit, but the strength of the blow pushed him off balance. As he righted himself with a cocky, "Your kind is the problem around here," he swung another right.

Major Auland easily blocked him and grunted as he hit Terbose's jaw with a straight right. "Stupid fuck!" the major contested. "Maybe that will keep the shit from running out of your mouth." Terbose lay sprawled on the floor, unconscious. "Excuse me, sir, I'll be leaving now."

A couple of minutes later, when Terbose came to, the CO and the major were gone. A couple of his fellow officers, who had not seen the fight, helped him to his feet. "What happened, Louis?" one of them asked. "We heard shouting. I thought there might have been a fight. How does the other guy look?" Terbose's face was starting to discolor.

Louis responded angrily, "He went out the back door with a broken nose." There was no way he was going to say he was beaten by some black prick.

Without an outside witness, the CO would no doubt have had the major court-martialed and fired for having the effrontery to attack the CO's Brethren, but the local politician had both heard the argument and seen Terbose instigate the physical hostilities toward the major. Therefore, when the major was paraded before him on Monday morning, the CO merely gave him the "boys will be boys, but don't do it again" speech and sent him back to duty. Terbose was not disciplined because he was a Brother, and, secondly, because he could not be found.

A week later, the orderly officer, doing his regular rounds early on Saturday morning, discovered a body lying twisted in a bed of flowering hibiscus that decorated the grassy area between the mess and its parking lot. Six months later, Terbose still couldn't be found and the army wrote him off their books.

* * *

Through his contacts within the Brotherhood, Eugene den Kamp heard of Terbose's exploits. Terbose had become quite a hero to white supremacists. A man who could gun down a black in cold blood and escape punishment was exactly the kind of recruit den Kamp was looking for. He sent out word through the Brotherhood that he would like to have a friendly meeting with Terbose.

3

David saw the flashing blue lights before he heard the siren. He checked his speedometer—85 klicks. After slowing down and pulling over, he glanced back in his only remaining side view mirror. The young constable who climbed out of his car looked as if he could take care of himself—white, about five-ten, and two hundred pounds, David reckoned. He rolled down the window and steeled himself for battle. David was in the open now. His unarmed combat experience could be brought into play without the restrictions of a crowded and policed airport terminal.

The constable stood a good three feet away from the open window. "Sir, I'm going to ticket you for doing 120 klicks in an 80 klick zone." The sarcasm in his tone was obvious.

David thought of a smart aleck response—something like, "How is that possible, officer? I've only been driving for half an hour," but ultimately decided comedy would get him nowhere. He glanced in the rearview mirror as the officer leaned to one side to get a look in the back seat. He saw no one in the police car stopped on the gravel verge about twenty yards behind him.

"License," demanded the officer, his countenance one of complete confidence.

"Certainly, officer," David replied meekly. "But I was only doing eighty-five to ninety tops."

"Get out of the damn car. Now!"

"Okay, relax, this isn't—"

As David left the car, his flattened left hand struck the young constable's windpipe like a truncheon. The officer went down, grabbing his throat. A few seconds of pressure on his carotid artery put him temporarily out of commission. David eased the officer into a sitting position in the Fiat's driver's seat so as not to attract too much attention from passing motorists.

As he removed the officer's Smith & Wesson and slipped it into the waistband at the back of his pants, a white Mercedes 300D heading in the opposite direction pulled a one-eighty and skidded to a stop twenty yards ahead of the Fiat. The well-dressed Afrikaner had police written all over him. As he strode toward them, he hauled a small Beretta out of his belt. "What the hell's going on here?" he demanded. "What have you done to that officer?"

"Put the gun down, sir," David demanded in his faltering Afrikaans. "We don't need any trouble."

"Like hell I will. Step away from the car."

"I was just stopped by this policeman for speeding, and when he got out of the car he collapsed. I'm trying to revive him."

"That's not the way I see it. Get away from him." The officer David had disabled was beginning to groan.

The other policeman was too smart to get close enough for David to disarm him, so David hit the deck, grabbing the Smith & Wesson. The policeman's first shot whistled harmlessly over David's head. As he was taking aim for a second shot, David shot him in the leg. The policeman couldn't shoot another round; the pain froze him long enough for David to race over, kick his gun away, and land a solid right punch to his solar plexus.

David raced off, earning the ticket the constable had promised him. Piet Neiderhof hauled himself back to his Mercedes and called den Kamp on his cellular. "Sir, I just ran into Henson…He attacked an officer, then shot me in the leg as while I was detaining him…yes, sir." He then went over to check on the recovering constable.

Searching his memory for an alternate route to Klerksdorp, David decided that going to Parys and then travelling south down back roads along the Vaal River would be safest. He wondered who told the young constable to stop his Fiat. *How did that plainclothes policeman man show up so fast? And since when did constables start carrying Smith & Wessons?* These were not coincidences.

* * *

During the planning meeting David and Grant had in Yonkers, they neglected to discuss the best way to obtain a weapon. Their meeting had been arranged hastily, due to the urgency of getting into South Africa before December 15.

"Obviously I can't bring in a gun."

"No, but we could get someone in the African National Congress to meet you."

"I thought we didn't want anyone to know we're working for them."

"That's true. My friend in Harare was specific on that point. No contact with the ANC. Maybe you could buy one in South Africa. You look enough like an Afrikaner." They both laughed.

"Yeah, right. I'll try to steal one."

Had there been less concern about who to trust, Grant would have arranged for someone at the embassy to meet David at the airport and hand over a weapon, but Dominance could easily have connections within the Intelligence community or the State Department. Putting a member of the embassy staff onto the objective could be signing his death warrant. The constable and his would-be savior had solved the problem for them by underestimating David's ability to act decisively.

* * *

Nearing Klerksdorp, David decided to get off the highway and onto dirt tracks, used mainly by farmers in this bleak area of the veld. The fast, easy-to-handle Fiat was having trouble holding the road. At one point it hung up between the ruts, forcing its occupant to peel himself off the steering wheel.

When David got to within walking distance of Klerksdorp, he thought, *I better get rid of the car. Too many people can identify it, and I just shot a police officer.* When he got to a point where the road passed a gully, he stopped, took out his carry-on, and pushed the automobile over the edge. He watched the snappy little sedan plunge the five yards into the rock-strewn gully, flip onto its side as it hit a large boulder, and come to rest with a thin plume of smoke emerging from under its hood. David had a much-needed feeling of amusement as he thought about the hell the loss of the Fiat was going to play with Geldhart's credit rating. To improve the chances that it would not be found for a few days, he climbed down into the ravine, scavenged some brush, and did his best to hide the outline of the car.

Covering his tracks he made down the bank, David set off to find a hideout in Klerksdorp.

* * *

Louis Terbose had been in hiding in Windhoek, Namibia, since disappearing from the Oudtshoorn base. It was quite easy for a Brother to blend into the landscape. During the apartheid years, many South Africans had taken up residence there—both liberals to escape apartheid's evils and Bureau of State Security agents to keep tabs on the underground activities of the ANC, whose main headquarters was in Windhoek. The South African police had sent an arrest warrant for Terbose to their counterparts in Namibia, but the Namibians were neither inclined to waste time chasing criminals who had done nothing in their country nor eager to help a government that had treated them as second class for the past century.

On Terbose's second weekend in Windhoek he went out searching for a bit of female companionship at the Flamingo bar in the Safari hotel. He checked out the local talent and was not impressed that most of it was black, so he grabbed a stool at the bar and got a lager. About ten minutes of glancing around the room didn't improve his chances of getting laid, and he was about to get up and leave when a white man hopped on the stool beside his. He was a retired guide and chief salesman for Keiler Hunt, an organization that provided hunting tours for rich foreigners from all over the world. After a couple of drinks and a few tales from Terbose about his days in the army and his ability as a marksman, he suggested he report for an interview at Keiler's head offices on Monday. Terbose was hired on the spot as a hunting guide.

On his third hunt, the chief guide agreed to let him go off on his own with Wilfred Armbruster, an Englishman who very much wanted to bag a big cat. This prey was strictly illegal, but Terbose failed to mention the target of their hunt to his boss. A thousand Namibian dollars from the Englishman easily corrupted the already shaky morals of his neophyte guide. Six hours after they set out, a bedraggled and badly mauled Terbose turned up alone.

31

A search party was organized and set out the next day. After spending an hour in the area Louis said they were attacked, they found nothing. "Terbose, are you sure Mr. Armbruster didn't just get lost when you weren't paying attention?" the head guide asked.

"NO! This big ass lion jumped us. I tried to fight him off, but he knocked me out. You saw what I looked like when I got back."

"Where's the blood?"

"I don't know. One part of this fucking desert looks like any other. Maybe we're looking in the wrong place."

"Well, I don't believe your story."

"Why not? It's true. When I woke up, Armbruster was gone. After the lion attacked me, it must have dragged him off."

"Bullshit. When we get back, you're fired!"

Armbruster was never found.

Terbose was both surprised and suspicious when he received the word that the head of South African Police Services, SAPS, wanted him to return to the country and guaranteed him safe passage. The only reason he travelled to Pretoria was that a highly trusted Brother told him that den Kamp had a job for him.

Terbose arrived at den Kamp's home, looking like a retired British Naval officer, complete with cravat and handkerchief up his left sleeve. The disguise was a precaution against immigration officials who might have memories good enough to tie him to the man on their old wanted posters. His British passport said he was Wilfred Armbruster from Manchester, England.

* * *

Den Kamp lived on Volk Street in Pretoria's posh Linshoten suburb. The rambling single-level stone ranch house was protected on its flanks by tall aloe hedges which also sheltered a very pleasant flagstone patio raised about two feet above the dark green carpet of grass that stretched a hundred feet to the quiet flowing Wakkerspruit River. Flowering jacaranda trees also covered the yard. Their beautiful purple blossoms belied the ugliness about to be hatched below them. On this warm October afternoon, three members of the South African Dominance cell were just finishing their first drinks over small talk about Terbose.

"Top marksman, who lost his cool is what he sounds like."

"Don't have any doubts—he's a Brother. The fact he acted on his honor says a lot. The only reason they pinned it on him was his disappearance."

"That's another point in itself. He has evaded being detained by the military and local law enforcement. His ability to turn ghost could be critical to keeping our operation from being discovered."

"With our capabilities and resources, are we sure this extremist is the right choice?"

Den Kamp ended the discussion. "The choice is mine to make. You two will be supporting him to make sure this goes off without any problems. It appears he has arrived."

Terbose was ushered onto the patio by the most beautiful creature he had ever seen. Marion Aflect was clad in a flowing lime green wraparound that did little to hide her sensual shape. *Working with this goddess is going to be a very pleasant assignment*, Louis thought to himself.

"Lieutenant Terbose, glad to see you made it. Would you like a drink? Take a seat." Den Kamp motioned to a padded lawn chair right next to his. "I am Eugene den Kamp."

"Thank you, sir, I was intrigued to hear you needed my assistance."

33

"Talents like yours should not be wasted. Have you been keeping up on your weapon skills?"

"Of course, sir, even with circumstances the way they are, I have been able to keep a sharp eye and steady hand."

"This is one of my top personnel, Henry Jackman. He will be assisting in operations on this mission."

Marion began a sensual stride parading her figure in front on the conversing men. Terbose's eyes began to follow the ample swivel of Marion's backside as she went through the open patio door.

"Keep your shit straight and your mind on the mission," Jackman barked.

"Trust me, my shot is straight." Terbose glared at Jackman.

Louis was not a handsome man. His face was craggy in a way that could be considered interesting, but it was also pinched, his eyebrows thin, and his eyes close together with a habit of darting. He had the look of a ferret, about to spring down a hole in the ground to trap an unsuspecting squirrel. He was strong and well built and had maintained his army conditioning even in exile.

"There will be no problems between you two," den Kamp thundered. "Save it for the enemy, boys."

Both men had been brought up in a regime based on hatred and fear of the black man. They learned at an early age that the way to treat anything that vaguely resembled a threat was to hate it. Louis realized that Henry was a rival—for the affections of Marion and for a place of honor in den Kamp's eyes. He sensed resentment oozing out of Henry.

Terbose was distracted once again by the flowing green outfit returning to the patio with fresh drinks. *I could get used to this.* As Marion bent over to hand him the Glenfiddich, he felt a tremendous stirring.

* * *

Den Kamp was a handsome man in a hard way. His features were as strong as his body. He carried himself like a Boer cavalry officer—which he might have been had he been born fifty years earlier. Den Kamp gave the impression, both through strong language and will, that he was a man to be reckoned with. Those who served under him, such as Henry and Marion, had tasted the venom in his piercing remarks.

When den Kamp was a young constable in Cape Town, his friend and partner, Forest Burton, had brought in one of the most dangerous ANC rebels who operated in the Cape area. Not one to miss a chance at notoriety, den Kamp had been first in line when the press arrived. From the published newspaper article, one would have thought that it was den Kamp, not Burton, who was the hero.

During their shift the next day, Burton faced den Kamp. "My so-called friend...you seem to be quite a hero. Just had to take the credit, didn't you?"

"Forest, don't take it so hard, man. You're the hero. The M&G reporter just misquoted me."

"Sure he did, you power hungry prick."

"Now, now, no need to get abusive. You'll get your day of glory." The steely stare in den Kamp's eye said the argument was over. He would get the credit and Burton would have to deal with the loss of prestige. It was not long before the two made an uneasy peace. Their partnership depended on it, but the loss of face festered inside Forest.

Den Kamp had risen quickly in the Bureau of State Security, often referred to as "BOSS," and was appointed its head by President De Klerk just prior to free elections. Now he controlled all of South Africa's police forces. In his view, such power was designed to protect the rights and privileges of the white man. He gave lip service to Truth and Reconciliation, but in his heart he wanted to return to the official racism of apartheid rule.

A few leaders in his forces, particularly in the central part of the country, shared his views about the proper use of police power. In time he planned to bring many of them into Dominance.

When his ex-wife, Sylvie, first introduced them, Eugene, like most men, thought that Marion Aflect was one of the most attractive women he had ever seen. A modeling agency in Alberton discovered her as soon as she completed high school in Pretoria. Shows for major designers in Cape Town and Johannesburg brought her face and figure to the attention of fashion magazines throughout the country. Marion and Eugene began an affair soon after den Kamp hired her as a constable in the force. She felt drawn to his power, physical attractiveness, and the fact that he had helped in advancing her career. He, in turn, was overwhelmed by her beauty and sensuality. It was not long before their affair became known to other police officers and to den Kamp's wife.

Henry Jackman was a tall, dark-haired, slim man with a toothbrush moustache and military bearing. He had been a policeman since leaving the University of Witwatersand in 1970. After three years on the beat in Cape Town, he came to the attention of Eugene den Kamp, who at that time was head of the Cape Town detachment. Henry's notoriety derived from the absolutely ruthless way he prosecuted those blacks who broke the Pass Laws that maintained apartheid, and in his brutal handling of captured ANC guerrillas. Jackman had reached the rank of captain before being wounded in a raid on an ANC cell in the town of Shrank, just east of Cape Town. After his recovery, he was rewarded with a posh administrative assignment as deputy to the chief in the Cape.

Den Kamp had thought about how to approach Terbose for quite some time. He wondered if he should feel him out to see if his racist views still held, or if he should just come out and ask him to join them. Though he had the power to slap Terbose in jail, he decided on the latter approach. If Terbose arrived of his own volition, then he would probably not refuse to take the job. He could not really put Henry or Marion on it. They were used to being on the other side of the law—keeping a high profile to scare criminals. If one of them tried to assassinate Mandela, the whole plot would probably be exposed, and they with it. He needed someone like Terbose: someone who could kill at a distance, then escape.

Marion stood with her back slightly arched against the railing of the patio, sipping a Caipiroska.

"To fill you in, Louis," den Kamp began, "we asked you here to join our plot to assassinate our beloved president."

"Sir? Are you serious?"

"Deadly. I am not in the habit of having ex-military officers to my home to drink my Scotch and tell jokes."

"Sorry, sir. I mean no disrespect." Terbose was starting to understand where he fit into this plot. He knew what his job was going to be and wondered what the beautiful people on the deck would be doing.

"Lieutenant…You are here today to align and plan the execution of President Mandela when he visits Bloemfontein on the fifteenth of December."

"That's less than two months away, sir. Can everything be set up in such a short time?" The shock of den Kamp's proposal was wearing off for Terbose.

"Oh, we'll be ready, Louis," Henry remarked. He had been told by den Kamp that he would not be the one to carry out the execution, and it still stung. "Will you?"

"I never miss my mark, Henry…"

"Henry and Marion, your first job will be to take out Henson if—"

"Who's Henson, sir?" Terbose pressed.

"Don't interrupt. You two will head to Bloemfontein to make sure the local cops don't pick Lieutenant Terbose up."

"How do we do that?" Henry asked.

"You're cops…Figure it out."

"And how do I get out after I kill Mandela?"

"Details, details. I'm sure all of us can work something out." Den Kamp was getting tired of the details.

"Terbose, do you think you're capable of hitting this mark?" Henry stammered.

"Sir, details are what will keep me alive after I pull the trigger."

"Your ability to disappear is part of the reason you are being contracted. Will you be able to accomplish this task, or do I need to contract someone else?" Den Kamp said as he took another drink of scotch.

Terbose hated the new black president almost as much as he had hated his previous black boss. In fact, he hated all blacks. He did not need any incentive to assassinate Mandela. "Of course, sir. Now who's this Henson?"

"We think he's a rogue CIA agent. You remember how the CIA was involved in the Inkatha scandals?"

"Vaguely. I was more interested in trying to stop the black officers from getting promoted in the army then. Didn't pay much attention to politics."

"Well, the CIA never liked the ANC. Thought of the lot as the communist scum they really are. So they sent in a couple of agents who put up some cash to help the Inkatha Party beat the ANC, but they screwed up and got caught. It's unlikely the CIA will risk another scandal, but they can deny knowledge of their agent Henson."

"Does that mean the CIA now supports the ANC?"

"Apparently, but that's beside the point."

"What do your intelligence officers know about this Henson, sir?" asked an intrigued Louis. He wanted to know how much information the head of the South African Police actually had. "Do we have someone inside American Intelligence?"

"That's no concern of yours, Lieutenant Terbose."

"Do you think he'll try to stop us?"

"I don't. But the head of our organization in Germany tells me this guy had been getting in the way of operations for years. He apparently annoyed the Russians by stopping the assassination of Lech Walesa in Poland in '83."

"I didn't even know there was an attempt on Walesa." Marion was learning something more now that she had another man vulnerable to her charms. Even though he was quite ugly, she fed off the energy.

"Neither did I," Terbose added.

"Neither did most of the world. Henson also exposed a group of Aryans out in Idaho five years ago. They were agents of our American representative and were helping some rancher in an uprising to get control of the whole state for their own country. This guy Henson got to the FBI director and turned them in." Den Kamp began to think he was talking too much.

"That surprises me too, Ge...Eugene," Marion interjected. "Didn't our US member tell you he couldn't let Everett go ahead or it would blow his cover?"

"Mr. er...he had his reasons for letting that story out." It was a prime directive of Dominance that the names of members in other countries would never be disseminated except to the heads of the organization. Den Kamp sent Marion a piercing look.

"Who's this leader and organization you keep referring to?" asked Terbose as he continued to stare at Marion.

Den Kamp went on to describe the goals of Dominance and how it was secretly set up to get stronger by adding highly placed operatives in cells in all Western countries.

When he finished, Terbose whistled. "Jesus, do you think we can do that? That would make a hell of a lot of headway."

The "we" sounded good to den Kamp. "Of course. I have the greatest confidence in our group and its illustrious leader. This little assassination we are planning is merely an exercise to show our leader you are capable of greater things."

"Anyway, Louis, you get the idea," Henry interposed. "This Henson has screwed up too many of our plans, and our leader wants us to take him out. If we come across him."

A loud buzzing came from the open patio door. "That may be word from our leader." Grabbing his drink, Den Kamp went into his study, motioning for the other three to follow him. After fifteen busy seconds during which his phone continued to ring, he responded, "Forty-seven here...yes, we're discussing it now...he will be? How do you know? We'll take care of him, don't worry...yes, Two." As he hung up, a worried look spread over his face. "Looks like we will have to deal with Henson. Apparently there's a leak somewhere."

"Do you mean we still go ahead even though the ANC are on to us?" Terbose began to wonder why he had got mixed up with this bunch of lunatics.

"Of course, Lieutenant Terbose. You've been in the military too long. The ANC always knows the Brotherhood is up to something. They think that local and presidential security can protect Mandela."

Henry began to wonder if den Kamp had made a mistake by recruiting Terbose.

"Okay, tell me how this Henson is getting involved."

"How the hell should I know?" Henry responded.

"Gentlemen, gentlemen, no need to get upset with each other. You're with us now, right, lieutenant?"

There was never any question in Terbose's mind about whether or not he was in. Here was his chance to get back at a system that had forced him out of the country. Not only could he get back to his home, but he also had a chance to do something great, something to increase his own stature and improve the future of whites not just in South Africa but in the whole world. "Of course, sir," he responded enthusiastically.

"Now, let's get on with the job we came here to do. I know you haven't had much chance to think, Lieutenant Terbose, but let's get together here next weekend to discuss your finalized plan and assure you have full access to Dominance resources."

"That should suffice, sir."

"And you two?"

"We'll be ready," Henry replied for them both.

"By the way, sir, what's my take?" Terbose asked.

"You'll be well rewarded."

"I require half up front at our next meeting. And what's your organization called?"

"Dominance."

Dominance, that sounds about right, smirked Louis.

After the three left, den Kamp went back to his library and dialed Dieter's number. He got his leader on the tenth ring. "Two here. What is it?"

"Forty-seven. We are ready when you approve the operation."

"I approve. Beware of Henson. I will try to get you his itinerary before he arrives. Do not fail."

"The president is as good as dead."

* * *

By the time David reached the outskirts of Klerksdorp, he was having trouble seeing straight. One thing he didn't account for was the absence of water in the Northwest Province. There were no streams, no ponds, and not even a roadside ditch with any moisture in it. *Welcome to Africa!* The Orange Bar and Grill appeared to him as a lifesaver. Using every fiber of strength he had left, he climbed up the four steps to the entrance. As he slipped in, he prayed that the alarm that he raised for his assault and escape on the highway had not penetrated this secluded suburban oasis.

"Afternoon, mate. You look like you've been out in the sun too long."

"Yeah, I could sure use some water."

The surly-looking Afrikaner bartender with graying blond hair and a rose tattoo on his right forearm brought over a glass of water without ice and asked, "Want anything to drink?" as he plopped down a menu in Afrikaans.

"Yeah, bring me a Castle, please." After finishing the water, he began to feel alive again.

When the bartender returned, he plopped down the beer, spilling a bit on the Formica table, and asked, "Want anything to eat?"

"Is this a steak sandwich?" David asked, pointing to number 4 on the menu.

"Yeah, that's it. Where you from, mate?"

"England." David wanted to avoid getting into a conversation—nothing that made him memorable, especially to someone as redneck as this bartender.

"Okay. Be about ten minutes. Should I keep the beer coming?"

"One more when I finish this one and another glass of water with ice." He never knew when he would need to be sharp, so staying sober was essential. The second beer arrived right away, and the bartender went back to watch a football match on TV.

* * *

As David finished his steak, the bartender ambled out from behind the bar. "Want another beer?"

"No thanks. Can you call me a cab?"

"Hey, you're a cab," was the reply, followed by a rough laugh.

David laughed, too. Maybe he was being overly suspicious of this guy. There were only two other people in the place, both sitting at the bar and watching the football match.

Before he left, David made a quick trip to the washroom to get rid of the dust and grime that had accumulated on his clothes and body—that gritty layer that only sun and sweat can lay down. As David went out to the waiting cab, he glanced back to see what the bartender was up to. *He didn't even leave the bar. I'm not in the clear yet; this could get ugly any minute.*

* * *

He had decided to stay at the Protea Golden Lodge in downtown Klerksdorp, but taking no chances, he had the cab drop him off on Barend Street, about two blocks from the Lodge.

The small, well-appointed lobby of the Protea felt cool to David after his walk in the searing summer sun. He was still tired and dirty, but at least he wasn't hungry.

A warning bell sounded in a small recess in the back of his mind. It was only a faint tinkle, but he had learned not to ignore it. The warning kept his inner temperature near boiling and his senses on edge. He could not shake it. It had met him at the airport, put bullet holes in the car he had abandoned, and stopped him on a main highway only because he was in the country to save Mandela from assassination. All seemed calm, but David had learned that just at the point where you seemed to be safe and free from an alert enemy, terror could strike—quickly and without warning.

The lobby was empty except for a well-dressed man who had his gaze fixed on the bodice of the tight suit the registration clerk wore over her sheer yellow blouse. He felt awfully exposed standing in the open, two yards behind the man who showed no signs of giving up his front row seat. "Ahem . . ." he cleared his throat without any apparent effect on the ogler.

At least the girl looked up from her computer screen. "Be with you in a moment, sir. This man needs to change his room, and we're having trouble finding one for him on the quiet side." To her visual assaulter, she said, "No, sir, we don't seem to have any second floor rooms at the back. I have an executive suite at the opposite end of the building from the bar. It's beside the conference rooms, but there's no convention right now, so it should be quiet."

"That'll be fine. Make sure I get it at the same price as my present room over the bar."

"No, sir. It will be twenty rand more per night."

David foresaw a long argument to prolong the visual contact the man had with the girl's bosom. "Excuse me. I need to be at a meeting by two. Do you have any rooms available?"

"Bloody well wait your turn, man. Who do you think you are?" David did not need any dispute; he needed to get out of the lobby.

David's appearance as a dusty farmer did not help to intimidate the self-important roué, but something made the man back off when David replied in his broken Afrikaans, "Sorry, mate, but I'm in a bit of a hurry. What is your cash deposit, miss?" It was the piercing eyes and tone that yielded the man's stance just long enough for the lady to answer.

"The deposit is 500 rand if you don't have a credit card, and yes, we have a few rooms left on the first floor." She placed a key on the counter and smiled. "We'll do the paperwork later."

The man moved aside, allowing David to plunk down the deposit and scoop up the key to room 127 with a lightly spoken, "Thanks, and sorry about butting in," as he dragged himself and his well-worn and dirty carry-on down the Hunter green carpeted hallway.

His room, like the lobby, was quietly decorated, the furniture and drapes a tasteful russet above teal carpet and checkered counterpane. After the bone-tiring activity David had been through since six that morning, the counterpane looked as welcome as a downy pillow. Without undressing, he flopped onto the bed. The exhaustion caused by intense physical activity, adrenaline, and emotional stress hurt behind his eyes. He fell asleep immediately.

David did not wake up until he heard the sound of a key being inserted into his door lock.

4

On the Monday morning after his meeting with Terbose, den Kamp was back in his plush office on the seventh floor of the SAPS headquarters building on Pretorious Brand Street. He sat in his burgundy leather high-backed swivel chair at the polished mahogany desk, hands pressed against the sides of his face. He had removed his gray silk suit jacket and rolled up his linen shirt sleeves. His work today had nothing to do with making the country safe for all its citizens.

He wondered if Terbose was too big a nut to send out alone to assassinate Mandela. Terbose had met with him dressed like a foppish Englishman but spoke and acted like an uneducated skinhead. There was no room for error. *Perhaps I should have had Henry keep an eye on Terbose and let Marion handle Henson.* He had to stop his thinking from going negative. *I'm just being paranoid.*

These thoughts were monopolizing his mind when he received a summons from the minister. *What does Bertel want and why didn't he just call me?* he thought as he shrugged on his jacket and started out to the minister's office on Church Square, three blocks away.

Parliament was not in session for the last six months of the year, so Crane Bertel, Minister of Safety and Security, was with his department heads in Pretoria. Den Kamp found it rather inconvenient having his boss so close. He enjoyed much more freedom to act from January to June, when the legislature was sitting in Cape Town and he could deal mainly with the minister's deputy and cabinet secretary.

* * *

Bertel's office was surprisingly plain considering the immense status that Safety and Security enjoyed in the new cabinet. Since free elections, crime and general unease had still not significantly abated. People—especially blacks—desperately needed jobs, housing, and clean water. They needed to move about, assemble, and enjoy their newfound freedom. It was Safety and Security that had been given the task of reducing a crime rate that was among the highest of developed nations.

The decor reflected the background of the man who had spent ten years of his life as commander of Umkhonto we Sizwe, Spear of the Nation, the ANC's guerrilla army. A plain blue wool twist carpet, matching drapes, and simple oak and fabric-covered chairs provided a quiet, businesslike atmosphere. Bertel gained his status through personal strength and self-confidence. He lived in a large home just outside Pretoria with his new wife and three youngsters—pleasures denied to him during his years underground—but needed no trappings to enhance his ego.

When den Kamp arrived, he flashed a smile at Bertel's gorgeous secretary. "How are you this morning, Jewel?"

'I'm fine, Mr. den Kamp. Would you like a cup of coffee?"

"That would be lovely. Is the boss in a hurry to see me?"

She got up and got a plain mug of coffee from the carafe in the corner. "He is, but there's always time to have a coffee. You just take one sugar, right?"

"Yes, thanks. We're certainly getting a lot of hot weather, aren't—" but before he could finish the sentence, Bertel shouted from his office, "Is den Kamp here yet?"

Jewel replied, "Yes, sir," and den Kamp nodded to her as he headed for the door.

As soon as den Kamp was seated in the straight-backed chair facing his desk, Bertel began, "I hear that the officer who murdered the major at Oudtshoorn has not been caught. What have you done to bring him to justice?"

"In spite of great efforts, my men have been unable to find him, minister."

"Tell me, do you think he would have been found guilty if we had brought him to trial?"

"I'm not sure. There was no direct evidence, only words overheard by a local councilor who said there was a strong disagreement between the two."

"So, he may not even have been found guilty?"

"He might have, but without a proper trial, sir, I can only speculate on the outcome." Den Kamp knew that fifteen years ago he would have been found innocent. "He may have left the country to evade my efforts to apprehend him."

"That is possible, but I want you to renew your efforts to find him. He needs to be brought before the Truth and Reconciliation Commission.

We can't let such men kill innocent officers and get away with it. If you need more resources to find him, let me know."

"I will try, minister."

"Do not try! Do it! He has been free for too long. This is a major mark against us!" Bertel thundered, banging his fist on the desk and making the coffee cups jump. He was tired of hearing his subordinates say they would *try* to make Truth and Reconciliation work. "I want action!"

Den Kamp's face reddened and his jaw clenched. He straightened his back, leapt out of his chair, turned, and strode toward the door.

"Den Kamp!"

"Yes, sir?"

"Your opposite number will be contacting you. It is imperative you meet with him."

Why did Arnold Graham want to talk to him, and why send him the message through Bertel? *Last thing I need is Bertel poking his nose into my business!* thought den Kamp.

* * *

Den Kamp and Arnold Graham stood on opposite sides of the racial supremacy issue. Graham arrived at his present, powerful position as deputy director of security through academia. He had been teaching military history at Witwatersrand University before being hired by Bertel five years ago. Den Kamp resented the fact that Arnold had little operational experience in security or intelligence and that he was an antiracist liberal, but he coveted his keen mind and highbrow social connections.

Arriving back in his office, den Kamp started to plot his next move.

"Get Graham on the phone."

"Yes, sir. Should I contact him on his desk phone or—"

"Just get him on the phone!"

Den Kamp shut his door with such force that the sound emitted through the entire floor. Arnold was on the line before he reached his desk.

"Graham, you needed to speak with me?"

"Eugene, with the president's tour coming up there is much to discuss."

"I assure you, my department is taking every precaution necessary."

"Can we meet for lunch today, Eugene?"

"Certainly, Arnold, but what's the hurry? We have our regular meeting next week, and as I mentioned, we are on top of the plans for the president's tour."

"It's important, but I'd rather not talk on the phone."

"If that's the case, today is fine."

Graham was not as naive in operational matters as den Kamp thought. Since coming into his present position, Graham had developed very good working relationships with the South African Army, NATO, and other intelligence services throughout the West.

Recently, Graham had noticed strange happenings in den Kamp's department. A ministerial order to replace racist officers such as Wilhelm Bradoer, chief of police in Ventersdorp, had been ignored. While it was SAPS's responsibility to produce minutes of meetings between the two departments, records often failed to show certain information, and that reflected poorly on the various police forces charged with enforcing the dictates of the Truth and Reconciliation commission. He realized that a head-on approach would just make den Kamp more cunning and deceitful. Den Kamp's force generally supported the Truth and Reconciliation commission, but there were still a few bad apples and Graham suspected his opposite number to be one of them.

Graham knew Minister Bertel would support him in weeding out resisters. To this end, he had secretly tasked Jon Mjaren, once a student of his and later a colleague at Witwatersrand, to keep his ear to the ground— or more specifically, to Den Kamp's door.

Mjaren had been a token, a black administrative assistant, on den Kamp's personal staff for the past five years. During Mandela's years in prison, Mjaren had worked tirelessly as liaison between the ANC and liberal elements at Witwatersrand and had been a faithful follower of Mandela and Bertel since democratic elections were first called in 1994. At first, Mjaren had been suspicious of the overtures from his old professor, but Graham was very persuasive and much admired by his former student and colleague, and Mjaren found the call impossible to refuse. He was well aware of the problems that den Kamp had been making for the ANC.

It was dangerous work; timing was important. The release of information had to follow an event that was fairly public. More people than Mjaren had to know about it so that a direct link between himself and the leak could not be established by den Kamp. Most information transfer was done during quiet weekend meetings between Mjaren and Graham. This morning, Jon had reported the possible assassination of the president. He felt he could not wait until the weekend and risked a call from a pay phone near his home on the way to work.

* * *

The Chez Patrice was famous for the French cuisine both men preferred when they had a chance to dine at government expense. Graham had made the arrangements. Their table was secluded, and the waiter seemed somehow familiar to den Kamp as he took their wine order. After a meal of pate de foie gras, vichyssoise, coq au vin, and crème caramel, all washed down with half liters of the appropriate Riesling, Sauvignon, and Merlot, the two men got down to business.

Den Kamp was anxious to find out what Graham was up to. "A wonderful lunch as usual for this little dime of a place. It's going on your expense budget, though. Now why all this mystery? Why couldn't it wait 'til next week's meeting?"

"I think there's a problem somewhere in your department…Wouldn't want that in an open meeting, would we? I didn't even want to discuss it on the phone."

"You sure? I personally screen all my headquarters staff…Of course we can never be sure what goes on in the back-veld can we?"

"It's not in the back-veld."

"You think one of my people is causing a problem? Don't tell me one of my staff is bending the Truth and Reconciliation rules or something as dire as that."

"No. Someone's plotting to kill our president."

"The hell you say! Where in God's name did you hear that?"

Den Kamp's feigned surprise threw Graham off for a moment. "You mean you've heard nothing?"

"Of course not…."

"Have you located this Louis Terbose?"

"As to this point he has eluded all of our efforts to detain him. What's he got to do with this?"

"I don't know. Let me tell you what I heard. As you know, the president will be making a series of speeches in the Free State and Northwest in December."

"Yes, yes. As I said on the phone, we're all set for that."

53

"Well, I think Terbose is going to try to assassinate Mandela sometime during that tour."

"Where did you hear this?"

"One of my sources."

"That's outrageous. What in God's name are you doing with a source in my department? Do you have any evidence that Terbose is even in the area?"

"My source is not in your department." Since leaving academe and entering the secret world of espionage, Arnold had learned how to lie effectively.

"But you just said I had a problem in my department."

"Yes you do, but my source is external."

"What kind of bullshit is this?" Den Kamp always felt that attack was the best defense. "If you have information about my department, I want it and I want it now!"

"Keep your voice down, Eugene. People are starting to stare."

"So you're telling me…someone has told you that there is a plot to kill the president?"

"Yes, I think you better increase security for the fifteenth in Bloemfontein—and the rest of the tour while you're at it. Drag in all your right wing Neanderthals."

"Security has been increased; you don't need to tell me how to do my job. Who else knows about this?" Den Kamp now knew of at least one.

"Just me."

"And your source."

Graham nodded and hoped he hadn't said too much. He knew den Kamp was clever, but he had to shake him up so that he would perhaps give himself away.

"Leave it with me, Arnold. Thanks for the tip."

As the two men parted ways, den Kamp couldn't hold back his growing hatred of Graham. *If Graham knew of my involvement, he wouldn't have approached me with this. Or does he know and is trying moving his chess pieces to lock me in a checkmate? To bring down Dominance? How the hell would he know about Dominance?*

Arnold took a leisurely stroll back to his office. The beauty of the capital was not lost on him. Spring sunshine, the blossoming jacarandas, and beds of yellow and orange tulips contrasted sharply with the evil he suspected was being plotted in the elegant dining room ahead of him.

Den Kamp took a cab back to his office. He was in such a hurry, the beauty of the season passed unnoticed by him. His thoughts were of much darker things. *It was obviously Graham who set the minister on him that morning.* There was also the ultimate concern—if the rumored leak was exposed in his outfit, Dieter would have a fit. Den Kamp had three choices. He could warn Bertel, leak a story to counteract Graham's, or forget about it and let the thing play out. If he warned Bertel, the minister would probably call out so much security that Terbose would never get to Mandela. He might even cancel the tour. But if he did nothing, Graham could blow the whistle and Dominance might be exposed. Den Kamp decided he'd better get to work on a story.

* * *

It was a hot day in Pretoria. The late spring swelter was cooking the jacaranda blossoms off their colorful perches. Church Square was nearly deserted as the two men strolled in quiet conversation. The importance of their words mirrored the beautifully manicured lawns, the magnificent sandstone Raddsaal, the Palace of Justice, and the dominating presence of the ten-meter statue of Paul Kruger, hero of the Boer War. The only clue that this was not a simple lunchtime chat between two friends was the unassuming presence of two powerfully built, well-dressed men who followed the pair at a discrete distance.

Crane Bertel was a leader. Just one look into his eyes revealed his power. His performance as head of the ANC underground army and support of the political aims of Mandela for the last ten years of Mandela's imprisonment had been rewarded with the Safety and Security portfolio in Mandela's first freely elected government. Bertel was a large, athletic man— over six feet tall and weighing 250 pounds, very little of which was fat. He thrived on eighteen-hour days and was loyal and tireless in his defense of the conciliatory approach being taken by the ANC, but God help those who broke trust with this determined giant. He could become an implacable enemy for those who failed to clear the bar he set for conduct in his Ministry.

Bertel's immediate concern was that three weeks had passed since he had ordered den Kamp to find Terbose. There had been no report. "You took precautions to make sure your chief has no idea we are speaking?"

"Yes, sir. Den Kamp's in Jo'burg for a couple of days. His secretary thinks I'm home for lunch."

"Good, I don't wish to put you in danger, but this is too important to discuss on the phone. Arnold told me this morning that you called him yesterday. I wanted to get the information firsthand. I am concerned for our president's safety. Your superior has done little to find this Terbose and bring him to justice."

"I overheard a few conversations in the office about how the Brotherhood considered Terbose a folk hero. I didn't want to expose myself by making charges through normal channels."

"That was wise. It seems den Kamp is doing all he can to ensure Terbose is not caught. What's going on?" The minister's eyes flashed. He sensed den Kamp was up to something and wanted Mjaren to confirm it.

"I'm not sure. What I fear is that the Brotherhood plans to assassinate the president during his tour through the Free State."

"Do you have proof?"

"No, just talk in the office. Assumptions I have made from overhearing scraps of his conversations. Nothing definite, sir."

"The visit to Bloemfontein will be well covered?"

"Of course. The local police will be out in full force, but there is still a chance a man like Terbose could slip through. He has shown himself to be quite elusive. But why do you think the attempt will be made in Bloemfontein?"

"Thirty years of experience—and a conversation with an evasive den Kamp three weeks ago—make me sure something is going to happen; if not at Bloemfontein, then sometime during the tour." Bertel anticipated Mjaren's next question. "The president is adamant about making the visits, even over my warnings. Nelson is a brave man."

"We will do all we can. Most of the staff is loyal."

"I think we need to call in outside help, but I don't wish my name associated with the call."

"You can't mean the CIA—or another African agency. We can't trust them." Both men recalled the CIA had sided with Inkatha against them.

When the minister had set up their meeting, Jon had assumed he merely needed to mention the threat and the tour would be cancelled. He was now becoming concerned about his president's safety. It emboldened his speech.

"I have an acquaintance in Harare," continued Bertel. "He's ex-BOSS and can find someone to assassinate Terbose, if you need it."

"I thought we had given up killing those who oppose us and threaten the party, sir."

"We have. Hopefully Terbose, or whoever is responsible, can be apprehended without violence. The party does not want to be involved. As you say, we have given up violent methods, and killing a Brother would put us in a very bad light. We may need someone we can trust to help find Terbose—someone who has no association with the Party."

"Do you really believe that we are not capable of protecting our president?" Jon asked defensively. "He is so popular with the people. Surely the Brotherhood, even this elusive Terbose, would not be able to get near enough to kill him."

"Terbose killed the major at Oudtshoorn from over three hundred meters. There are many hiding places in and around Free State Stadium. He need reveal himself for only an instant. I don't doubt your department's ability, but the old regime still has friends willing to hide him. Some officers would still rejoice that the enemies of peaceful reconciliation struck a blow for the racism of the past. Think a minute. Can you afford not to ask for help?"

"How do I get in touch with this man from Harare, sir?"

"I have written the details on this card. Destroy it before returning to the office. Den Kamp would like nothing better than to know the name on it."

"I will call him, sir. Who should be his contact?"

"Ensure it is no one in the ANC."

"I will make sure the party is not involved, but I will not act myself."

"Why not?"

"I have no concern for my own safety, but there would be a great risk to the party if we were exposed."

"You're probably right. Perhaps it would be better if the agent acted alone. Then no one would risk being exposed." This plotting reminded Bertel of his days in the underground. It would be enjoyable if not for the danger to the president.

"Can you not remove den Kamp, minister? He seems to be the one working against us."

"I could, but that would not stop the Brotherhood. It would also make us appear arbitrary. Den Kamp has many friends and an excellent record. Removing him could stir unrest inside his force. You would like his job, wouldn't you?" The minister laughed. It was rare he did so these days. So many vestiges of the old racism remained to be eliminated. So much of the force, including the Chief, hated the fact that they reported to a black minister.

The minister sighed. His task of turning the Department of Safety and Security into a force for protecting, rather than repressing the citizens of South Africa, was proving more daunting than he had originally thought in 1994, when Nelson Mandela first approached him to run this most difficult of ministries.

5

Grant Weldman represented the CIA at the Counter Terrorism Center. It was not a popular post for intelligence agents. Most preferred to gather intelligence, infiltrate terrorist organizations, and catch spies without interacting with other agencies. As a newly appointed manager at the bottom of the executive food chain, the role of CTC representative fell to him.

Grant felt deeply for the problems facing agents operating alone and unsupported in foreign locations, not least because of their importance; in his view, input from field operatives was more critical in uncovering and preventing a terrorist threat than any computer analysis.

It was a brilliant Saturday morning. Saturday seemed to be the only time Grant could get his head out of the mass of paperwork his position required. The maples and birches were painting the well-trimmed lawns with brilliant reds and yellows. He leisurely strolled to the Pickle Factory, as it was less-than-fondly called by its inhabitants. It was 7:00 a.m. and he had left his car in a lot a half-mile from the entrance in order to enjoy the cool November sunshine. A slight breeze flapped at his London Fog topcoat as he pulled it back to get the coded pass out of his inside pocket.

He had recently made an ugly discovery. A threat to international security that, until now, had only existed as a suspicion in David's and Grant's minds, had proven serious. As soon as Grant entered the office, he took off his coat and jacket and hurried down the hall to find his CTC boss.

"Come in, Grant," came the answer from the office of Francis Edwards, the Center's chief, when Grant rapped firmly on the door. The view of the maple scattered lawns from the window was so magnificent that Edwards could not stand the distraction. Important things happened inside, not outside, the office. He kept his expensive oak desk angled toward the door. "I see you're still on about this new terrorist organization." He was reading from a memo Grant had left on his desk Friday afternoon. "Nobody has ever heard of them."

"Don't you mean nobody in Washington?"

"I mean just what I said. I had NSA run the name through their intercept files. They drew a blank. That means that this group doesn't communicate with one another, so how can it be a threat?" The NSA was the federal government's communication monitoring watchdog and, in theory, should have caught any communication between members of a group such as this.

"Maybe they communicate in person or by mail. Maybe they have developed a radio system that NSA can't monitor, maybe—"

"—And maybe pigs can fly. Our people came up blank in our own computers too, so I really can't see why you keep insisting this organization exists. The FBI had nothing either, but that doesn't mean much. They have trouble finding their backsides with both hands."

"Just because we are not aware of an organization, doesn't mean it doesn't exist." Grant paused. "I think that's a double negative," he said with a laugh. "These guys have been working under strict silence, and that only shows their true strengths."

Edwards was not laughing. "What makes you think this outfit is a threat to us? If a name did not show up in the records of the NSA, it should not exist."

"I talked to one of my agents who was in Germany last week."

"Which one?"

"Sorry, sir. This one's a secret."

"What do you mean a secret?"

"I've never let anyone know who he is."

"But I should know." Edwards was used to Grant's evasiveness about David Reasons's identity, but the fact that he had been unable to wheedle the name out of his subordinate still rankled.

"No, sir. There's a leak somewhere in our organization, and I will not tell anyone my source's name."

"Damn conspiracy theories. What makes you think there's a leak?"

"For one thing, somebody tipped off David Koresh that we were going into his compound."

"Shit, that was years ago. And we're not sure he was even tipped off."

"I'm sure."

"Never mind the past. What did this *secret agent* of yours say?"

"He overheard two men talking in the bar at the Frankfurter Hof. We had a conference there in '93 with NATO."

"I remember."

"My agent was following a Belgian who had shown a great deal of interest in moving some electronic components over here without having to clear customs. The guy claimed detonators and fusing mechanisms produced in his country were a generation ahead of anything in the States."

"Where does this Dominance fit into that?"

"I'm coming to that in a minute. I just thought you'd be interested in this upgrade in bomb technology that could be coming in."

"Have you let Curstan over at FBI know?"

"Yeah. He didn't seem too interested. I thought I might bring it up at the next staff meeting. Get everybody revved up."

"For Christ's sake, don't do that. I'll get on it." Edwards looked back down at his notes. "Now, about that Dominion outfit..."

"My agent heard the other guy say he could arrange a slip through Customs. Then he started talking about a new terrorist organization from Germany."

"This isn't just the Baader-Meinhof going active again, is it?"

"No. My source thinks it's much bigger than that."

"You think there's a connection between the bomb threat and this organization?"

"Hard to say. The funny thing was his reaction when the other guy made the same connection you just did. He damn near went over the table. Told him to mind his own business or someone high up would take him out."

"So this new organization is called Dominion?"

"*Dominance…*"

* * *

Heinz Volmar, Dieter's father, had made his fortune rebuilding commercial property destroyed by the Allies. In countries whose infrastructures had been devastated during World War II, reconstruction was a lucrative business. Financing these developments were sales of a considerable number of French and Italian art pieces to various private collectors throughout the world—those who did not ask too many questions concerning their provenance. Heinz obtained these pieces as a thirty-year-old colonel acting as Herman Goring's aide-de-camp in the final days of Germany's destruction.

When money had bought him all the material things he had wanted, Heinz was still not satisfied with his life. He realized power was his true desire, so he turned to politics. By the mid-1980s, he had reached the pinnacle of his second career—Minister for Economic Development—although it was with some regret that he realized he would never become the most powerful politician in Germany. His somewhat plebeian upbringing and known association with the Nazi party prevented him from ever attaining the post of chancellor.

At that point in his life, Heinz turned his considerable energy to a third career—the acquisition of real power. He had never ascribed to the platitude that power derives from "the people." That was a myth perpetrated by dictators, democratically appointed or otherwise. Power came from the ability to wield personal influence over others—to bring them around to your way of thinking and control both their minds and their actions. To manipulate the masses is to be master of power in all its forms: militaristic, economic, and political.

Hitler had real power. Through fear and intimidation, he controlled the German mentality. Few were able to resist the strength of his personality. Heinz Volmar had admired the Führer greatly, but he wanted to maintain the power that eventually slipped through Hitler's grasp—keep it, relish it, and pass it on to his son.

The road to that power came—if the terrorist credo were to be believed—from the "barrel of a gun." Governments do not surrender power by choice. They only do so when overthrown. This was the basis for Heinz's theory of world domination. He would control strong leaders in powerful countries, mold them to his way of thinking, and use them to develop a terrorist organization like none the world had ever seen. Hitler had been defeated because he tried a frontal assault on too many enemies. Heinz would mount his assault from within, one country at a time.

Heinz was shrewd enough to appreciate the impact of a few terrorists. In small, concentrated cells, the Palestine Liberation Organization had spread fear in the eastern Mediterranean and much of Europe. The 1972 Olympic massacre was a brilliant example of the ability of a small group of well-organized fanatics to wield power over his country.

Heinz had watched various minor terrorist movements in several countries grow and die according to their quality of leadership. Public acts of terrorism tended to mean the end of these groups, and Heinz began to realize that these organizations failed due to their lack of coordination. They simply did not think on a large enough scale. The Baader-Meinhof, Red Army Faction, Neo-Nazis, KKK, Aryan Nations, and a number of others were all regarded as simply a lunatic fringe. They needed to grow, to amass resources, and to train and organize until they were in a position to do something on a grand scale.

They also needed a higher level of leadership, and Heinz Volmar had answered.

Heinz had also learned that high-ranking and ambitious government mandarins were generally frustrated by their lack of any real authority. Power tended to gravitate to strong political centers: Bonn, Washington, Paris, and Rome. Those outside the presidential or prime ministerial circles, who felt there might be a better way to achieve national goals, tended to go unnoticed.

By late 1990, Heinz had seduced powerful, disgruntled bureaucrats in NATO countries, and many others in the Middle East, to his way of thinking. Through them, he controlled small but strong and growing groups of well-trained and highly motivated terrorists. He was also severely crippled with emphysema, confined to a wheelchair, and mechanically given oxygen.

For the past five years, since his son had comfortably wielded leadership qualities as Executive Vice-President of Renaissance Developments, Heinz had been teaching Dieter to be a leader of Dominance as well. Dieter was an apt pupil. He loved to dominate people, especially women, but Heinz taught him to dominate men as well—to control their thinking and seduce them into wanting greater glory. The conversion of his son was another remarkable achievement for a man whose life had been full of achievement. He had only had custody over Dieter since he'd turned fourteen, an age when most parents start losing control of their offspring.

Dieter had been born and raised in a whorehouse in Baden. Until Dieter reached puberty, Heinz was not aware of his son's existence. Heinz had a loveless marriage and little time or interest in returning it to normalcy. He preferred to visit Elsa Ramsfeld, an alcoholic prostitute at one of the many houses near the Kurhaus in Baden. Dieter grew up to be extremely handsome, pampered, and spoiled. He was smothered constantly with love and affection by attractive ladies. After his father discovered him, Dieter learned a taste for power as well as for feminine affection.

As Dieter grew in both Renaissance Developments and Dominance, he was able to convince his father to test the mettle of the Dominance leaders. Except for a few minor operations, Heinz had been content to recruit and train, waiting for the time when his groups were strong enough to take on a large and effective operation.

Dieter had recruited Eugene den Kamp on his own. Heinz had been so delighted with this find that he allowed his son to run a couple of small operations, even though the South African group was not fully integrated into the Dominance structure.

6

David's father and mother, Ted Reasons and Edna Mason, met during registration the Tuesday before classes started for their first year in medical school at Ohio State University. They married surreptitiously three weeks later.

David was born into a dingy but happy world. The rooming house held seven students, some with small families. They all took turns minding each other's offspring. David learned to be flexible, using different ploys to get what he wanted from each surrogate caregiver. The constant impact of clever and inquiring young minds hardly produced a deprived environment despite the poverty and their occasional bouts of hunger pangs. It seemed that one friend or another was always available to take David for a stroll around the Oval, to feed the ducks at Mirror Lake, or to wrestle on the manicured lawns of the campus. But among the beautiful, ancient brick and stone buildings and the stately oak and beech trees of the campus, David learned to forget the poverty at Chittenden Street.

One Saturday night, three-year-old David sat in a warm bath. Mr. Wack and Turk Turtle bobbed precariously as he scooped handfuls of soapy water over his flattened curls. He loved the feeling as it flowed over his chest and back.

Edna and Ted were at the library. They went there almost every night. Final exams were fast approaching. In Ted and Edna's cases, these were the final, final exams. Both had been accepted into residencies at the Medical Center. Janet Marsden, who shared the third floor with the Reasons and had been charged with David, had left to answer the phone in the downstairs hall. David did not notice how long she had been gone. He loved his bath.

"You look funny, 'Nett." David smiled as his favorite sitter squatted, her eyes red and knuckles white where they grasped the side of the yellowing tub. "Can I stay in tub? Getting cold."

"Oh, David."

"It's a'right, 'Nett. Don' cry."

"David, dear little David," she sputtered.

"When Mommy and Daddy be back?"

On their way home, David's parents had been killed by a drunk driver.

"Come, dear. We'll get dry now and go to bed."

"No go bed. Wait Mommy, Daddy." He started to cry and shake.

It took Janet an hour of cuddling and soothing to get David to sleep. Then she had to make the dreaded phone call. She knew the Reasons had disowned their son, Ted, but she had to deliver the sad news to his parents and Edna's.

Sam Reasons, Ted's father, took over David's upbringing. Edna's parents were no match for Sam in the struggle for control of their grandson. David grew up under the same vicious discipline that had alienated his father. There were no more walks on the common or ducks at Mirror Lake. Life became harsh. He loved his Grandma Grace. They played together and she read to him when Sam was away at work—*Winnie the Pooh* and *Wind in the Willows* were his favorites—but the stress of trying to protect her grandson from the same verbal and physical assaults that had been meted out to his father by her husband were too much for her.

After Grandma Reasons died, Sam remarried within six months. His new wife, Elinor, quickly convinced Sam that the only place for David was the Virginia Military Academy, an institution that had done wonders in bringing a semblance of order to the life of her younger brother. David was happy to get away.

He discovered that life at the academy was preferable to that at home. He had a rigid schedule and tough academics and discipline, but all the cadets received the same treatment. In his years living with his grandparents, he found that none of his school friends were singled out for the same discipline as he had been by Sam. When he was tired or upset because he had been punished for not dusting the top of his wardrobe, it was nice to remember that his roommate would receive the same punishment for not having his boots shined to the proper luster.

The strong discipline allowed him to develop attitudes and strengths that he hoped he could use one day to wreak retribution on his abusive grandfather. Even after being away from the tyrant for three years, David despised him so much that he wanted to do him physical injury.

David graduated from the academy with a three-point-eight grade point average—enough to get him into Michigan's business school. His grandfather was quite happy to pay for his schooling and separate accommodations, but David hated to be dependent on them for anything and applied to get into the ROTC education program. He was accepted just before his first year and felt overjoyed when he called his grandfather to tell him what he could do with his money.

After completing college at Michigan and basic infantry officer training at Fort Benning, David began regular army life as a lieutenant in General Wayman's headquarters in Saigon. His commanding officer was Colonel Manley, director of planning. The first job Manley assigned him after he had finished his "in routine" was to make sure senior staff had prepared a plan for an attack on the village of Dak Kon in accordance with divisional directives. The attack was designed to prevent the Cong from interfering with the Vietnamese breaking siege at An Loc. Though he was fresh out of school with no combat experience, David's ROTC training told him that the plan was terribly flawed. He headed for Manley's office.

"Colonel," David started after being invited into his commander's air-conditioned office, "I think the staff has made some mistakes in preparing these plans."

"Really, lieutenant, and what makes you an expert on military operations?" Manley responded sarcastically.

"Well, sir, there's no reinforcement plan, no air or artillery support, and the enemy strength has been underestimated. And the plan calls for a daylight approach. The attacking force will be cut to pieces before they even reach the town."

"That's quite a mouthful from someone with only a few weeks in theater. Besides, it sounds as if it was prepared to my precise instructions."

"But, sir," David objected, "those men don't stand a chance."

"You were to review the plan for form, not content, Reasons." Colonel Manley disliked being told about his apparent lack of knowledge by a young lieutenant. "Get out."

"Yes, sir." David saluted, turned, and left. He didn't leave it at that, though. Someone with operational experience would take a hard look at these plans.

David next visited the office of Lieutenant Grant Weldman, who worked in Intelligence. Grant had made David feel welcome to Saigon when he had first arrived, and they had formed a sort of kinship through work and social activities at the officers' club.

"Grant, I wonder if you would take a look at the plans for the attack on Dak Kon." David pushed the Top Secret folder across the desk.

"I saw an earlier draft, David, and prepared a reply to Manley for my colonel. Didn't you see it?"

"No, I just came from Manley's office. He reamed me for telling him how stupid his plan was. He didn't mention your memo. Tried to make me look like a fool for questioning him."

"You're not a fool, my friend. We told Manley about the force level, timing, and support problems. I'm sure he won't try to sell it to Brigade."

"I think he plans to. Shouldn't we do something to stop him?"

"Pretty hard to do without sacrificing your career. If you knew someone at 3rd Brigade who wouldn't drop you in it, you might get away with it." Grant might have been a friend, but with a wife and two little ones back home, he was reluctant to take on a full colonel. "My suggestion, though, is that you forget it. General Marks at Brigade will see it for what it's worth and send it back to Manley for reworking."

David took his friend's advice but kept his eye on the Op Orders that routinely came through Planning. He wanted to make sure a disaster at Dak Kon was avoided. To his dismay, two days later, General Marks's helicopter was shot down while he was doing a personal recon of the Dak Kon area. David wondered if the general might have had it out with

Manley, then gone to the front to reconnoiter the situation in person. Two days later, Marks's 2IC, Colonel Braddock, sent though the Op Order exactly as Manley had planned. David felt the need to do something, and it looked as if that something would land him in trouble—perhaps even end his career before it began.

First, he went to see Manley at his office. The colonel made him cool his heels for ten minutes before calling out, "Well, lieutenant, what do you want this time? I hope it's not about the Dak Kon plans."

"It is, sir."

"Oh, for Christ's sake. Same old story, or do you have something new?"

"Sir, I still believe reinforcements and both air and artillery support are needed."

"Listen, lieutenant, I've had enough of this from you. First, the attack goes ahead as planned, and second, you can expect transfer orders out of planning as soon as I can get to it."

It took three phone calls to Craddock's HQ for David to finally find a lieutenant who would talk to him about Dak Kon, and he went to meet him at Brigade HQ in Pleiku. The lieutenant didn't want to talk around the office, so the two of them took a walk up a jungle trail.

"Is there any way I can convince you to try to get the colonel to change his mind about the attack?" David asked.

"Why would he change his mind? We're all gung ho about it. Going to kick some ass."

"But there's not enough support. You guys may get your ass kicked."

"Come on! There's always risks. You know Braddock's new. He'd jump down my throat if I tried to stop him. Christ, I'm only a louey."

David realized this wasn't going to work. Maybe his only option would be to openly challenge his superiors in public—and in print. Then he got an idea. If he couldn't change his superiors' minds, perhaps he could change the enemy's.

"Colonel Manley, could I have a word with you?" David asked, sticking his head in the boss's door.

"As long as it's not about the Dak Kon attack, or you staying in Planning," was the gruff reply.

"No, sir, I was wondering if I could take a week off, considering I have to leave anyway."

"Sure, I'll let you know where you're posted when you get back."

"Thank you, sir." David saluted and left.

The next stop was Stores. He convinced the supply sergeant that he was being posted to the 3rd Brigade, and was issued full battle gear. Then he scrounged some face and body paint and a few other items that were not in the kit.

The next part was a bit tricky. He needed some detailed maps of the Dak Kon area and transportation to get there. It was Friday afternoon—the attack was scheduled for the following Wednesday—and Dak Kon was three hundred miles from Saigon. By 3:00 p.m., he was sitting in Grant's office.

"Grant, can we have another look at those Dak Kon plans?" David asked. "Maybe the colonels are right. We haven't seen the area."

"David, you're just like a dog with a bone. Can't you leave this thing alone?" Weldman chuckled. "I looked at the plans and the detailed maps of the area when I sent the memo to Planning, and there's no way the thing is going to work."

75

"Maybe I could look at them again," David pleaded. "I know Manley and Braddock think they can do it. Maybe I can ease my conscience if I have one more look at the maps. Besides, I'm leaving Planning—Manley tossed me out—so I'm not even involved anymore."

"Okay, David, but only because you're a friend. The folder's in the top drawer. Make sure you put it back and lock the cabinet when you leave. I'm going now. Got some errands to run before five."

The final requirement, a jeep for the journey, was simple. He merely used the same excuse on the transport compound's master sergeant he had used on the stores sergeant, promising to return the vehicle after he was moved. The transport staff was not too worried about losing one jeep.

The attack at Dak Kon went off without a hitch. Braddock and Manley never truly understood why. The only clues were a very worn and unreadable copy of the Op Order taken from a Cong colonel captured in the attack, a jeep that was found to have two bullet holes near the spare Jerry gas can during its next inspection, and a very tired young lieutenant, who required an extra day of leave before reporting to his new post in Intelligence. Braddock and Manley were too egotistical about their own success to ever think that they might have received external assistance. The battalion commander was too flushed with victory to wonder how they trapped the enemy from the rear with his artillery aimed in the wrong direction. Only Grant Weldman remembered the events of the previous Friday afternoon and understood their significance. David Reasons had thwarted the efforts of a conniving authority figure. His career as an anti-terrorist had been launched.

7

Forty-five minutes after they left Johannesburg International, Henry Jackman and Marion Aflect were uncomfortably seated in the rich brocade armchairs facing the large mahogany desk of the chief of the South African Police Services. Marion kept crossing her left leg over her right, then reversing the process. Her left hand hurt and the restless leg movements seemed to make it feel better, but the accompanying view was distracting to Henry. He nervously stroked his moustache and smoothed back his hair with his left hand. "Sir, will you give me that file on Henson?"

"Why? And why did you miss Henson at the airport?" Den Kamp slammed down the file in front of Henry. "Are you really into this operation, or do you think it's just a game? Now I have to call Volmar and tell him we screwed up. If he ever comes down here, you'll find out it's not a game."

Henry opened the file on his lap. "I'm sorry, boss, but how were we to know Henson would use a decoy? Who told you what Henson's name would be and what he would look like? I think the screw-up might have started in Frankfurt."

"You two are supposed to be trained for this shit. *You should have spotted the difference!* I don't give a damn where it started, it's still happening and we are the ones who'll pay if he finds Terbose."

"Should we warn Louis?" Marion asked. The file in Henry's lap was making her forget the pain in her hand.

"On the tenth, Louis was going to ground in Bloemfontein and no one was to know where he was. There's a leak somewhere. That's why I told Louis not to let anyone know where he was—not even me. Christ, now Henson and the ANC will be after him."

"We'd better get on our way." Henry wanted to catch Henson and needed to get away from his irate superior.

"Not so fast. I have some good news, too. Piet Neiderhof is joining us in Dominance."

"When did this happen?" Marion asked. "I knew you had talked to him, but thought he wasn't interested."

"While you two were on your way to Jo'burg this morning, he called to say he had changed his mind and would like to join us. I told him about Henson, and he agreed to take the Kimberley–Klerksdorp route to get here. That's the way I suspected Henson would take to Bloemfontein. I was right. Piet found Henson between Klerksdorp and Jo'burg."

"You mean he has him in custody?" Henry could see the glory slipping away.

"No. Henson shot him in the leg."

"Christ, that's not a good start." Marion was sympathetic.

"Oh, but it is. Do you know how badly he wants Henson now?"

Marion marveled at how callous her boss could be about someone's injury. "He'll be a great help in finding Henson. He can call out the whole Bloemfontein force. Henson also took out a cop and stole his gun. Piet was trying to help when he got shot."

"You mean he killed the policeman?"

"No, no, just knocked him out. Henson's dangerous and now he's armed. Better get him in Klerksdorp before he gets to Bloemfontein. He'll probably disguise himself as soon as he gets there."

"We're on our way," Henry responded. He was ready to go. Renewed contact with the target and thoughts of getting back into action had reinvigorated him.

"Good. Get the police looking for him, but I want you two to find him first. We now have a good excuse to pick him up. The locals can't know why we want him and why I'm interested. Think about a cover story for them on the way."

Marion was a bit worried. "Maybe we shouldn't even let the local police know we are coming, Eugene. They may ask too many questions."

"If you contact the police, instead of me, it should keep down their curiosity. I'll leave it to you. By the way, Marion, do you still know anyone in the Harare police department?"

"Sure, why?"

"This whole episode has the trademark of Forest Burton stamped all over it. I'll bet he's the one who called in Henson. Get someone to keep an eye on him?"

"No problem, boss. Consider it done." They left their chief's office with renewed determination.

* * *

At home that evening, alone and confident of success, den Kamp carefully dialed Dieter's number on his encrypted phone. He had gained a new recruit who would be a great asset in controlling the police in Bloemfontein. Henson had been spotted and den Kamp's two lieutenants were hot on his trail and filled with enthusiasm.

Dieter Volmar was still in his office. He unlocked the noisy drawer, turned three knobs, and lifted the receiver. "Two here."

"Forty-seven. Good news. Today I recruited one of my police chiefs. He is hot after Henson."

"You're telling me you haven't caught him."

"No, he had an accomplice on the flight and changed his appearance."

"Fool. I should never have approved the operation."

Den Kamp was becoming hot. He wondered himself if he should have joined this egotist. "Your agent should have noticed the subterfuge. He failed to mention an accomplice."

"Find him, Forty-seven, or he will ruin your action. When you do, I want to be involved in his demise. Don't blame others for your shortcomings."

Den Kamp slammed down the receiver.

8

Marion returned to her office and called to Henry as she shut the door, "I'll set up that tail on Burton. Just be a minute. Meet you at the car." She made a quick phone call to an old flame in Harare whom she had enchanted during their two-week vacation in Madagascar last summer. After assuring her he would keep an eye on Forest Burton and any other person who might interfere with her activities, Marion hung up and headed for the underground garage

"Okay, Henry, where do we start?" Her hand felt better when she rested the arm on the back of Henry's seat. As they sped out of Pretoria, she gently curled his dark hair around her forefinger.

"It looks like Henson was staying off the main road. Like the boss said, he's probably headed for Klerksdorp. We should start there." He desperately needed to find a place to assuage the terrible tension he felt building. Keeping the car in the lane was becoming problematic. A patch of grass behind some aloe bushes just off the road near Krugersdorp served to take the edge off until they reached a motel in Klerksdorp.

* * *

The Blossom Motel proved to be a much more comfortable place to renew their enterprise. As he roused himself and started to pull on his working clothes, which in his case consisted of a one-thousand-rand gray suit, white shirt, and maroon and gray striped tie, Henry asked rhetorically, "Where would he hide?" Henry had two reasons to get out of bed and dressed. First was his strong desire to be the one who captured Henson, and second was his desperate need to get away from the sexual appetite of his companion. He knew if he remained under that spell, they'd never catch Henson.

"If I were him, I would find a cheap motel, rest, disguise myself, then move on to Bloemfontein. He has no reason to stay here." Marion rolled onto one elbow, letting the sheet fall away from her left breast. The sight nearly made Henry forget his newfound resolve.

"We could search for the Fiat."

"If he still has it." His cell phone rang. "Jackman," Henry growled as he snatched it up and flipped it open after the first ring.

"Den Kamp, Henry. The Klerksdorp police just found Henson's Fiat in a ravine, about five klicks north of there. Is Marion there?"

"No, sir," he lied, "but I can get her."

"Never mind. Just get that bastard Henson."

Henry flipped the phone shut and turned to Marion.

"Let's start with the motels."

"I wonder how den Kamp found out about the Fiat. He must have alerted all the police forces between Jo'burg and Bloemfontein to be on the lookout. I thought that was to be our job."

"At least we know Henson's here."

"Shit, Marion. Do you know how many hotels and motels there are in this city?"

"Not that many. We better get busy. By the way, thanks for not giving us away to Eugene. He'd be mad if he knew."

"He probably knows anyway. Look, you use the room phone to call hotels. I'll use the cellular to cover car rentals. He'll need transport."

It took Marion fifteen calls to get to the Protea Hotel. When the clerk answered, she said, "Afternoon, did a man named Henson register today?"

"I'll check." After two minutes of silence, "I'm sorry, no one by that name is registered." The answer Marion expected.

"Have any foreigners registered today?"

"Oh, maybe. A guy came in and was in a hurry to get a room. Said he had a meeting. In fact he didn't even register yet."

"Thank you." She thought, *Henry, we got him.*

* * *

At the sound of the key in his hotel room door, David leapt from the bed and positioned himself against the wall beside the door so that the intruder would not see him when he opened it.

When Henry entered David's room, he noticed that the bed was empty. He went straight to the open balcony door, opened it, and looked out. David knew he could not escape without disabling his adversary. Backup no doubt lurked close by. Before Henry realized he should have given the room a good search before rushing to the window, David was on him—right hand hacking the wrist of his gun hand, left catching him full force in the neck. Henry went down. David rushed to the window and cut the drape cord with his pocketknife. He tied up Henry tightly and left him bound—hands behind his back and feet connected to them.

David wondered where the man's backup was as he raced from the room. *He couldn't be alone, could he?* He flattened himself into a doorway down the hall from where the back stairs were located. He heard a door smash open ten seconds later from down the hall. He did not see who rushed to his room as he slid along the wall toward the stairs that Marion had just left.

* * *

Henry came to with a sore neck and drape cord expertly binding his limbs. He could not move a muscle. He could not even shout. A pillowcase was tied across his mouth. *Where the hell is Marion?* The answer came in a hammering on the door.

Marion had to stifle a laugh when she finally got in and saw him. Her frivolity was short lived.

"What's so god-damn funny? You didn't do any better. I don't see Henson stretched out in the hall."

"You looked pretty funny, Henry, dear, trussed up like a turkey. We better get moving. Den Kamp will be really pissed if we miss him again."

"He's probably still in the hotel. All his stuff's here."

"You mean this crap. He'll just leave it." Marion turned the dirty carry-on out on the bed and came up with two pairs of beige socks, the same quantity of gray underwear, and a blue shirt.

"Okay, where do you think he's gone?"

"He needs a disguise. Let's check the chemists and department stores within walking distance."

Henry went to the washroom and threw cold water onto his face and neck. His neck hurt like hell. It felt like someone had turned his head around like Linda Blair's in *The Exorcist*. After five minutes of listening to Marion's calls to hurry up, the pain had begun to diminish. He straightened his suit and tie and joined Marion, and they rushed out to renew the search.

In ten minutes they were showing David's picture to Amelia Petra, cashier at Beardsley and Son, Chemists, on Margaretha-Prinsloo Street. "Yes, he was here but he left a few minutes ago. You must have seen him when you came in." Amelia looked toward the storeroom as she told the lie David had asked her to. He had relayed his sad tale about being chased by cops because they thought he was someone else. His haggard, handsome face and pleading tone, along with her long-standing mistrust of white police, moved her to David's support.

Marion caught her glance and raced down the twenty-meter aisle to a door marked "Employees Only." She was through just in time to hear the back door to the store open and slam. Her view was blocked by rows of well-stocked shelves.

Henry rushed after her, but she yelled, "Go back out the front door and check the main street. I'll cover the alley."

She raced down the row of stock, knocking over a towering stack of Revlon shampoo cases, yanked open the door, and cautiously stuck her head out. There was nothing in the alley but a dozen or so dust bins. She knew her enemy had a weapon and felt extremely exposed. Rather than risk being cornered at the end of the alley that was blocked by a two-meter chain link fence, she slowly backed out to the street, ten or so meters away. "Henry, have you seen him?" brought a response from around the corner.

"Not yet."

Together they cautiously entered the alley. "Maybe Henson is hiding inside one of the bins," Henry suggested when they got to the fence without sign of their quarry. The bins were those large green metal ones the garbage trucks pick up with long forks.

"Jesus, Henry, these bins smell awful."

"Yeah, and the garbage we're looking for probably smells bad too. At least it did when it hit me back at the hotel."

"And we will too in about three minutes." They failed to find their target, and they gave up after about ten minutes.

On his way out of the store, David picked up the three packages she had kept hidden for him under the counter. On his hurried way out he told the clerk, "If the police come back, just tell them I threatened you with a gun. They aren't nice police. You understand?"

"I sure know. There aren't too many nice police nowadays...."

Two minutes after David left, Henry and Marion were back at the counter. "Where did he go?" Henry was standing with his nose about an inch from her face. She bent backward over the waist-high counter, forcing the lower portion of their bodies into contact.

"I don't know. He said he was going back to the hotel."

"That's a lie."

"No. That's what he said."

"YOU'RE LYING! I DONT HAVE TIME FOR YOUR GAMES!"

She began to sob. "He went to the right out of the store. But I don't know where he went, just that he told me he had a gun."

He would have been foolish to tell her. "Well, *miss*, if you can't tell us where he went, tell us what he looked like. No lying this time or we'll take you to the station and book you for obstruction."

The girl began to sob. "For Christ's sake, stop sniveling. What does he look like?" Henry had not seen the man who had cold-cocked him at the hotel.

Marion struck the countertop. "We mean now!"

"He had reddish brown hair, a dirty gray shirt, and brown pants, I think."

"You have to do better than that. How tall was he?" Marion demanded.

The girl nervously looked from one to the other. She pointed to Henry and then Marion. "He was a lot shorter than you," she sniffed, "about the same as you."

"That's better. Was he light, or heavy?" Marion knew they were now getting the right answers. With about two more questions they had a pretty good description of David.

"It looks like he is headed back to the Protea," Henry said after they left the girl.

"Why do you think that?"

"It's in the direction the girl gave us."

"And why do you think she's now telling the truth?"

"She knows we're police."

"You didn't even threaten her like we should have if we had jurisdiction here."

87

"For Christ's sake, Marion, we don't want to get involved with the locals. What if I took her in? Then we'd have to explain to some lieutenant why we're stepping on his turf. You're right, though. He probably went left, toward the center of town."

"Okay, let's try the car rentals."

* * *

Eight o'clock p.m. EST was the agreed time for David to call Grant at his office in the CTC. It was now nine-thirty and there had been no call. Grant was not particularly worried. David had been late with calls before and invariably had a good reason. He was just about to leave the office for a cold dinner at home when his phone let out its long awaited ring. This was not his regular phone. No one but the agents he ran knew its number. "Fieldstone Enterprises," he answered after the third ring. "How may I be of service?"

"Your shipment arrived safely as expected, but there were several problems with the paperwork." They knew the call would be eventually heard, so no names or locations were given. There was no use in giving the enemy, or the NSA for that matter, more information than necessary. The difficulties of identifying unknown voices and useless information might just give an agent an hour—or even just ten or fifteen minutes—head start. It would also keep the Washington security agencies from finding out who Gregory Henson really was.

Grant knew "as expected" meant that David had run into some sort of ambush. "Do you know who caused the problems? Was it our competitors or the client?"

"I'm fairly sure it was our competitors. They seem to have a branch office in this country now with substantial ties with local vendors."

"Do you require further instructions or funds to get the parcel to its final destination?"

"No, I can manage. Will update you at the usual time."

"Thank you."

Since David had spoken of further problems, Grant assumed the interdiction of the assassination was still on for the fifteenth and that he could expect to hear from him the morning of that day. Grant doubted this would happen. He would get the results off the wire from South Africa.

The next morning, at seven-thirty sharp, Grant went up to his boss's office. He needed to know something. Edward's secretary told him that Art Curstan from the FBI was in the office, but Grant just went past her and opened the door. "Francis, have you got a minute?" he asked, wondering if his request would even be heard over the heated discussion that was going on.

"What the hell is it?" was Edward's loud reply. "Can't it wait?"

"It might be good for Art to hear what I have to say, if you don't mind my interrupting."

"I mind. We're meeting about Cuba. You interested?"

"Yes, but not as much as I am in South Africa."

Art and Grant never saw eye-to-eye on any subject. Art was old school FBI. He had even known Hoover and agreed with the way he used to run the organization. It hurt him to see the liberalization of attitudes toward subversive elements that threatened the American way of life. He and Grant had spent many a long lunch hour discussing such things as allowing gays into positions of authority in the security establishment. They were bitterly opposed on this and most other issues of the present day. Grant saw the need to have a more flexible and representative work force in all departments. Art preferred the old WASP mentality. They were both drinking coffee, but Francis made no offer to get Grant a cup.

"I'm pretty sure Dominance is operating in South Africa." Grant watched Art's face when he made the announcement.

"What the hell is Dominance?"

Grant thought Art was a pretty good actor. He doubted Francis really had kept Dominance a secret. "I thought Francis would have told you about them."

"You know damn well I haven't. Why would I? They don't exist."

"Well, well, I guess all is not rosy in the spook empire. Do I detect a note of disagreement?" Art enjoyed a joke at the expense of his CIA counterparts.

It was time to lay some cards, maybe even an ace face up on the table, if Grant was to get any closer to the leak. "I have it on good authority that an organization is being developed in Germany that threatens many countries."

That got Curstan's attention. "Why am I just hearing about this now? At our last interdepartmental you didn't breathe a word."

"I wasn't sure then."

"You're not sure now." Francis was most anxious that they not look bad in front of the competition. If he let Grant get away with exposing an organization that did not exist, they would lose face with the rest of the security community. Better to wait until there was proof. "What's happened that you bring this up?"

"A source in South Africa has encountered difficulty from a force outside the normal SAPS and Intelligence."

"I haven't heard about anything going on in South Africa," Art commented.

"We think…"

"You mean, *you* think…"

"Okay, *I* think someone will attempt to assassinate President Mandela."

"Is that so? Why is it that I hadn't heard about this before now?"

"Of course you haven't. Neither has NSA. It's just one of Grant's pipe dreams."

"Okay, boss. I just wanted you and Art to know. Now, what's this about Castro?"

Edwards was so mad he could hardly sit still in his chair. He was curious as to why Grant would keep bringing Dominance up. "I think we should leave that for another time. Stay for a minute after Art leaves, Grant."

Art left the office with a smile on his face. He just loved it when his competition couldn't figure out what they were doing.

9

After his call to Grant, David walked along back streets in Klerksdorp, pondering his next move. He did not want to go straight to a car rental company; sure that would be where his pursuers would expect him to go. Also, going back to the Protea would be suicidal. He was trapped in this country, so if he was caught, it would be jail and probably torture. The enemy had his description by now, so he thought he had better change it.

David had spotted two police cars slowly cruising the side streets and assumed they were looking for him. Each time they passed he had ducked into doorways to avoid their scans.

The bus station was nearly deserted. The sterile gray walls were matched by the chrome and plastic bolted down rows of seating. Decor consisted of taupe drapes on large windows that overlooked the bus assembly area, which was just off Church Street. With his limited Afrikaans he was able to learn from the ticket agent that the daily Translux, Johannesburg to Cape Town bus, would be along in about three hours. It did not stop in Bloemfontein, but that was just as well.

One scruffy old rubby with a rumpled paper bag was having a rest in the corner of the washroom by the washbasins. It looked like he was asleep. As he came in, David heard a toilet flush and almost ran into a burly T-shirt clad Afrikaner who seemed in a hurry. "Watch where you're going," the rough-looking character shouted as he shouldered the smaller David out of the way.

It was one of those events that David absolutely hated—a bully thinking he could do what he wanted because he was bigger than the person he faced. It flashed through his mind what had happened one Sunday afternoon while he was a sophomore at Michigan.

David had been dating Emily Farquarson, a cheerleader and one of the most attractive girls on campus. It was funny how they met. David played safety for the Wolverines. One cold, dark, November evening, the team was practicing for the big game against Ohio State. The winner would get a Rose Bowl invitation as Big Ten champs. The cheerleaders were practicing late as well. David was covering the wide-out who was running a down and out pattern. Just as he tipped the ball away, David stumbled sideways, rolled three times into the end zone, and cut the legs right out from under Emily. The field lighting was turned down for the practice and she never saw him coming.

They saw each other every weekend for the rest of the season. As soon as he began going out with Emily, David noticed that Greg Olsen, the second-string tight end, had been going out of his way to dish out punishing blocks whenever the play went to the weak side. They were dirty hits, below the knees, with an attempt to roll over his ankles on each one. In the locker room after practice a week later, David faced off against Greg.

Greg was six-foot-three and weighed two hundred ten pounds. David was about five-ten and one-ninety. He remembered Greg's snarl when he asked him what his problem was. The reply had nothing to do with Emily. "You think you're so good. I thought you needed taking down a peg or two."

"Just lay off the dirty stuff in practice."

Greg took a swing, which David easily avoided. "Take it easy, man. We don't need this on the team."

Another wild right brought a physical response from his smaller adversary. David swung for his face and connected dead center on Greg's collar bone. As soon as he gained his breath, Greg gasped, "*You stay a...way from Emily!*"

Now, decades later, in a lonely bus depot, another bully seemed to think his size gave him the right to push David around, but David stopped himself in time. The last thing he needed was a scene that would bring the station attendant into the washroom. The man did not even notice the tension as he slammed out the door.

David seethed as he entered a stall as a dirty-looking farmer and came out as an unshaven tourist. He had purchased a colorful linen shirt and a pair of Dockers on a quick foray into Jan Fredrik's on Hendricks Polgeiter Road. Applying the makeup he had bought at Beardsley's brought no reaction from the rubby in the corner. Ten minutes at the basin took care of the unshaven part.

* * *

A frustrated Marion announced, "Well, he's not at any of the hotels or rooming houses. Maybe he has a contact here."

"I doubt that. A contact would have met him at the airport. He hasn't rented a car. The son-of-a-bitch seems to be invisible," Henry declared as he joined his partner in the soft armchairs in the Protea lounge. They had been on the phone for two hours and were both upset. Henry and Marion were out of practice in tracking and eliminating subjects. They were more interested in the political and sexual influence they wielded from

95

their positions close to den Kamp's power, than they were in operations. Henson was a good learning experience for them as future members of the Dominance group, but they realized their boss was not particularly interested in their learning.

"Let's think where else he might go," Marion suggested.

"He could have bought a car."

"Yes, or gone to the rail station. There are all sorts of places there to disguise himself."

"The bus depot too."

"That's it, let's go…"

* * *

When Henry walked in through the east entrance to the depot, David was sitting quietly reading the *Johannesburg Star* on one of the hard seats in the waiting room. Twelve other passengers awaited the Translux bus that was due in from Johannesburg in ten minutes. As Henry approached the row of seats, David's pulse shot up to two hundred beats a minute. Henry was showing his picture to each passenger and getting very poor responses. The people of Klerksdorp, like most natives of Northwest Province, were reluctant to talk to the police, particularly ones dressed in thousand-rand suits.

"Have you seen this man at this station?" A frustrated Henry shoved the photo into the well-dressed tourist's face.

In his best Afrikaans, covered by a feigned raspy cough, David declared, "Never seen him."

"Where are you from?"

"Fish Hoek," David squawked.

Henry turned his back in disgust and went over to a charming-looking older woman who sported a long dress and broad-brimmed hat. David's heart slowly left his throat as his pulse lessened.

When he finished the row, Henry went into the men's room and David got up and left. Just outside the depot was a door that led to the second floor offices of the Translux, Greyhound, and Intercape bus companies that used the terminal. At the end of the tiled hallway there were two doors, one a unisex washroom and the other a janitor's closet. The simple lock on the closet door yielded easily to the blade of David's pocketknife as he slid it between the catch and the jamb. In seconds he was inside and had relocked the door.

The room was only about five by six feet. It contained some cleaning and washroom supplies and nowhere to hide. David was about to leave when he noticed that the block wall between the closet and the washroom did not go all the way to the ceiling. There was a two-foot gap between the roof slab and the drop ceiling in the washroom. Several wires, pipes, and air ducts for the washroom ran into the space.

David moved the green plastic dustbin from the back of the closet over to the wall and climbed up on it. He grabbed the two ducts and lifted himself off the bin. The pipes held his weight. He hoisted himself into the space, slid on top of the ducts, and found he was quite comfortable, although his nose was only about an inch from the concrete roof slab. His senses told him it was a good place to wait out a search.

Within minutes, his heart rate and adrenaline flow subsided, and the numbing tiredness he felt at the Protea returned.

* * *

As Henry cleared all the stalls in the bathroom, his attention locked onto the rubby.

"Have you seen this man?" Henry shouted as he dragged the rubby to his feet.

"Hard t'tell. I seen lotsa men come in here"

Henry produced a five-rand note. "Does this improve your memory?" he snarled.

"Longtime go, guy came in luked bit like that."

"Where'd he go?"

"Donno." At least Henry knew Henson had been at the station. As he turned to leave, the rubby asked, "S'that all you want to know?"

"Why, what else can you tell me?" The greedy hand went out again.

After the five rand were safely stowed, the old guy said, "He w'nt luk t'same as picture. He changed. New clos'n hair."

* * *

David was startled when he heard the door to the janitor's closet open. His heart went into his throat, and his cramped muscles tensed further. The search went as far as the dust bin and shelving. Henry slammed the door as he went back into the depot to call Marion, who had been looking for their quarry at the train station.

It had not been a good day. Henry was looking forward to a better night.

Their search would now have to turn to Bloemfontein.

* * *

David sat alone in the backbench seat of the ten o'clock Intercape bus for Kimberley; he would otherwise have disturbed a fellow passenger with his rapid, almost convulsive movements. His dream centered on a time long past, a time when he was under the vicious care of his grandfather. He saw a long road, winding into the distance. The road was covered with leaves and filled with potholes. At the end of the road he knew there was a toy store, although he couldn't see it. His feet wouldn't move toward the store, and he dodged bats and lions that charged at him out of the woods on either side. He awoke in a sweat just as he had to jump into a deep, wet ditch to avoid a Model-T that came straight for him.

Sitting breathless and only half awake, David tried to figure out what the dream meant. It seemed simple enough; *I was dodging the enemy here in South Africa to save the president who was the toy store at the end of the road.* He wondered, *why was my grandfather was involved? Was he driving the Model-T? And why am I still trying to get away from him?* It was terrible to think that his whole life was being driven by negative emotions—hatred of his grandfather, hatred and loathing of tyrants like Milosevic, and now hatred of his new enemy, Dominance.

After three stops—Bloemhof being the only one for which David was awake—and four and a half hours, the bus pulled into the Shell Ultra Service station, which served as the bus depot in Kimberley. It was two-thirty in the morning and nothing moved. A few cabs were hopefully parked behind the bus, their drivers gathered in the air-conditioned, all-night diner in the depot.

David kept one hand inside his sweater on his stolen Smith & Wesson as he scanned the dimly lit area around the bus, including the faces in the diner. No sign of the man who had spoken to him at the depot in Klerksdorp. *Since he did not find me at the depot, he must have assumed I split and took some other way.* David realized they knew where he was headed. He took the first cab.

"Where do you want to go, man?" the cabby asked.

"Oh, you speak English. How did you know I was English?"

"You get to see these things. Where are you from?" He started the Opel and pulled away from the curb.

"England. Do you know a quiet hotel, kind of out of the way?"

"Sure. The Savoy's plain and quiet. You must be beat after that bus ride, eh?"

"Yeah, I need a rest. Where did you get the 'eh'?"

"We get some Canadians here, as well as Brits, looking for the diamond museum or the 'big hole.'"

It was nice to be able to relax with a man who was obviously not the enemy. "I hope they have a room."

"Oh, they'll have one. Don't worry."

* * *

Marion and Henry arrived in Bloemfontein at around midnight. They left Klerksdorp as soon as the search of the bus depot proved fruitless and had a miserable five-hour drive through the Transvaal. There was little to talk about. David had them confused. They almost had him at Dolphin Car Rentals, but he escaped. They found him again at the Protea, but he lost them again. He had been in Beardsley's but left without a trace. They also knew their sexual activities were not aiding the task of finding Henson and would no doubt soon be discovered by den Kamp.

When they stopped for supper in Allanridge, Henry stated blatantly, "Marion, I think we should stop the sex until we catch Henson."

"You're probably right. I think better after a good romp, but it seems to slow you down."

"Well, thanks for the vote of confidence. If you're so much smarter, maybe we should carry on."

"No, let's stop. Gene's going to find out if we don't, and we'll get bored. Now how do we find this elusive bastard?"

About ten minutes after Marion's head finally hit her pillow in the luxury room at the City Lodge hotel in downtown Bloemfontein, her cell phone warbled. "Yes, Eugene…No, he wasn't at the train station, and Henry didn't find him at the bus depot either, but he thinks he was there and left before he could find him…You don't have to shout…No, he's not here…I'll get him to call you tomorrow…Okay, I'll get him to call you now. He has a cell phone…No, I wasn't being impertinent. It would save me making another call and let me get some sleep." Two minutes later, Henry's cellular, which was on Marion's bedside table, responded. Their resolve to give up sex hadn't lasted very long.

"Yes, sir, I nearly had him. He must have spotted me and left the terminal as soon as I came in. I never saw him…I know it's not much of a report, but Volmar will just have to accept it. Henson's a slippery bastard…No, we haven't seen Louis, but we only arrived here at midnight. Security is awfully tight. The army stopped us coming off the N1. I'll call if anything comes up…Yeah, you too…No, we're not sleeping together. What gave you that idea?…Good night."

10

President Mandela would be in the City of Roses in two days. His speech would be made in the Free State Stadium, which was already fully guarded. Three companies of the Kimberley Rifles were billeted in Grey College High School about a kilometer from stadium. These troops had been dispatched to assist the Bloemfontein police with sweeps around the entire stadium area: Konigspark, Springbok Park, Loch Logan, and all the streets through and around them. Not even a mouse could move without someone asking it for identification. Crane Bertel had gone above den Kamp's head and set up all the security he thought his president would need. Nothing must happen to the wonderful man he had revered and served for so many years.

Terbose thought he could find a place outside the stadium, blend in with the crowd, and take a shot when Mandela went in or out. Every hour an armed patrol would set off down The Kingsway and cover the park and stadium in ever widening circles. Others manned the main entrances to the city on a two-shift basis. The police and army had been briefed on what to look for. The army had been warned that Louis Terbose—the man who had killed the black Major at the Oudtshoorn training base—was the would-be assassin. The police had been advised by their chief that a foreigner, probably an American, would be making an attempt on the president's life. Pictures of Terbose and Henson, resembling neither, had been circulated to both organizations.

Terbose watched the security activity from his room at the Roberta Hotel. He realized that it would be very difficult to move about with a rifle on the day of the speech. He couldn't get into the stadium, but a cooperative agent there had given him details about the visit he didn't yet know—namely, that there would be a parade to the stadium, arriving at noon.

The Grey's Old Boys Club was only fifty meters from the stadium grounds, and he was sure the nooks and crannies in the clubhouse would give him a hiding place for his weapon. Terbose thought he'd pay them a visit.

Just inside the front door, a secretary sat at a curved reception desk. "Good morning, sir. How can I help you?" asked a fiftyish-year-old lady working a computer behind the desk.

"I was a member of the club years ago. Been in England. I was wondering if it would be possible to have a look at the old place."

"I'm sorry, sir—you probably saw the soldiers outside. They're worried about someone trying to kill the president. We've been told not to let any strangers in the building."

"But I'm not a stranger, I'm a graduate. Surely it wouldn't hurt to just let me have a quick tour."

"They said…"

"Who said?"

"The police said only staff and members were to be allowed in."

"But you could make an exception for me."

"Sorry, sir, no exceptions."

Terbose stomped out with a curt, "I'll write your president."

Terbose's day of glory was getting closer, and he was becoming more and more desperate. Where could he hide, get off a kill shot, and get away without being captured? He had been over the grounds near the stadium a half dozen times. There had to be a place that would meet his needs if he just looked hard enough.

It was late Wednesday afternoon. Terbose strolled around Kings Park with a handful of breadcrumbs to feed to the Eider ducks in the lake. To all appearances he was another wealthy, English-looking tourist who had planned his visit to Bloemfontein to coincide with Mandela's speech. His passport and international driver's license were in perfect order. In the last three days the police had stopped him twice and the army three times. Each time he had been welcomed to the city and told of the president's upcoming speech.

But he still had not found a place from which he could get a shot at the president. The late afternoon sun was just dropping behind him and he was ready to pack it in. *There has to be some place safe where I can take a shot from*, he said to himself. Looking up at the twenty-six-story building just across the Loch, he spotted his post. Everything in Terbose's military past told him he would have little chance of survival after shooting the president from the top of a high building. It would take the guards about thirty seconds to determine from where the shot came and would have the building locked down within another minute. But there was nowhere else. *Maybe there's a way off the roof after I kill Mandela*, he thought as he threw the last of his crumbs into the water. He'd caused quite a flurry among the ducks. He strode off purposely toward the Kingsway.

As he approached the building, a young black corporal faced him on Eerste Street. "May I see your papers, sir?" he asked with a friendly smile.

"Of course. Here they are." Louis was getting a bit tired of this.

"Thank you, sir. They seem to be in order."

"Of course, corporal. Tell me, what is the name of that building over there?"

"That's the CR Swart Building, sir, tallest in the city. It has a revolving restaurant on top, too."

"And what is the name of the restaurant? Is the food good?"

"I don't know, sir. Corporals aren't paid enough to be able to eat there."

Terbose flashed the large eighteen-carat gold pinky ring, set with a carat of diamonds. He had found it necessary to buy it for himself with the large bonus den Kamp had paid him. "Well, I think I'll have supper there anyway."

"Yes, sir." The corporal's smile was falsified. He had been told to be pleasant with tourists, but this Englishman was almost too much.

The Acropolis Restaurant was somewhat less impressive than Louis anticipated. When he had finished dinner, which started with the traditional Greek hors d'oeuvre, Spanakopita, and a mediocre steak, Terbose called the waiter over. "Before you bring me the bill, I would like to personally thank the chef for such a wonderful meal. Do you think that would be possible?"

"Yes, sir. One moment. I will get him."

"No, no. I'm sure he's much too busy to come out of the kitchen. I'll just go in and thank him."

"But, sir, no one is allowed—" Before he could finish, Terbose was out of his chair and on the way through the swinging door to the kitchen. The waiter merely threw up his hands and went back to his station beside the bar.

The kitchen was very quiet. One cook was stirring a large pot of soup, and another was slicing carrots and celery at a large butcher's block. Neither paid him the slightest attention. There was a small office off to the side of the kitchen where the chef probably was, but Terbose headed for the door at the far side. The door that led to the roof.

The door was not locked. Louis found himself in a hall about twenty meters long which followed the curve of the kitchen wall and ended in a long, curving flight of metal steps to a landing and a door marked "Emergency Exit Only." He quietly climbed to the exit door, found the alarm easy to bypass with his pocketknife, and opened it a sliver. Elation flowed over him. He had found his site. Now all he needed to do was smuggle in the rifle.

*　*　*

At six in the morning on the fourteenth, in his comfortable office, away from all the tiresome stress that was going on in Bloemfontein, den Kamp was planning a call to Baden. He was almost ready and had just finished his third cup of coffee when the phone buzzed. *I guess our glorious leader struck first*, he muttered to himself as he went through the rigmarole of answering. "Forty-seven here."

"Two. Report, please."

"Our enemy is still at large. We narrowly missed him in Klerksdorp yesterday. Our efforts are now concentrated on the target city."

"I shall be there today."

"Shall I meet you?"

"Yes, I leave now for Johannesburg. It's a long way to your country from mine; the flight will take ten hours. I want to talk to you firsthand. Get this operation back on track. Meet me at the airplane." Dieter hung up.

Damn, den Kamp thought. *With Dieter here things are going to get even more complicated.* The phone rang again. He answered in a record fifteen seconds. "Forty-seven here, De—"

"Eighteen, here. Be more careful, Forty-seven."

"What can I do for you this morning?" Eighteen was the Dominance representative from the United States. *I hope he's not coming too,* den Kamp thought.

"I have information. Rumor 'has it there is an operation in your country. You should beware."

"What is your source?"

"Our intelligence service."

"Reliable?"

"I'm not sure. Advice is not universally accepted. I am taking no action pending the outcome on the fifteenth. Just a warning...There will probably be some outside interference." Dieter had briefed all heads of Dominance on the pending action in Bloemfontein.

"Thank you, Eighteen. I am aware of the threat."

As he hung up, den Kamp got a premonition of disaster. It was a new feeling for him. He always felt in control. Things were slipping. He could not contact Louis to stop the hit, Henry and Marion could not find Henson, and the president's speech was to be made at noon tomorrow.

He had to get to Bloemfontein after Dieter's visit. The failing pair of agents needed to be motivated, which only could be done in person.

* * *

108

David awoke at ten still feeling groggy. Sleep seemed to relieve his subconscious of its need to remain vigilant. He rubbed his eyes to get his mind and body into action.

The day had dawned less brilliant than the day before. The pale sky filtered through flowing, flowered drapes and painted the room the same reddish gray color. His hotel room was attractive, and he remembered why he picked it. Then he remembered the cabby. *That man was the only one I'd met in this country who was the least bit friendly*, he thought as he sat upright and stretched his arms and legs. He had to take that back as he thought of the girl at Beardsley's who had saved his life. *I hope they weren't too rough on her*, he grumbled. Efficiency kicked in after five minutes of this thinking. He was showered, shaven, and dressed in another fifteen. *No time to waste.*

The lobby looked attractive and expensive with its dark oak paneling and crystal chandelier. The main dining room appeared similarly costly. The maître d' showed him to a quiet table in the corner where he could watch the people passing on Old de Beers Road. They carried umbrellas, perhaps in the chance of rain from the overcast. All of them were in a hurry.

David had not eaten since the lunch in the bar in Klerksdorp. Because he was used to working as an agent in foreign countries, he had learned to satisfy his hunger when he could. He had trained himself to be like a lion. Hunger was irrelevant when danger was present. All his nervous energy became concentrated on the task at hand. There was no time to think about hunger, or thirst, or sleep. Thoughts of sex were even further away, but in a now familiar pattern when he let his mind wander, reminiscences of childhood crowded into his consciousness as he waited for his breakfast.

When he was growing up in Dublin, eating had been an activity to be enjoyed. Sam Reasons's cook, Isabel, though she was a very strange person, prepared the most sumptuous meals. He smiled as he recalled the time she was nearly ready to take a knife to him for messing up her salad arrangement before a dinner party with a very important client of his grandfather's. Usually she was kind and joking, telling him stories that made him laugh about her life in Poland.

He never did tell his grandfather about the near attack. Looking back, he felt it was only motivated by the same fear David had always felt. Her mistakes resulted in unreasonable punishment doled out by her boss, so she lashed out at the first person available: David.

After a hearty South African breakfast of fried eggs, boerewors, fried tomatoes, bananas, Brinjal , toast, and coffee, David ventured out of the lobby to get to the shops on Jones Street and Market Square, only a couple of blocks from the hotel. He wanted to be in Bloemfontein before dark. The president would give his speech at noon the next day, and he had still to scope out the stadium and pinpoint the location the would-be assassin would take the shot from. It would normally be a two-day job when he had freedom of movement, but he had neither the time, nor the freedom.

* * *

Eugene and Dieter were comfortably seated in deep, cushioned leather swivel chairs anchored to the floor of the latter's custom-built Challenger aircraft. A beautiful brunette had just served them Courvoisiers after an excellent lunch of poached salmon and German spargel. She had since retired to the crew section of the aircraft.

Dieter realized his constant haranguing of Eugene was not improving the chances for the mission's success. "Do not trouble yourself too much about Henson. He has been a thorn in my side for some years now. I would like to see him eliminated so that this operation has a better chance of success and our long-term goal of world domination made simpler, but the success of your little operation is much more important at this time." Dieter spoke excellent English with a slight British accent. He found den Kamp's clipped South African accent a chore. Den Kamp was used to using Afrikaans in both business and social settings.

"I'm glad you aren't too concerned with our failure…"

"Oh, I'm concerned, but not devastated. Better men than yours have failed to eliminate him."

The slight hurt. "You will see. We'll capture him. When we do, I presume you would like to be involved in his elimination."

"Oh, yes. When you catch him, keep him for me. Do you want me to take over control of the operation?"

"Certainly not. I don't see how you could anyway. I have no idea where the assassin is at the moment."

"You would do well to keep better control in the future."

"I felt that by having him go to ground without anyone knowing where he was, there was less chance of other security people finding out. There is a leak—" As soon as he said it, den Kamp knew he had made a mistake. He had opened himself up to criticism, a commodity he was used to handing out, not receiving.

"A LEAK?! *Where?*" Dieter's conciliatory attitude had not lasted very long.

"I'm not sure. Someone called in Henson. Whoever it was must have found out about our operation. My boss hauled me in some time ago and accused me of not being enthusiastic enough about finding Terbose, who I am using on this operation." Den Kamp was becoming defensive. Dieter had that effect on people. He was used to unwavering obedience in his own company and expected the same from his Dominance members.

Dieter realized this was not the time for nastiness. He sensed den Kamp was ready to admit defeat and must be motivated.

He responded enthusiastically, "It does not matter, my friend. Henson can wait. You get Mandela. Now there's something that will further our cause, not to mention you if you manage to pull it off."

The way Dieter talked, den Kamp was tempted to, and very nearly replied, *Ja, wohl mein Führer*. "Don't worry about Louis Terbose. He has killed before. He *will* eliminate Mandela. Would you like to go to Bloemfontein to meet my team?"

"Not yet. After they show some signs of competence I will be pleased to meet them and welcome them into the organization. For now it would be better if we didn't meet. I do not want incompetents in my presence."

"Perhaps a motivating talk now will improve their performance."

"I leave that to you. Now, I think we have finished."

Den Kamp enviously watched Dieter's Challenger take off. He felt a bit better about the mission and was anxious to get down to Bloemfontein to motivate his subordinates. He also missed his encounters with Marion. Before he left, however, he thought he had better try to throw Bertel off the track

* * *

In two hours he had his story ready and was seated in the straight-backed chair facing Bertel's plain, uncluttered desk. Striking first was den Kamp's strong point. "Why did you call out the troops in Bloemfontein, Minister? My police are quite capable of protecting our president."

"I had word that an attempt would be made to assassinate the president. I will not have that. The troops are extra insurance. Never mind that. Where is Terbose? Have you done anything to catch him?"

"We almost caught him, sir. He was at Detrusburg yesterday. I had our police chief from Bloemfontein there. I believe you know Piet Neiderhof?"

"Yes, I met him at your annual Meeting of Chiefs last winter." Bertel rarely forgot a face. "I seem to recall he was somewhat reluctant to accept the concept of reconciliation."

"Well, that's all changed, minister. Piet put a large force of his men out to find Terbose. They have been stopping cars for two days and have checked out every hotel and guesthouse in the city. Piet arrested an old Boer, who knew Terbose and got him talking."

"So you found him. Is he in custody?"

"Not exactly. Piet Neiderhof was right in the van of the search, and was shot in the leg by Terbose while trying to bring him in."

There has to be something wrong with his story. Bertel had been listening to lies for enough years to know when he heard one. He knew there was an outside agent who was in the country trying to eliminate the threat of Terbose, although he did not know his name. *Maybe that is the problem! Neiderhof and den Kamp are looking for the person Burton had called in, not Terbose. The threat they wanted to eliminate was to their assassin, not to the president.* Still, he could not prove that den Kamp was not actively hunting Terbose. All reports he received from his many sources in Bloemfontein and the surrounding towns and villages indicated a lot of police presence. Den Kamp was wily. "I want you to keep trying. I will be in Bloemfontein with the president on the fifteenth. Make yourself available here if I need you."

With a quiet, "Yes, minister," den Kamp left. *You don't know it yet, my friend,* he thought, *but I will be watching our president's assassination from Bloemfontein. Perhaps a stray bullet will find you.*

As den Kamp was returning by cab to his office, he kept trying to find holes in the story he had just made up. Bertel didn't seem too enthusiastic about it. He realized he had to be wary. *I don't need to go down for this!* When he got back to his office, he personally ordered a charter for the trip to Bloemfontein at 8:00 p.m. and a room at the City Lodge Hotel.

11

Henry rang room service. He and Marion were sprawled comfortably in the queen-sized bed in the City Lodge Hotel, just opposite Kings Park in Bloemfontein. He realized there was no getting away from the desire he had for his partner, even if it meant failure of the mission. He ordered a couple of omelets from the hotel's extensive menu. As he hung up the phone, he turned toward her and almost gasped at the sight of her profile. Her lips stood slightly agape, and her still hardened nipples pointed toward the ceiling. "God, Marion, you certainly know how to wear a man out."

"The pleasure is all mine. I'm glad we're bad at keeping promises."

All the same, Henry realized they had better get moving. Den Kamp would be annoyed if he discovered their affair, but would be irate if they didn't catch their prey. "Maybe we'd better get dressed, have our omelets, and go after Henson. It would be great to have him for den Kamp when he gets here tonight. He might forgive us our transgressions of the flesh."

"You worry too much. We'll get him. I know we didn't find him this morning, but that may be because he hasn't arrived yet."

As they ate and washed their delicious meal down with a bottle of fifty-rand Cape Chardonnay, Marion began to think. Sex, and her ability to control men, always did that to her. She thought better on a satisfied id. "You know, we are really up against a pro in this thing. I've never seen anyone disappear so completely and stay out of sight. God knows how many people Eugene has out looking for him. You and I have gotten close several times, but he always slips away. Do you think there's another tack we should take? Like getting into the stadium itself and waiting. Surely Henson has to show up at the stadium."

"How'll he get in? The army has the place completely covered. I'm more worried about what may happen to Terbose. I can't see how he'll get in either."

"Terbose doesn't have to get in. All he needs is a hiding place where he can get a clear shot at Mandela. That will be tough, though, with all the army around. Maybe one of us should have helped him instead of chasing Henson."

"The best way we can help him is by stopping the one guy that's capable of stopping him. You know Dieter wants him badly too. We can make some points with den Kamp and Dieter if we get him."

* * *

With each step through the downtown shopping area of Kimberley, David watched for a shadow, a head turned in the wrong direction; something to indicate the enemy was still after him. After about an hour, he realized they weren't on his trail. By lunchtime, he had made the purchases he thought necessary to change himself from the tired farmer who had checked into the hotel, to a rich British tourist, in town to take in the city's beautiful roses and, by happenstance, catch the president's speech. He had bought spare clothing, a suitcase, a briefcase, and a pair of 70 power Bushnell binoculars. He returned to the Savoy and converted himself into his new persona with a white cotton cable knit sweater, beige linen slacks, Rockport deck shoes, and a Greg Norman Shark golfing hat.

The last item he required was an off-road vehicle. There was no telling what kind of roads he might have to take if they got onto him again. Renting might be problematic, as he had no papers as his English alias, but cash usually kept mouths shut if there was enough of it.

He checked out and got a cab from the front of the hotel. The desk clerk had assured him that Dalham Road was the best area to find a used car.

"There's one," said the driver, pulling his Opel over to the side of the road. David had asked him to check the north side lots for SUVs while he checked the south. There was a blocky white Land Rover on the small lot.

David didn't want the cabbie to know which car he bought. "Those things are pretty expensive, aren't they?"

"They sure are. We can keep looking if you want."

"No, that's okay. I'll have a look at that one, and I'm sure he'll have others if I can't afford it. Thanks very much. I hope this covers the search." David handed the driver one hundred rand.

"That's way too much, sir. I know you don't understand our costs here. Perhaps that ride would cost more than ten pounds in London, but not here."

"I understand your rates quite well. Let's just say the tip is for your helpfulness and discretion."

117

"Thank you, sir. Good luck." The cabbie could not understand why the Englishman didn't just rent a car. He figured his passenger was up to something.

By one-thirty David had bought the Land Rover and was on his way out of Kimberley. He had two choices for the journey to Bloemfontein: the fast and direct route on the main highway through Detrusberg and De Brug, or the R64 which was a few kilometers longer and much slower. If time had not been pressing, he would have chosen the less direct route.

Driving toward Bloemfontein through the arid countryside, he marveled at how the South Africans could have built such a strong nation out of the dry and barren soil. Only large kaffirboom trees and struggling aloe broke the openness of the flat landscape, sparsely covered with scrub grasses. The trip was only a bit more than two hours. His actions in Bloemfontein would be fluid. As he drove, his mind wandered back to a mission in Idaho. Back then, his plan had been just as simple: find out who the bad guys were and find a way to stop them.

* * *

By the late-eighties, Grant and David were well aware there was a leak somewhere in the US Intelligence services. Secret weapon transfers to moderate Contras in Iran became embarrassing public knowledge. But Grant had no idea where to find the leak. He met David in Fargo, North Dakota, to devise a way to draw out the mole.

Their second day there, the two of them were having lunch in the coffee shop at the Holiday Inn. They were completely alone except for a bored waitress who was trimming her nails at the cashier's position. Grant had just told him about a rumor that the Aryan Nations were planning a big convention at Everett James's dude ranch near Hayden Lake, Idaho.

"I think your infiltration should be known only to the FBI," said Grant.

"Isn't that a bit dangerous for me? Kind of like walking back the cat."

"Yeah. Old Littell loved that one. Make sure only one person knows, then; a leak identifies the source. But can you remember a mission that wasn't dangerous? I haven't let anyone in the Center know about the op, so if your cover is blown, it has to be someone in the FBI or at the ranch. These guys don't take kindly to people other than white supremacists attending their meetings. But they won't know who you are. I know a guy here in Fargo who has pretended to be an Aryan for years. He'll introduce you to James."

"But what if some Aryan gets onto me? Don't those bastards want the whole state for their own country?"

"Before you go in, I'll leak it that I heard someone from the press is trying to get right inside the movement. The bureau will be covering it pretty closely. If they know someone from outside is there, they're likely to tip their hand by letting James or one of his cohorts know about the infiltration."

"What if the leak is your boss?"

"I'm pretty sure Edwards is okay."

"How do you know?"

"He's hardly ever out of the office, so he probably isn't passing out secrets. Spies who do, generally travel a lot. To make sure, I went through his filing cabinet."

"How did you do that? He wouldn't leave the cabinet open when he was out of the office, and I'm damn sure he wouldn't let you go through it while he was there."

"No, but he leaves his lock on top of the cabinet after he opens it in the morning. I just changed it for an identical one on Friday afternoon when he wasn't looking. When he left, he locked his cabinet with my lock. So all I had to do was go in after everyone left and open his cabinet."

"And you didn't find anything that could tie him to the leak?"

"No. I thought maybe I'd find some secret codes or numbers, but if he has any, he doesn't keep them in his cabinet."

"Smart bastard, aren't you? I guess you just locked the cabinet with his lock when you went home."

David recalled the visit to Idaho vividly. He was shot at while returning on horseback from a scouting mission in the Coeur d'Alene Forest, lost his horse, had to walk around all night, got attacked by a local cop who seemed to think what was going on at James's ranch was none of David's business, and had to steal the cop's car to escape to Spokane and a flight back to Columbus. *What a trip that was…*

* * *

An hour out of Kimberley, David wished he had taken the slow route. The main highway bypassed Detrusburg, but just at the off-ramp, uniformed police officers were waving over just about every other car. His heart leaped into his throat, and sweat began to trickle down his neck as he searched the road for some place to escape. None. He might have to answer their questions. David hoped they wouldn't ask for papers.

A young black constable eyed the well-dressed man with Kimberley plates on his Rover and waved him by. Slowly, the clammy feeling began to leave, his pulse slowed, and the twitch that had started in his left eye subsided.

David wondered why he hadn't been pulled over. Could the cop just be going through the motions? Perhaps the police hadn't been told who they were looking for, or that there could be an assassination attempt. Perhaps they had a picture of Henson that didn't look like him. *The closer I get to Bloemfontein,* he thought, *the tighter security is going to be.*

David used his time on the road to steel himself for a possible escape. *Whether or not I stop the assassin, I still have to get out.* He remembered Poland nearly two decades earlier. That escape had presented all sorts of surprises.

* * *

David had not been aware that his diplomatic status as Henson expired the moment Aeroflot Flight 213 left the tarmac at Chopin Airport in Warsaw. He hadn't even thought about it. When they were well into East German air space, a man seated about ten rows ahead of him slipped out of his seat and headed down the aisle toward the mid-cabin washrooms.

On the way by, in perfect Oxford English, he said, "Good afternoon, sir. That arm of yours looks quite painful. I am a representative of Aeroflot. Perhaps I could have the stewardess get you something for the pain."

David was scared to death. He suddenly realized how vulnerable he was at 35,000 feet over East Bloc territory. This agent or one of the crew could easily drug his food, wait until he went to the can, and eliminate him in the galley area, or even assault him in his seat. He thanked God they had given him a warning.

"I'm really feeling quite a bit of pain," he responded much more bravely than he felt. "Perhaps a couple of aspirins would help me get some rest."

"Fine, sir, I'll tell the stewardess." The agent continued on to the galley.

When the stewardess brought the pills, David pretended to take them. With a sigh of apparent relief, he sank down against his skimpy airline pillow and seemed to drift off to sleep. All the time he kept his right eye open enough to give him a sliver-shaped view up the aisle. Ten minutes later his seatmate leaned over and felt his pulse.

Here he was, seated next to an enemy who was now aware that the pills hadn't killed him. David feigned unconsciousness. The seat belt light had been turned on. The man must have only been a lookout, because he made no threatening move. He couldn't leave his seat without attracting attention. David had about ten minutes to devise an escape plan.

As soon as the plane touched down, David was out of his seat and headed for the forward exit. Before either the airline representative or the crew realized it, he had moved into a defensive position with his back to the exit door, where he could only be approached from a short, narrow aisle between the crew compartment bulkhead and the metal side of the galley.

The stewardess who had served him lunch and brought him his pillow and aspirin blurted out in heavily accented English, "Sir, you must stay in your seat until the aircraft has come to a full stop in front of the terminal building." David ignored her.

The Aeroflot representative was harder to ignore. Before they had turned off the runway, he was at the front of the plane facing David. Not a word was spoken as the two eyed each other. Magically, a six-inch, double sided blade appeared in his left hand. "You have interfered in the politics of our country," he snarled. "It is my duty to take you into custody and return you to Warsaw."

"But I have diplomatic immunity," was David's reply. "I realize this aircraft belongs to the Polish State, but we are now in West Germany, where you have no jurisdiction."

"This is all the jurisdiction I need," hissed the agent as he flashed the knife toward David's throat.

David blocked the stroke with his left forearm and nearly fell over an empty seat. The man quickly jumped back and launched another attack.

This time David was more prepared. He leapt sideways to avoid the blade, and with his left hand assisted his opponent's head into the tightly closed exit door that was designed to withstand atmospheric pressure. The force of the blow spun David painfully around, jamming his injured shoulder into the galley bulkhead. The agent's head was no match for the door, and he collapsed in an unconscious heap.

The Il-86 slowed as it approached the sweeping concrete of the terminal building's apron. David had no fear of Frankfurt airport security but was very concerned about the dangers that still lurked inside the aircraft. The crew was moving cautiously toward the body of David's attacker. The aircraft suddenly jerked to a stop. He had to move fast.

Turning his back to the three agitated flight crew, who seemed immobilized, he managed the two-handed door release with his one good arm and a painful assist from his right elbow, swung the door open, and dropped the twelve feet to the concrete. The force of the fall reverberated in his right shoulder. It also turned his left ankle, so that he staggered toward the still turning, port inboard engine that was beginning that high-pitched growl that showed the throttle had been advanced.

He desperately dodged toward the shelter of the port wing. His left hand got too close to the intake. The rush of air was so strong that it slapped his wrist against the cowling with enough force to stop him in his tracks. As he pulled it away, he felt the searing pain of a round entering his damaged right shoulder. A heavy jerk got him free of the nacelle minus his watch, which made a clanking ping as it went through the engine, doing what David hoped would be some serious foreign object damage.

The sudden release of force toppled him, and he was forced to roll away from the shooter at the aircraft's door. It briefly crossed his mind that they could have killed him, had his assailant merely jumped from the aircraft, but his attacker probably did not want to be found on the tarmac by the police. His only problem was to stay away from the sight lines of the open door. At this point, the pilot released the brakes and the aircraft started to roll. Now he had another problem. After the nacelle passed over him, the exhaust would fry him.

Rolling away from the shelter of the nacelle would briefly expose him to a shot from the still open door, but that was preferable to being fried. David started his roll toward, rather than away from, the aircraft to cut down his exposure to fire from the door. Blinding pain from his doubly injured right shoulder almost caused him to pass out on his first revolution. Another shot passed two inches from his right ear and hit the pavement as the large fuselage, relative safety, and unconsciousness swept over him.

It took an operation and ten days in a Frankfurt hospital before Gregory Henson returned to Dublin.

* * *

Nervous tension increased and thoughts of past successes receded when he hit Bloemfontein proper. David was approaching the western bypass of the Johannesburg–Cape Town highway. The off-ramp had a barrier on it manned by two infantry soldiers. They were not stopping cars on Haldon Street, which David needed to take to get to downtown, but had backed up traffic for about a kilometer on the N1. It seemed to David that they looked more serious than the ones near Kimberley.

As he crossed over the highway, the band that had kept his head in its grip so many times in the past two days tightened even further. *Would there be a barrier on the other side of the overpass? How can I get off this road and onto a side street?*

Topping the ramp, he noticed soldiers on the other side of the road were also checking out cars exiting the N1, but not on his street. He wheeled the Land Rover off to the left into a Shell station. He needed gas and a map.

While having the car filled, he studied the map for the most strategic hotel. He chose the Brandhof. It seemed to offer a location that was not too close to the stadium, yet close enough so that a quick getaway was possible if necessary. It was also within view of the stadium area.

He used the map to find a hiding place for the car—the suburban Universities Hospital. He drove in, took his pass at the automatic gate, and left the Rover in the visitor's parking lot. He then dragged his suitcase and briefcase out of the car and headed across the Orange Free State campus, using trees and shrubbery for cover. He waited in the shadows while an army jeep went whizzing by on Zastrroon, and then David crossed the street quickly to the hotel.

There was no lineup for registration at the desk where a clerk with blonde hair and pretty blue eyes smiled welcomingly at him. "Good evening, sir. How may I help you?"

Remembering he was a British tourist, David imitated an appropriate, midlands accent. "It is a good evening, my dear, and even a better one since seeing you. I wonder if you might have a room overlooking King's Park?"

The blonde blushed. "Certainly, sir, could I have your credit card?"

"Never use them."

"I'm sorry, sir, we need a five-hundred-rand deposit, then."

David flashed a wad of cash and peeled off five, one hundred rand notes. "That should take care of that. By the way, are you free later this evening?"

"Oh no, sir," she stammered as she handed him the key and paper work to fill out. "I'm meeting my boyfriend after shift."

"That's a shame."

* * *

Den Kamp spent most of the flight from Johannesburg to Bloemfontein pounding on the armrest of his seat. He was the only passenger on the twin Beechcraft, and the two pilots were used to strange behavior from high-ranking political figures and company executives. It was normally panic time for those who used charter services.

He had not perceptibly calmed down by the time he got to the hotel. The more he thought about how Dieter had handled him, the angrier he got. The specter of Marion and Henry's probable sexual activities also flashed through his mind, making him even more irate. As soon as he got into the limo from Tempe airport, he called Henry on his cellular.

"God-damn, Henry, I hope you've caught Henson."

Henry stiffened when he picked up and turned red in the face. Another part of him lost its stiffness.

"Sorry, sir, we haven't. I've been trying to find him all day with no more luck than we had in Klerksdorp."

"I'm on my way to the hotel, now. I want you, Marion—I hope you two are not together—"

"Of course not. What gave—"

"—and Piet waiting at my room when I get there."

Henry was almost ready to explode with a "Ja wohl, mien Führer," but he replied simply, "We'll be there."

* * *

Den Kamp checked into his hotel room at about ten thirty, and the three were waiting for him in the hallway. When they all entered and took seats in his room, he wasted no time with small talk. "Henry, report! What are you doing to find Henson?"

"I will find him. He has to be somewhere in the city."

"Not good enough! Use your training to figure out where he is hiding. Piet! You have the whole police force here. Why haven't you found him?"

"We've stopped hundreds of cars and hundreds of people. I don't know what else we can do, but we'll keep at it."

"Be sure you do. Go back to your station and get your troops moving."

"Yes, sir."

Neiderhof got up to leave, but den Kamp ordered, "Sit down! I'm not finished."

"Henry and Marion, you look tired. I hope it's all from losing sleep over Henson."

They had separate rooms at the inn but had not yet recovered from the sexual Olympics of the past two days. "We've been looking for him day and night, Eugene," Marion replied. "The bastard is invisible. We'll find him, though."

"I just finished meetings with the minister and our Dominance leader. Bertel thinks we're up to something, and Dieter's pissed off because we can't get rid of Henson. Now let's get moving. I'm sick and tired of you three making excuses about why you can't find Henson. You're all officers, but your efforts to find one man are laughable! Don't you have any discipline? How can you say you're members of Dominance, when one man can dominate *you*? Bloody well find him. Our futures in Dominance depend on it. And Neiderhof, make sure your people don't find Terbose."

* * *

Den Kamp calmed down a bit and turned on the cable to learn about the next day's activities. There was no mention of any problem—no assassination speculation. But then again, if there was, it wouldn't be mentioned on public television. The local newscaster, an attractive East Indian lady, merely applauded the president for his initiative and iterated her hope that soon the entire nation would support his efforts for equality among the races. After she predicted that, through similar actions like the present tour, Mandela would soon gain even more foreign and domestic respect. Den Kamp swore, grunted, "Like hell," and turned it off. He felt

127

his speech might have motivated them a bit. "All right, do you all know what you're supposed to do tomorrow?"

"I'll be in the stadium with the president and the mayor," Piet volunteered. "They might think something's out of order if I don't show up. Tonight, I'll be after Henson."

"Of course. Keep an eye on Bertel as well. Take a cell phone and let me know what he's up to as it gets close to the time for the speech."

"I'll keep looking for Henson," said Henry. "I don't see how he'll move around; the army will stop and search him. I was searched three times today myself." Henry did not hold out much hope of finding his adversary. Two days of failure had made him believe that Henson really was a will-o'-wisp. He did not want to be near den Kamp if something went wrong.

"Marion, I want you to stay with me. As backup."

"Okay, Eugene. I still think you worry too much. Terbose will hit his target and, like Henry says, Henson's stuck wherever he is. He won't move around much."

"I don't know. He's slipped away often enough."

"My men will find him," Piet added. "I can brief any number to look out for him."

"For heaven's sake, no, Piet, don't even think of increasing the number of people who know about Dominance."

"But I needn't say anything about Dominance. Just show them Henson's picture again to remind them and tell the shift sergeant to look out for him."

"Risky. What if he asks why you want him? I know he shot you in the leg, but if you go around telling that story, you have to explain why he isn't on the wanted list."

"I suppose you're right, but I still think we should be able to find one man, especially an American. He should stand out like a sore thumb."

"He should, but he doesn't. He's good. Just let things go as they are. As Henry says, he won't be able to move around much...All right. Why don't you all go find him? No one kills him, though. Our German leader wants to have that privilege."

"And how is our German leader?" Marion wanted to know. Den Kamp was the strongest man she knew, and any man who could intimidate him was of great interest to her.

"He would be happy if we caught Henson, but killing Mandela is a higher priority."

Piet made the final summary. "I wouldn't mind meeting a man who can control power like this guy does. We better make sure this assassination is a success."

Amen, murmured den Kamp to himself.

* * *

Piet went to the station to motivate his troops and renew their efforts to find this thorn in his side. Internally, he was more insecure, but he sure wanted to get the bastard.

Marion went back to her room. There was no way she was going to stay the night in Eugene's bed. Not after he'd been so condescending to her. Hopefully she'd get some sleep to prepare her for tomorrow's events.

Henry left the misery of den Kamp's room for the streets. It was after midnight, and he was tired and frustrated by the elusive Henson, but ambition spurred him on. As he left the room, he had to admire his boss. All they needed was a little motivation. He was determined to be the one to find Henson. He figured the bastard would wait until everyone was in bed before he started his hunt for Terbose.

12

Grant sat nervously at his desk. It was early evening in South Africa, and for the twenty-sixth time he considered calling Arnold Graham, head of South African Intelligence. They knew of each other by reputation but had never met. What bothered Grant was whether or not he could trust Graham. His reputation in the security community was one of progressiveness and desire to work toward a better future for his country, but Grant, out of habit, never trusted reputation.

He had not heard from David for nearly twenty-four hours. Had he been captured? Was he in danger? Had he reached Bloemfontein? Grant picked up the phone and called Forest Burton. At least he could get some close-up knowledge of what was going on. The American papers and newscasts told him nothing about Mandela's speech tomorrow.

Forest answered quickly but wasn't sure how to respond to Grant. "Hello?"

"Jackson, from Fieldstone Enterprises. Can you tell me anything about the package we sent to South Africa?"

"Not much, Bill. I heard some rumors that the competition might try to block delivery, but no definite info. Do you want me to check on it?"

So at least David had not been caught, or Forest would have heard about it.

"No need," said Grant. "Let me know if you hear anything."

"I will."

The line went dead, and Forest put down the receiver. He hadn't wanted to add to Grant's fears by mentioning that he felt as if someone were watching him.

* * *

At 6:00 p.m, the Free State Stadium underwent a thorough search. Even though dusk was still three hours away, lights showered the rugby pitch with brilliance. Extra searchlights, provided by the army, were being trained into every nook and cranny. A cat would neither get in nor move about inside unnoticed. Bertel would take no chances.

David chewed on a chicken wrap he got from room service and sat backwards on the straight-back desk chair at the window in his room on the third floor of the Brandhof Hotel. It was a long way from the stadium, but at least he could study the grounds to the north of it in private. He had his binoculars focused on the west entrance. The brilliance from the overhead lights dilated his eyes, but he could make out a pair of metal detectors and a welded structure designed to stop heavy vehicles from making an unwanted incursion into the stadium. The stands were higher than his present vantage point, so he couldn't see inside the stadium itself.

He knew at least two things. First, the assassin would not be able to shoot from the Brandhof. David couldn't see the field where the president would be standing, even from the roof. Second, the assassin wouldn't be going in or out by the west entrance. He'd have to either be in the stadium or in one of the tall office buildings near it. A sharpshooter could make the shot from three-quarters of a mile away, but David suspected he would be closer, to be certain of the kill. It was time to string his camera and binoculars around his neck and go for a stroll.

As evening approached, the sky cleared and the dinginess of the morning disappeared. Tomorrow would be a typical high-sky day for which the Transvaal was famous. David thought it was strange how the weather seemed to cooperate with terrorists. Fog or heavy rain would have made a hit on the president all but impossible.

As he turned from the window to leave the room, something caught his eye. A jeep stopped at the corner of Parfit and Henry Street, and a corporal got out to talk to someone. David had originally thought the army was only looking after the entrances to the city. As he watched, they stopped a man waiting for a bus. David pulled the binoculars back up to his eyes. He saw the man reach in his coat pocket and hand something to the soldier. The papers received about a minute's review before the corporal gave them back with a nod, just as his bus was pulling away from the stop. David would have loved to hear what he had said to that corporal.

David slumped back into his chair. His papers were no good, and he wasn't going to find the killer without leaving this room. He went over to the desk, picked up his street map, and started to work out a way.

* * *

The President of South Africa sat in his office with his Minister of Safety and Security going over the soon-to-be delivered speech.

"It is a good speech, Nelson," said Bertel. "I particularly like the references to the importance of the Free State in the development of this country and the bravery of its citizens in the British Wars."

"You don't think I'll come across a bit too sugary? They may get the idea we are only trying to appease them—hoodwink them into joining us."

"I'm surprised at you. You don't feel you're trying to mislead them, do you? Surely you still believe we can eventually turn all the Boers around to supporting the cause of democracy."

"Who's making this speech, you or me?" The president laughed the same hearty chuckle that had won him so many supporters during the recent election. He was a strong, happy man with a huge heart. He only came up to Bertel's shoulder, but they were of equal stature in each others' eyes. The years Mandela had spent imprisoned had not broken the bond between them, so strongly welded during their early years of fighting apartheid. Since his release they had become even closer—a closeness that would frighten many men.

Bertel laughed too, and then the big face became solemn. "You know, I still wish you would cancel this speech tomorrow. Put off the tour until I can get to the bottom of this den Kamp and Terbose thing. I'm certain they are going to attempt an assassination."

"No, my friend. I will never give in to hatred and racism. We fought too long against those two devils to let them beat us now. I will give the speech at noon tomorrow, as scheduled. What do you hear about attendance?"

"I can check. I'm sure your idea is popular with the citizens of Bloemfontein. You've been there before. Most of them support us, you know that."

"Please check and let me know on the flight down tomorrow. Is there anything else I need to know?"

"I don't think so. The army has beefed up security, and I made sure the local police chief is aware of the threat. Apparently he was injured trying to bring in Terbose. Den Kamp assures me he has called out sufficient force to protect you." Bertel did not want to burden the president with his doubts about Neiderhof and den Kamp.

"And you too, my friend. If they are after me, they will likely try for you at the same time."

"You and I have been through many threats before. It would be unfair though if someone got to us now that we are free."

"It would be, but are we ever free? We serve a different master now. The hate of apartheid was a cruel but understandable force. The enemy now is subtler. We cannot see its face."

Bertel stopped himself from making the obvious reply.

* * *

Both the lobby and the front entrance to the Roberta Hotel were busy and noisy. Terbose sauntered out just as the streetlights were turning on, their slow orange glow gradually turning to amber. Busloads of tourists had just arrived and were looking for information about when the president would speak tomorrow; how far to the stadium and would they need tickets? The desk was so busy that no one noticed his departure.

"Things have changed so much since I use to live here. Is that still Louis Botha Tech?" Terbose asked a lone private who was checking papers at the corner of Victoria and Harris Streets.

Casually looking at his papers, the young black private replied, "Yes, sir. Did you go there?"

"Yes, many years ago. Is the school still segregated?"

"Oh no, sir. A lot of blacks and coloreds go there now. Thank heaven for the new government."

"Could you show me how to get in? Just for old times' sake."

"I'm sure everyone has gone home now. The dormitories will still be open, though. Maybe you could visit them."

"They must be new since I was here. Can you show me them?"

"I couldn't leave my post, sir."

Terbose looked around. No one else seemed to be out on the street. "I think you could," he hissed as he shoved the six-inch blade right up to the hilt in the private's side, covering his mouth with his left hand. The private was dead in his arms as he carried him, as he would a drunk, into some shrubbery on the west side of the main academic building. A rich green juniper thicket became the interim coffin for the private and Terbose's natty attire. *By the time the army finds him this will be all over*, he said to himself as he straightened the black beret and tugged at the tight waist of the Private's fatigues. *Now, back to the hotel for my weapon.*

The Sako TRG-21 .308 sniper rifle he had ordered from a supplier in Harare had been modified to be broken down and stowed in what appeared to be an ordinary briefcase. As Terbose strode boldly past the front desk on his way out of the hotel, the clerk did not even look up. He marched out the front door and headed for President Boshof Street and the Swart building.

* * *

It looked to David that it would be nearly impossible to leave the hotel. Twenty minutes after the streetlights turned on, he was still staring out the window, trying to find a possible route he could take to check out the stadium and surrounding area. He couldn't sneak around unobserved. He'd be caught for sure. Then it struck him: if he were a policeman or a soldier, he could move freely—even ask others for their papers. After five more minutes of thought and a trip to the washroom, he picked up the phone. "Sergeant, I've been robbed." He was speaking to the desk sergeant at the downtown Charles Street police station.

"Are you sure, sir? People sometimes misplace things."

"I didn't misplace my money belt. It was in a dresser drawer when I went to supper and now it's gone."

"We're pretty busy with the president's visit tomorrow, sir. I'll get someone over as soon as I can."

David hoped it wouldn't be a woman as he hung up and went back to watching out the window.

* * *

"We have lots of room, private. Will you be dining alone, or is someone else joining you?"

Not many army privates frequented the Acropolis. The waiter thought perhaps a more well-to-do guest might be accompanying Terbose.

"A Major Krause may be joining me for drinks in the bar after dinner. Come to think of it, he knows I am here and may join me for dinner. Perhaps I should just have a drink and wait."

"Very good, private. What would you like?"

"Castle lager."

The order didn't surprise the waiter. What surprised him when he returned was the sudden disappearance of his guest. He wondered if the man had gone to the men's room as he set the glass and bottle down and went back to his station. Fifteen minutes later he went to the washroom and called out but got no response. He shrugged as he returned to the dining room, picked up the untouched beer and glass, and returned to the bar.

Terbose easily disabled the alarm on the door to the roof with a screwdriver and a small shunt. He wondered if, given the run-down condition of the door, the alarm would have sounded anyway, but there was no use taking any chances. He had to stay close to the windows so that no one looking out would see him unless they stuck their nose right against the glass. As he looked over the coping on the edge of the roof, his heart soared.

There, fully lit and in full view, approximately five hundred meters away, was the Free State Stadium. Police, soldiers, and dogs patrolled the stands. He could even make out the color of the seats. *My God, what a spot,* he said to himself. The only problem he could see was that the dais, where Mandela would be speaking, was covered by a canopy. *I guess they didn't want the bastard to get sunstroke,* he mumbled to himself.

It was a simple matter for Terbose to pick out his sight lines to the entrance, where the president would leave the car, and the point he would emerge from under the stands up to the dais. Terbose would have several chances to shoot Mandela. He knew his first chance would be when the president left the car and stopped to acknowledge the crowd before he headed toward the stadium. If he got him there, at least the people would be saved the drivel he would spout. If he couldn't get a shot, he could still get him on the way out.

Terbose hunkered down under the restaurant's overhang for the night.

* * *

It was ten-thirty when Constable Joseph Webb arrived at David's room. Webb was a bit curious at first as to why this particular Englishman was robbed. It was not a luxury hotel, but it had a good reputation for safety. "How much money did you have in the money belt, sir?" He decided to at least go through the motions.

"A couple thousand rand, officer. There was a bit more than that in travelers' checks as well."

"And you're sure it is not still in your room."

"I've looked everywhere, constable. I am a frequent traveler and know the perils of leaving money around. I hear it is—" David was interrupted by the squawk of Webb's radio.

"Excuse me, sir. Four eighty-two, control."

"Webb, your wife wants you to call as soon as you're done there."

Jesus, David thought. *Why did she have to call him now?* "Why don't you call her from here, constable? Then you won't have to remember it later. If you're anything like me when I'm at work, I always forget to phone my wife."

"Thank you, sir." Webb dialed the number and took down a list of three items to bring home after his shift. "Now, sir, I just need a few more details before I leave. I don't hold much hope in finding your money, but we'll do our best."

"I'm sure you will." David drew back his right hand and unleashed a vicious jab at Webb's midsection. As Webb was going down, the constable lashed out with an ineffective left at David's solar plexus, but David merely absorbed the blow and landed a right cross to Webb's jaw. The officer hit the carpet, unconscious. "Sorry, fella," he said. "I hope I didn't hurt you too much." David removed the constable's uniform, badge, nightstick, keys, radio, and weapon. "I'm afraid I couldn't make you believe why it is important that I find someone who wants to kill your president."

David tied the constable securely with sheets from his bed that he had torn into strips. He hoped that would keep him until he found the assassin.

Before he left the room, David did one more thing. "Control, four eighty-two," he called in his poor Afrikaans while holding a piece of torn linens over his mouth.

"Four eighty-two, you're garbled."

"Control, need to go home for a couple of hours. Over."

"Roger. Be back by one. Come here to the station, but call before you leave home. It's quiet now, but you never know when it might get busy."

"Roger that."

David now had a car and a gun but no idea where the assassin was. He realized he only had until one or one-thirty to use his present disguise. He thought his first trip had better be to a shopping center. When they found Webb, he had better not look like the man the constable would describe.

13

Bright stars and a first quarter crescent moon did little to warm the gravel on the Swart Building's roof. Terbose began to wish he had worn something more than a light singlet under the attire he had exchanged for the private's summer fatigues. It was nearing midnight. A strong breeze began to blow out of the northwest. It made an eerie whistling sound in the antenna farm standing on top of the restaurant. Terbose hoped that the wind would die down by morning.

Terbose figured that the gorgeous creature and the skinny bastard who was screwing her must have been doing their job. He hadn't seen any sign of Henson. He wondered if Henson had actually arrived in the country, or if he were just a figment of den Kamp's imagination. He consoled himself with the fact that in roughly twelve hours it would be all over for the president. Terbose hated what Mandela was trying to do. Maybe when he got rid of him, they could go back to the old way, with whites in their rightful place as masters. He wondered if den Kamp's real goal was to set up a state inside the country where whites could get on with their lives without having to kowtow to the blacks. If it was, Terbose would be with him.

Terbose tried to get some sleep. He used his beret as a pillow and the flashing below the dining room window for a heating pad on his back, but sleep would not come. He thought of Henry. *I'll have to watch that bastard*, he mumbled to himself. *Henry will be my rival for head lieutenant in den Kamp's new state.* Den Kamp was a man he could follow. A strong leader who picked the best and let them do their job. *He doesn't put up with any crap either*, thought Terbose. *Look at the way he handled that Dieter. Took all the bullshit and moved on.* He thought of Marion. *My god, she was some piece.* The next half hour brought him some feeling of relief from the cold.

* * *

"Piet, den Kamp here." Den Kamp wanted action. At least he wanted to know that others were taking action.

"Yes, sir." The sleepy voice did nothing to reassure the South African head of Dominance that everything possible was being done to stamp out Henson and ensure Terbose's success.

"What's the status of the search for Henson?"

"As you directed, Henry's out hunting for him. I haven't alerted more forces to look for him specifically, but my men know that they're to report anything suspicious to me."

"I think you should be with your men. They will then see how urgent it is to find Henson."

"They also may find Terbose."

"That's possible, but I want you to get down to the station and report to me the moment you hear something. Maybe I should join you at the station."

"What would my men think? I need the head of SAPS to do my job? I'll get down there and call you the moment I hear anything." He no sooner put down the phone than it rang again. He peered at the clock. One-fifteen. "What is it now?"

"Sorry, sir," came the voice of his shift sergeant. "I thought you wanted to be briefed when something went amiss."

"Yes, Paul. I was just awakened needlessly a few moments ago and thought it was the same person. What's happened?"

"Our Constable Webb went out on a robbery call and didn't come back."

"Is he still missing?"

"No, he's not missing, but his uniform, gun, radio, and car are gone. We found him in a room at the Brandhof all tied up. The man who you thought might try to assassinate our president is probably impersonating him."

Piet needed to think fast. The sergeant could be right. It could be Terbose, using a police uniform to move about. "I'll be right there. Double your patrols." He slammed down the receiver. Terbose was smarter than den Kamp would give him credit for. Impersonating a policeman was a sure way to move around without getting picked up. *But it could just as easily be Henson.*

Piet swung his bad leg painfully out of bed, threw on his clothes, and was about to leave the room when his wife called from the bed. He hastily explained that someone was threatening to kill the president, and ran out of the room.

The station was mass confusion. Paul Brill and his deputy were both on the phone calling in all off-duty officers. Joe Webb was sitting beside Paul's desk dressed in sweats, a huge mug of coffee clasped in both hands. He was describing the man who had attacked him to another constable. The more Joe talked, the more Piet realized they were after Henson, not Terbose. He went to his office and called den Kamp again.

"Just because you have a description of him does not mean he will look the same the next time you see him," warned den Kamp. "He's a master of disguise."

"We'll find him. At least we know he's around the stadium now."

"Good. I'll let Henry know, too."

* * *

"Grant, can you come to my office?" Francis Edward's call came at 6:00 p.m. EST the day before Mandela's speech.

Grant supposed Edwards was going to want a report on the situation, but he couldn't tell him squat.

"What is the word on the Mandela case?"

"Not a damn thing," he answered. "I can't very well call their police or security people because we don't know who's mixed up in the plot."

"You mean you don't even have contact with your agent?" Edwards understood the rules very well. Regular contact was essential on a foreign mission to make sure goals were being met and dangers avoided.

"Yesterday he was headed for Bloemfontein and had avoided a couple of attempts to stop him. We agreed we would have no contact until after the speech tomorrow."

"That's two days. How do you know what's happening?"

"I don't. There was no time to set up regular links through an agent in South Africa. The threat may be from the very people we normally link up with. I could have set up a contact with the ANC, but they didn't want to be involved. So I'm in the dark. It's frustrating."

"It's damn stupid, if you ask me."

I didn't ask you, Grant felt like saying, but he bit his tongue. "I expect a call tomorrow morning. The speech is at five o'clcok a.m. our time."

"Let me know the minute you hear."

As Grant left the office, he wondered about the real reason for his boss's interest and resolved to keep better track of his infrequent trips. He thought about having someone tap Edwards's phone, but didn't think anyone would be stupid enough to do that.

* * *

David needed to survive without making anyone suspicious about his identity until about eleven the next morning. By that time, crowds of people would be streaming into the stadium, and it would be nearly impossible for the police and army to check everyone. They already had a poor description of him. When Webb came to his door, he was disguised in a wig he had purchased in Kimberley, long dark eyebrows, and a sheet wrapped around his middle under his sweater.

By one-thirty, David had ditched the police car, radio, and night stick between two dumpsters in the parking lot at the Fleurdal shopping center in the south end of the city, and changed from Constable Webb to David Reasons, alias Gregory Henson. He actually looked like the picture Henry had. He prepared himself for action and that old rush flooded his forty-four-year-old body. It was time to find the killer.

David stayed away from the streetlights on the three-mile walk back to King's Park. As soon as he reached it and looked across at the stadium, he saw where the assassin was likely to be hiding. Towering over the stadium lights and almost blocked from view by their brilliance stood an office building. He did not know that there was a restaurant on top, but he knew you could see into the stadium from the roof and that it was about five hundred yards from the assassin's target—a reasonable distance for a good marksman and a fatal one if the shooter was excellent. *Now, how could he get up there?*

David got to Loch Logan without being spotted. The night was cool, but he decided to go for a swim anyway. It seemed the most discrete way to get from the park to the building. He soon found that a channel went from the loch, right past the stadium, and almost changed his mind about the shooter's probable plan. They would certainly guard the banks of that canal tomorrow, but it would be fairly easy for a killer in a wet suit to surface, take a shot and dive below. That could be what he planned, though David couldn't see how he could know when to surface. It would have to be just when the president was leaving his car to go into the stadium, or just as he came out. Possibly he could have radio contact with an accomplice. The top of the building was more likely. The next problem was how the hell would he get up onto that roof? That street was crawling with patrols. There was no way to get there tonight.

David thought back to the tourist map he had studied in his room. He remembered there was an area to the north of the city center called Signal Hill. There would be plenty of places to hide there, and it would be closer to downtown than the shopping center to the south. He thought of buying some scuba gear and making his approach to the building from the canal but was not sure he could find the necessary gear being sold that late at night.

     * * *

Henry was beginning to get himself back into detective mode. When he left the hotel, he wandered about for about an hour trying to clear his mind of Marion, den Kamp, and the failures of the last forty-eight hours. Like David before him, he was eventually drawn to the loch. He found a sheltered spot where he could see the lights of the stadium and buildings around the downtown core. The breeze sang though the willows and brought coolness to both his body and mind. He wondered where Terbose was, or at least where he was most likely to be. It took him about three minutes of looking around to see the best spot. Just as he noticed the elegance of a shot from the roof of the Swart building, his cell phone jangled.

"It looks like Henson may be impersonating a cop. He ripped off a constable's clothes and car a couple of hours ago," den Kamp announced.

"Do you think it likely he's still a cop? He's smart enough to know we'd eventually catch on to him."

"I agree. At least we know he's not holed up in a hotel. Keep your eyes open."

"Definitely, sir." *What does he think I'm doing?* he grumbled as he snapped the phone shut. He was sure that Terbose would use the roof of the Swart building. He'd be high enough to see into the stadium and far enough away to have a good chance of escaping. *That would be the most important thing to that bastard*, he thought. *So, if Henson's as smart as we think he is, he'll be around the Swart building come speech time.*

To be keen and alert tomorrow morning, Henry knew he had better get some sleep.

* * *

Marion lay on her queen-sized bed, staring at the ceiling. She was sure things would fall into place. They hadn't caught Henson yet, but it looked like security had kept his head down. At least they hadn't heard that Terbose had been caught or eliminated. She hoped the prick got eliminated after he killed Mandela. Life could get a bit complicated if Eugene made him out to be a hero. Henry and Eugene were enough for her. She thought Dieter was interesting—a man of power. Her mind shifted forward, on to the days after Mandela would be killed and Eugene became a hero in Dominance. Maybe she should call Eugene and let him know she was going out to help Henry find Henson. Henry always took the straight forward, police approach. He needed someone to help him think like Henson.

"Eugene, Marion. Do you think I should go out and help Henry find Henson? I feel useless."

"Apparently Henson is now impersonating a police officer. Nothing to report on Terbose. Looks like he's safe. Why don't you come down to my room?"

"I don't think so, Eugene. You were pretty nasty tonight."

"Marion, that really wasn't meant for you. Sorry if it hurt you, but I understand if you don't want me right now. When we get Henson, we'll have a real celebration. You should probably get some sleep."

Marion was not excited about trying to sleep alone. She called Henry's cell after den Kamp hung up. "Marion, good to hear from you. I was thinking of calling. I think I know where Terbose will shoot from. Henson has surely figured it out by now too."

"Where?"

"The Swart building. You know that big office building across from the park with the restaurant on top."

"I know it. Are you there now?" She did not want to tell him that Eugene had already briefed her.

"No, I'm on my way back to the hotel…Just a minute. Here you are, sergeant. Yes, thanks…Just checking to make sure security is up to scratch. Are you still there, Marion?"

"I'm here. I guess I'll call it a night."

"I'll come join you."

"Don't bother." She changed her mind about sleeping with Henry. With their boss in the hotel it would be too risky. "You'll need your strength for tomorrow." She hung up. *Guess I will be sleeping alone,* she said to herself.

148

* * *

Things were settling down at the Charles Street station. The extra cops he had brought in had found no trace of Webb's attacker in the last hour. Sergeant Brill was ready to send them home so they would be rested for the morning's festivities when the phone rang.

"Sergeant, Lieutenant Meiring here. Have you heard anything about our private Maarten?"

"I don't have any report here. Why, is he missing?"

"He was on patrol in The Willows about three hours ago. When we went to pick him up, we couldn't find him"

"Let me check with my people here and get back to you."

"Right. I'm over here at Grey College."

Brill asked around the station and found no one who had seen or heard of the private. He went straight into Neiderhof's office. "Sir, there's something here that might interest you. The army just called about a missing private. No one has seen him. It could be our killer has changed from police to army."

And it could be that Terbose is as smart as Henson, Piet thought. "Why can't the army find him? Have they got as many people in the city as we have?"

"I don't know. They said they couldn't find him after his shift was over, and that was three hours ago."

"Maybe we should look for him. Is he from around here? Maybe he went home, or to his girlfriend's."

"I'll get back to the army and get the details. Then we can look for him."

"Thanks, Paul. Oh, on second thought, let me think about it. There's something funny here. I'll get back to you." As the sergeant left his office, Neiderhof thought to himself, *Terbose wouldn't leave the private around to answer questions, though. I wonder where he hid him.*

"Den Kamp, Neiderhof here. The army just reported one of their privates missing. Seems he disappeared about three hours ago. Now, that's before Henson took Webb's gear. Terbose must be dressed as a soldier."

"Well, well. Good for him. You can't have the police looking too hard for their private. They may find him."

"That's what I'm worried about."

"Tell them you're very busy with security at the moment and could they find their own soldier. That should keep things quiet for a while."

"Okay. I'll think of something."

Neiderhof went back to Paul Brill's office. "Listen, Paul. You're pretty busy, aren't you?"

"We sure as hell are. I've still got most of the crew out looking for this guy who took Joe Webb's stuff."

"This missing army private may be just a distraction dreamed up by the real assassin to put us off the scent. Are you sure it was the army who called?"

"The guy said he was Lieutenant Meiring."

"Well, call him back and make sure he really is army. Then, if he is, give him the, 'we'll get right on it,' routine, but don't take too many people off the present search."

"That's good, boss. I'll call him and let you know what happens." The sergeant forgot all about sleep for his reserves.

* * *

David had to pause a couple of times to let patrols go by on main streets, but he was neither stopped nor spotted on the journey from the streets of downtown to a thick cedar hedge about a half-mile up Signal Hill. It was cool in the hedge. His mind whirled around the probable action tomorrow. It did not rest on one subject for long. Was the assassin on top of that building? How did he get up there? Would the police look on the roof and make his job easier? Would they even think the assassin could kill at that distance? How would he get away tomorrow after the speech? Should he go to Cape Town to wait out the search, or through Johannesburg, Durban, or Port Elizabeth? He wished he knew how the South African police thought.

It was two o'clcok a.m. before David slept.

He awoke at six o'clock with a start. Helicopters were approaching from behind him. He hadn't thought about having to hide from them, and he burrowed more completely under the bush. They passed low overhead on their way to the stadium. It was full light, another beautiful, clear day.

14

Bloemfontein was ready for the president's visit. Red, white, and yellow roses hung in baskets from lamp poles on the downtown streets. The stadium was covered in banners and flags of South Africa, The Free State, and the city. In the larger centers—Johannesburg and Cape Town—there may have no shortage of crime going on, but Bloemfontein was full of enthusiasm and hope.

Terbose heard the whop, whop, whop of the helicopters' rotors before he spotted the two dots coming from the northwest. He crept over to the coping that surrounded the high roof and peeked over the edge. There was another roof below covering the south part of the office building. The restaurant overhung that roof and would keep him out of the pilots' sightlines. There was a twelve-foot drop. *Shit, that's a long way to jump,* he thought as he huddled out of sight of the helicopters.

Terbose breathed a sigh of relief as the birds moved toward the stadium. When they were flying dead away from him, he grabbed his briefcase, hauled himself over the coping, and dropped to the lower roof. The fall knocked the wind out of him. When he got his breath back, he felt a sharp pain in his right ankle.

In a couple of minutes he heard the sound of the helos increasing. He dragged himself to the shelter of the restaurant. They passed by on the north side of the building and banked to do a complete circuit. Terbose heard the sound of the rotors change as the pilots added collective to make the tight turn. If they hovered near the coping and below the level of the restaurant they could spot him. *I better get right up under the overhang*, he thought.

He quickly tossed his briefcase over to the side of the roof. As they whizzed around past the corner of the building, Terbose hauled himself painfully up onto the beams that supported the restaurant. *That was too fucking close*, he said to himself as the birds left to search the few other tall buildings in Bloemfontein's downtown core.

Terbose pulled up his pant leg to check his ankle. No real damage. In about six hours he was going to need that leg to get him out of there. He thanked God he hadn't been badly hurt in the jump, and, as he dropped back to the roof, he made sure to land on his good leg.

* * *

As Terbose took evasive action on the roof, David began his careful journey down Markgraaf Street from Signal Hill. One false step, one move that would mark him as a threat to the few people already out on the streets, one spotting by the patrols who, though now getting caught up in the spirit of the visit, were still looking for people without the proper papers, could end any chance he had to complete his mission. He still had the policeman's revolver but knew that using it, even in desperation, would likely spell the end to any chance of success.

Off to his right, just out of the park, a jeep went slowly north on Eerste Street, one block away. The driver and a young private were checking up and down all the side streets. Fast movement would catch their eyes. He backed slowly into the trees and held his breath. They must have spotted something because the jeep turned onto Barnes Street and accelerated toward him. David froze. *They couldn't have seen much.*

They slowed as they neared the tree behind which their quarry was hidden. "It was right about here, wasn't it?" David overheard the driver ask.

"I think it was the other side of Markgraaf." The jeep stopped at the intersection, then slowly went through.

David waited a full ten minutes. The jeep did not return. *Another hurdle cleared.*

The next major obstacle was two busy one-way streets. As he approached Zastron, he noticed with dismay that there was a lot of police activity a block away. The officers seemed to be going on and off shift, but none were particularly interested in their surroundings. He would not have worried as much had he known that these were homicide and robbery detectives and not actively engaged in presidential security. When the last of the detectives said their good mornings and disappeared either into the building or car parked around the back, he crossed the street.

Voortrekker Street was a different story. David didn't know it, but this street was on the route that the president would take to the stadium in a little less than six hours. As he watched the traffic from the entrance to a brand new Kentucky Fried Chicken franchise, he spotted a patrol of two policemen, three army corporals talking together on the south side of the intersection right across from where he was standing, and a lieutenant with a driver in a jeep checking out the ten or twelve people who were out early.

He felt awfully exposed. The building was locked. He could do nothing but stand and watch, heart in throat. Just as he thought the best plan might be to beat a retreat back to Signal Hill and await the midday crowds to hide him, a young man approached. He wore jeans and a white shirt, a new KFC button, with his name, Eldridge, proudly exposed. "We're not open for a couple of hours, sir. There's the Star Bakery, just a block down the street if you need something to eat."

"Thank you, but I'll just wait here for a few minutes. Do you know when the parade is coming through?"

"It should be here about eleven-thirty according to last night's paper. You're from out of town, aren't you?"

"Yes, from England, actually. I wanted to hear your president speak, so I arrived yesterday."

"It's quite an important speech. I think he wants us all to forgive and forget the past."

"That sounds like a good idea."

"Yes, but there still seems to be a lot of people who want the old ways. We coloreds don't get many good jobs yet. Excuse me, sir, but I have to get the place ready for business. We're expecting quite a crowd before and after the speech."

As he started out of the KFC entrance, he noticed someone familiar standing at the corner. It did not take long for his memory bank to dredge up the Klerksdorp bus station.

* * *

Henry had risen early. After a call to den Kamp for last-minute instructions and a call to Marion's room to make sure she was there, he headed out onto the streets. It was going to be a long morning. His search started at the front of the stadium and fanned out in ever-widening circles. His heart almost stopped when he saw the helicopters fly around the Swart building. Since they did not stay in the area, he assumed that Terbose was either not there or well hidden. He had been awake for an hour when he reached Voortrekker and Markgraaf streets.

His search would have been over had he turned and looked behind him. David closely resembled the photo that Henry had showed around. Henry was a good policeman, but he was no spy catcher or anti-terrorist agent. The ANC he had fought for so many years tended to be good at hiding and striking without warning, but were not particularly adept at subtle escape and evasion tactics, blending with crowds to go unnoticed and hiding in unlikely places. After ten minutes or so, each person he checked seemed to look the same, and no one had seen the man in the photo he showed them. They were all happy and waiting for their beloved president to appear—no threatening gestures, no scowling faces, and no Gregory Henson.

He crossed Voortrekker and headed east, away from the stadium. Time for a coffee and breakfast, he thought as he spotted an "Open" sign in the window of an office-building diner.

* * *

David's eyes followed Henry's progress. As soon he disappeared into the coffee shop, David stepped boldly out onto Voortrekker. It was still not safe to cross, but cross he must. If he stayed where he was, he would certainly be stopped by one of the patrols that were still thick on the parade route. Sweat poured from his hands and brow as he left the relative safety of the KFC outlet and into the intersection. Two heart-stopping minutes later, he was seated at a small round table in the back corner of the Star Café. He ordered a large muffin and an even larger coffee. Sometimes an agent needs eyes in the back of his head—that sixth sense that allows a man to know when danger approaches. It came from being in dangerous situations time after time until it became a part of his nature. David would need all of that sense to get him the final five blocks to the building where he was sure his quarry would be.

As he left the café, David sensed something was wrong. Something had happened that he had missed. He did not know what it was that made him do so, but he stopped beside the doorway to the Shell station, south of the bakery. He was able to see the street as a reflection in the clean window.

The feeling of danger—real, imminent, palpable danger—would not go away. He had to get off the street now.

He pushed open the door of the garage and went in but felt no more secure. He glanced out the window, just a peek, without turning his head. Two patrolmen, one of whom was Constable Webb, strolled slowly by on the sidewalk.

They glanced in. Webb grabbed his partner's arm and dragged him past the pumps. David left through the service bays out a side door into an alley behind the station as the two constables raced through the garage.

* * *

Mayor Daniel Oppermann was ready for the arrival of his president. He, like the majority of his citizens, admired Mandela. He knew there were forces at work in his city and the province that would like to return to the apartheid days, but did not know who they were. By eight o'clock he was seated in his modern, functional, but unpretentious office at City Hall. He knew the president had simple tastes—no great feast and fanfare for him.

He planned coffee and muffins in his office for the arrival at ten-thirty, followed by the closed car motorcade on a short circular route—east on Charles, north on President Brand, west on Voortrekker, and south on Eerste to the stadium. Daniel was most concerned about the president's safety while in the car. Anyone wanting to assassinate him could hide in a building along the route. Even though police and army would have swept those buildings by the time the motorcade arrived, a clever assassin could hide among the crowd and enter the building after it was searched. Daniel had served in army intelligence for ten years and knew the dangers.

To aid in the security arrangements, he had not let anyone, including the army and police and his own staff, know about the proposed route until the night before, when he released the news to the army commander, Piet Neiderhof, and the *Bloemnuus News*, the local Friday paper through which he hoped to attract a large crowd to the parade.

He picked up the phone and called Piet Neiderhof. When his chief of police answered, he asked, "Are you sure all security possible is in place for the parade and speech? Nothing can happen to Mandela on my watch!"

"My men are vigilant. The president will be well protected."

"I'm sure he will. How's the leg, by the way? Going to let you attend the ceremonies tomorrow?"

"It still hurts, but I'll be there." *I'll keep an eye open for what you're up to as well,* he thought as he hung up. *I better be there or den Kamp will kill me!*

* * *

President Mandela and his Minister of Safety and Security rode together in the presidential limo to Pretoria Airport where the ancient, but reliable, presidential *Falcon*, which would take them to Tempe Airport in Bloemfontein, sat, prepped and guarded on the tarmac. They were scheduled to leave at 8:00 a.m. The day was bright and clear. The chance to bring the country one step closer to real freedom and prosperity for all their people lifted their spirits. Today they would take one more tiny step down a road strewn with the potholes and debris left by decades of racism.

"Now that I've accepted the fact I can't change your mind about taking this risk, Nelson, I'm looking forward to this day. In spite of all the talk about assassination, I'm sure you will be well protected and make a great speech."

"Yes, it's good to get out of the office for a while. I enjoy meeting our people. I wish you would forget about the dangers. We're always in danger. Bloemfontein is probably one of the safer places we will visit."

* * *

"Any sign of Terbose?" den Kamp asked Henry. He was phoning from his desk in the war room at the City Lodge Hotel, close to the action. Marion was at his side. His first lieutenant was out on the street, and his

159

primary force, Louis Terbose, was near its target. The battle was about to be joined. It was nearly ten o'clock.

"I haven't been able to spot him, but I still think I know where he is," Henry replied. "No sign of Henson either. The police or the army could have him."

"Don't be a fool. Where are you now?"

"I'm just outside the Raddsaal. I have been over every street in the past two hours. I don't see how Henson can take out Terbose if he's not around."

"He's around. You said Terbose was probably on the roof of the Swart building. Go there!"

"I'm on my way, sir." Henry was happy to be given a direct order. At least now he wouldn't catch the blame if he didn't find Henson. *Den Kamp is probably right anyway.*

* * *

David sprinted to the end of the alley onto Elizabeth. Webb and his partner arrived at the side entrance of the Shell station just in time to see him turn left. There was neither time nor opportunity to get off a shot. And there were too many people out on Elizabeth Street. They raced to the corner.

Before the cops reached the main street, David was hidden in the beautifully manicured, stately cedars that guarded the walls of the Appeal Court, South Africa's center of justice. He watched the two officers run by on President Brand Street. By the time they realized he was not ahead of them, David was strolling calmly down Elizabeth toward the stadium as part of the thickening crowds and no apparent threat to anyone.

15

There were seven around the table in the city hall council chambers. All but one were upbeat about the prospects of a successful outcome to the day's formalities. The mayor was ebullient. He had never met President Mandela. He had only ever met Botha once, and only under the less than pleasant circumstances of a court martial.

Daniel Oppermann had been a young lieutenant, fresh out of the South African Military College at Voortrekkerhoogt. He was in charge of local security during one of Botha's visits to what was then the colony of Namibia. He did not know it then, and he did not know it now, but another man at the table played a vital role in his being court marshaled. Crane Bertel had set up an operation to capture Botha during the visit. One of Lieutenant Oppermann's corporals had saved the president by throwing himself at the ANC abductor and getting himself severely wounded. In a letter to the Chief of General Staff, Botha had been effusive in his praise of the corporal's bravery and scathing in his condemnation of the lax security. Oppermann's career ended almost as soon as it had begun.

Oppermann didn't know it, but the nervous man at the table was concerned about the same fate. Niederhof was in charge of the city police. He knew an assassin was out there and he would certainly be blamed—at least in part—if something happened to Mandela. He was much more concerned, however, with what might happen to the assassin, and with the wrath of den Kamp, if the attempt failed.

The mayor explained the security arrangements for both the parade and speech, the setup and timing of activities at the stadium, and other administrative details. When he had finished, he asked, "Minister Bertel, why was it necessary to bring in a company of infantry to help us with security? Surely there is no threat in this city."

"We told your Mr. Neiderhof the reason," Bertel explained. "He must have neglected to advise you. I have reason to believe there will be an assassination attempt sometime during the president's tour."

Oppermann looked at Neiderhof. "Is that true, Mr. Neiderhof?"

"Yes. I did not think it necessary to tell you. We are perfectly capable of protecting the president and have set up additional patrols."

"Let us not waste time now. I will speak to you later."

When the meeting ended, Bertel was left wondering about Neiderhof's motives, as well as den Kamp's. "I'm sorry to see you have had an accident," Bertel asked. "How did it happen?"

The police chief was well aware of den Kamp's explanation of his injury. "Well, minister, I was trying to arrest the man you wanted captured for that murder in Oudtshoorn last spring. He turned on me before I could get a shot off and hit me in the knee. I'm quite sure we scared him off, though, if you were concerned he might be a threat to the president."

"I was concerned and still am. I trust your failure to advise the mayor will not increase the chances he may slip through our hands." Neiderhof gave no sign he felt the criticism.

"It is time we left for the parade. Advise your people to be extra vigilant, Mr. Neiderhof. You may use the phone in my office." The mayor was not used to incompetence on behalf of his chief of police. The city's crime rate had dropped since Neiderhof took over more than three years ago. It was an interesting exchange between Neiderhof and the Minister. He would ask him about it when this was over. God, how he hoped it would end well.

The president, Bertel, and the mayor headed for the Mercedes that would take them to the stadium. It was parked at the bottom of the city hall steps.

Den Kamp's directive to keep an eye on Bertel could not be accomplished. Neiderhof was not invited to join them in the Mercedes and had to make his way to the stadium in his police Opel.

* * *

Henry did not have a schedule. He had one directive—find and eliminate Henson—and still saw no way to accomplish it. The cheering noises from the steps at city hall reached him as he crossed Henry Street a block behind the motorcade, but they only served to show him that others were enjoying the day while he was not. He started to wonder if den Kamp was right in trying to kill the president. Were they helping the return to the old ways or hastening the new ones by creating a martyr?

I better drop these thoughts if I'm going to find Henson, thought Henry. He decided the best place to watch for him was the fountain beside the canal.

* * *

Den Kamp and Marion watched out the window of den Kamp's hotel room. They were not involved in the festivities. "Eugene, how do we get out of this when Terbose completes his mission?"

"Simple. Bertel does not know where I am. He will call me at the office. Pretoria will have the call transferred to my cellular. I will tell him I will be there in a couple of hours. When I meet him, he will, no doubt, fire me. He won't be able to prove I had anything to do with the assassination. I made up a story to cover that. Then you and I will just disappear for a while."

"Good, I thought you would have a plan. Where do we go?"

"Marion, my dear, my condo in Durban has all the amenities we could possibly want. We can have a well-deserved rest. Then we may leave the country. Dieter will look after us financially, especially if we get Henson for him." It helped to talk of what would happen when they achieved success. It kept the wolves of failure out of his conscious.

"And if Terbose is not successful?"

"Bertel will probably just reprimand me for not getting Terbose before today. I'll probably be able to keep my job. Then, we'll have to answer to Dieter. He'll be abusive, but I can stand that. I will tell him we need more time and perhaps additional training for you and Henry in Libya."

Marion particularly liked the sound of "we."

"So this mission is not all or nothing?"

"It is for Terbose."

* * *

David watched Henry stride down Elizabeth Street. He wondered why he was in such a hurry. David was careful not to be in the line of sight if his enemy happened to turn around. He was nearing that point where continual concentration could lead to loss of focus. *On prior missions I overcame this—I will on this one.* Combat was approaching and he needed every ounce of strength to face the enemy.

He heard cheers. The parade had started. The president was on his way—on his way to the stadium and into danger. He thought it possible that the killer could attempt to hit the president in the motorcade instead of in the stadium. One could hide in a building along the route and open a window when the parade came by. But the car was likely bulletproof. The killer would be on that three-hundred-foot building down the street; he was sure of it. David just had to stick with his gut.

* * *

Terbose also heard the cheers. He opened his briefcase and removed the four parts of his weapon: barrel, stock, bolt mechanism, and scope. They fitted together smoothly—no glitches or burrs. He had sighted the rifle two weeks ago in a remote area of the mountains around Oudtshoorn. After three tries and adjustments, he had been able to pick an orange flower off a desert cactus at seven hundred meters. The flower was only one tenth the size of a human head.

When he had the rifle completely assembled, he limped in a crouched position from the shelter of the restaurant to the edge of the meter-and-a half-coping, rose up, placed his elbows on the lip, and sighted in the stadium entrance. It was the size of a barn door at seventy-power magnification, even though the target was over five hundred meters away. Terbose swung the sight back and forth. He needed a good aim point. The president would get out on the stadium side. His bodyguard might leave Terbose a shot.

The helos came back from the west. Terbose dove for the base of the restaurant, his sore ankle forgotten.

He had no time to climb up under the overhang of the restaurant before the deafening sound of rotors at high torque from only twenty meters above him burst into his head, shutting out all thought of movement. They did not descend. They did not turn. As he crawled back to the side of the roof, the pain in his ankle returned. Once again he sighted the entrance where the president would arrive in about five minutes.

* * *

David passed on the north side of the Swart building. He studied the top of the building while moving through the thick crowd. He noted the revolving restaurant. If the assassin could immobilize all the staff and patrons in some way, that would be a good place to shoot from. He'd have to break a window, though; there was no way to take an accurate shot through plate glass. The roof beside the restaurant was the most likely place. It was time to get up there.

He turned the corner at Elizabeth and Eerste just in time to see the motorcade round the corner off Voortrekker. The police, army, and all the citizens on the street looked toward the motorcade. No one watching the parade paid him any attention as he entered the lobby of the Swart building.

As David waited for one of the six elevators that daily take the hundreds of provincial government employees to their place of duty, Henry yanked open the entrance door. Again, David's sixth sense activated. It started him moving before he even heard the door close. As Henry was drawing his gun, David leapt to the right, yanked open the emergency door, and began the long ascent to the restaurant.

Henry got to the door just as it banged shut. By the time he reached the stairs, David was on the second floor landing and increasing his distance between himself and his pursuer. By the time Henry reached the fifth floor, he wished he had kept himself in better shape. He had slowed to a plodding one step at a time pace by the ninth, and began to think of other ways to stop Henson. Catching him in a foot race was not going to work. If he remembered correctly, the stairs didn't go to the restaurant. They stopped just below it for night security. Henson would have to use the elevator to get to the restaurant. He went out to the ninth floor lobby and took the elevator to the top.

David stopped at floor twelve. He heard no sound from behind. He guessed his pursuer had taken the elevator and would probably be waiting for him on the roof. Even though he slowed his pace and quietly ascended each floor, checking the flight above when he rounded each corner, it was a tired David who reached the twenty-fifth floor. He was also puzzled. The stairs stopped just above him in a metal grate that held air-conditioning equipment. He was trapped. The first thing he did was stop and listen to determine if his enemy had resumed the chase up the stairs. Not a sound. He raced back down the stairs, not knowing that his enemy was waiting for him just one floor above.

* * *

"They certainly seem enthusiastic about the visit, Nelson. I have only seen a more cheerful and rambunctious crowd in Cape Town, when I made my first public speech." That was not quite true, but Bertel was putting his concerns aside and getting caught up in the reception Mandela was receiving in the City of Roses. He could not quite forget his responsibilities, though. The looming chance of assassination pressed mercilessly into his consciousness. "Don't forget, when we get to the stadium, you stay in the car until I get out and make sure the police have the area well covered."

"But, sir," Mayor Oppermann objected. "The police and the army have the situation well under control."

"I'm sure they do, but I will leave first."

"Gentlemen, we are nearing the stadium. I'm sure the mayor is aware of possible threats. I will wait in the car until you both have left." Part of the reason Mandela was now president was his diplomatic ability.

As they approached the stadium, the din increased. Happy faces pressed close to the car to get a glimpse of their leader. Flags and banners waved. Police and soldiers were everywhere.

The Mercedes stopped right at the gates and Neiderhof pulled up behind. He thought this would be the best chance Terbose had. He swung his injured leg out of the car door and got painfully upright. Automatically he glanced up to the top of the Swart building. He saw a quick glint, perhaps off the sight, perhaps off a piece of jewelry. His heart nearly stopped. Quickly he averted his gaze. No one was looking at him. Some police were looking up at the surrounding buildings, but none seemed to notice the flash.

* * *

Terbose took careful aim at a point about three feet above the top of the back door of the Mercedes. The passenger door and the other rear door, the one on his side, opened and two men got out. The sight moved to both of them. Neither was Mandela.

The other rear door was opened by the huge black man who had gotten out on the street side. Terbose swore to himself as the man handed the president out and moved quickly—too quickly for Terbose to take aim and squeeze off a shot—between his target and the car. In the cross hairs of his sight, he followed the procession into the gate until they disappeared. He then swung the rifle to the point he predicted they would emerge onto the rugby pitch. They seemed to be out of sight for ten minutes. Every minute he stayed at the edge of the roof increased the chances of his being spotted.

Emerge they did. One last chance before they got to the podium. Two bodyguards and the black giant seemed always to be in the way. When Mandela's head emerged from the crowd for a moment, he tightened his pressure on the trigger. The steps to the podium neared. The head disappeared once again behind a bodyguard. He relaxed his right index finger. Mandela disappeared under the canopy. Louis disappeared under the restaurant and painfully hauled himself up on the protective beam. He would be able to tell when the speech ended by the noise. It was then he noticed his gun case on the roof below. He hoped the helo pilots wouldn't know what it was as they continued to survey the event from above.

16

As soon as the band major of the Grey College Cadet Band was sure all the VIPs were settled on the podium, he raised his baton and they struck up a loud and tuneful, if somewhat brassy, rendition of "Die Stem." A few of the trumpets missed the high notes and the cymbals did not clash on cue every time, but they made up for their lack of polish with genuine enthusiasm. The crowd added their exuberant musical talents to the happy din—"Uit die blou van ons se hemel, uit die diepte van ons see…" combined with, "Ringing out from our blue heavens, from our deep seas breaking round…" Two languages, many cultures, countless voices, proclaimed their belief in their land.

"You see, Crane. There's no danger. They love us here," Mandela whispered to his chief of security as the last notes died away and he, Neiderhof, and Bertel moved to their seats on the dais.

Mayor Oppermann began the ceremonies. "Citizens of Bloemfontein, I am happy—in fact proud—to be with you on this glorious spring day. We have been foremost in the search for peace in our great Free State and are honored to have our beloved president, Nelson Mandela, with us today. It is his first visit to our city, and we are most pleased to welcome him. President Mandela." A roar from the crowd brought the president to the microphone.

"Mayor Oppermann, distinguished guests, citizens of Bloemfontein, I salute you…" The crowd roared once again. When relative calm returned, he continued. "Mayor Oppermann and his staff and all of you have made me feel very welcome. Your beautiful City of Roses already seems a second home to me." Another roar. "These are troubled times in our great country. When I first became president, Desmond Tutu and I began a process of healing the old wounds of apartheid. My purpose here today is to tell you that my government intends to continue that process and remove the scourge of racism from our nation forever." As if on cue, the crowd erupted in loud applause.

And so he went on with his speech. They yelled and cheered at the appropriate places. The police and army security force, as well as the presidential guards, kept a sharp look out. Terbose could not hear every word, but he could hear the approbation of the crowd. He cursed the man under his breath. *I must get rid of him.' He's too popular. If this continues, we'll be stuck with black rule forever.*

* * *

By the time David got back down to the twenty-second floor, he realized no one was chasing him. He still had to get to the roof. He got out, called the elevator, and took it to the restaurant.

Henry was ready when the doors opened—Beretta drawn but hidden, in case it was just another customer. He waited a second for Henson or whomever it was inside to come out. No one did. He carefully stuck his head and shoulders in. David grabbed his arm and jerked. The force drove Henry's head into the back wall. Just as he passed out, he looked up and saw Henson step over him. As David left, he punched "G" on the elevator console.

The restaurant was nearly deserted. The maitre d' was on the phone at the bar. Two bar customers got off their stools and headed toward David, who held the gun out in front and yelled, "I need to get to the roof!" They froze, but there was no response, just awed silence. "Put that phone down," he ordered the maitre d'. "There may be an assassin on the roof. How do I get up there?"

The men at the bar had been watching the speech on TV. One of them got back his wits to ask David, "How can he be killed from here? We're nearly a kilometer away from the stadium."

"No problem for an expert shot. Besides, we're a lot closer than that. How do I get to the roof?" David noticed that the maitre d' had hung up the phone, but assumed more police were on the way.

"Are you police?" the maitre d' asked.

"Yes. Hurry. How do I get to the roof?"

No answer.

David grabbed him by the collar and dragged him over to the window past the slowly revolving floor where the tables were located. They both looked out on the roof. Nothing was there. He was about to drag his hostage back to the bar when he noticed the lower roof. They both sidled around the moving floor to the south side and peered over the edge. No one. David was just about ready to give up and make a break for the stadium when he spotted Louis's empty weapon case. "See. That's a weapon case. Now, how do I get to the lower roof?"

"You'll have to get down from the upper one, or go down two floors and out the roof exit." The maitre d' finally realized the danger. "We could wait for more police. They'll be here any minute."

"No time. How do I get to the upper roof?"

"Through the kitchen."

* * *

"...I thank you for coming to meet with me today, wish you every success in the future, and pray that the day will soon come when we all can live together in the peace that God intended for us." The crowd roared its approval. Bertel, Mayor Oppermann, and Piet Neiderhof joined him at the podium. Mandela basked in the applause for a full three minutes, waving to the crowd.

Bertel was first to speak. "Time to leave, Nelson. Mayor Oppermann, would you please lead us to the car." The four left, Mandela still waving. He was happy. It was a good start to his tour. He knew that Bloemfontein was mainly loyal to the new regime, but he did not expect such an outpouring.

Now it will happen, Neiderhof thought.

Bertel knew they must not relax. His eyes darted around the stadium's roof. He signaled to the security men to form a cordon around the group as they made their way through the crowd, now streaming onto the pitch.

* * *

Terbose lowered himself from his perch, raced in a crouch to the edge of the coping, raised his Sako sniper's rifle to his shoulder, and sighted in the stadium infield. His ankle felt much better. The crowds around the official party left no opening for a shot. *It'll have to be when he goes to his car*, he thought, and sighted in the exit.

* * *

David let the maitre d' go and pushed through the swinging doors. The roar from the TV announced that the speech was over. David raced through the kitchen and followed Terbose's route to the roof. He noted the bypassed security and increased his pace. He pushed open the door and stepped out.

David got to the edge just as the official party came though the exit. He saw Terbose, rifle at his shoulder and eye pressed to the scope. Even though he could not see Mandela, he knew there was no time to jump down to the lower roof. He would have to take out the assassin from where he stood. Terbose had sighted the crosshairs on Mandela's forehead. The .357 Magnum slug from David's weapon did not stop Terbose's right index finger from reflexively squeezing the trigger, but it did kill the marksman before the round intended for the president's head left its cartridge.

The .308 slug from Louis's Sako went high and right of its target, flattening itself on the steel frame of the stadium exit door.

Bertel forced his president to the ground with one scooping movement of his powerful right arm. They both lay panting on the sidewalk as the crowd closed in around them.

It was only moments after the sounds of the shot ringing off the stadium door that the police and army personnel realized what had happened and swung into action.

* * *

Henry awoke propped up between the elevator doors in the lobby. When his elevator car arrived with its unconscious cargo from the restaurant level and the door opened, there was no one to notice the passed out policeman. After the usual minute delay, the door closed again. It was a full five minutes later, just as Terbose was taking aim at Mandela, that a man who had decided to get away from the stadium ahead of the crowd and a good table at the Greek restaurant pressed the call button.

Henry was groggy but had enough sense to ask the man for a report after flashing him his badge. The man had missed the assassination attempt. The sound of the shots had not penetrated the steel and glass of the building. "I don't really know, sir. I came in from the stadium, just as the speech was about over and saw you out cold."

"Find a phone and call emergency. I think someone may have tried to kill our president."

"My God. There's police on the street. I won't need to phone."

"Okay. You get them. He's inside this building." Henry went back into the elevator.

The man turned and ran out to alert the officers he saw standing guard as he left the stadium.

* * *

The ten people in the restaurant were glued to the window after they heard the muffled sound of two nearly simultaneous shots. What they saw was Louis and his rifle slumped against the wall of the lower roof. What they did not see was David Reasons racing back into the kitchen. They heard him knock over a rolling steel tray of dirty dishes as he painfully banged his shoulder against it. One or two moved back into the restaurant just as he burst through the kitchen door. "What happened?" the man who had asked David about the extreme range of the shot asked. "Is the president all right?"

"I hope so," was David's response as he rushed over to the elevator doors and jabbed a button. "I must get to the stadium to find out," was all the explanation the startled group received.

When the elevator arrived, David expected at least one, and maybe more, policemen to rush out. He stayed flat against the wall beside the door to at least have a moderate chance of escape.

No one was in the car. David rushed in and pushed "10." When the doors closed he quickly removed a ceiling insulation panel, the emergency exit cover, scrambled onto the top of the elevator, and replaced the hatches in the same order in which he had removed them.

* * *

"What happened, Neiderhof?" Den Kamp had been watching the festivities with ever increasing disgust on the room's TV. Mobile cameras had been quick to pick up the action outside the stadium, but it was not clear from either the pictures or the explanation by the commentators what had really happened. Neiderhof's call came just as he was about to leave for the stadium.

"Terbose's shot missed the president. Mandela appears safe. We have failed."

"Are you sure Mandela wasn't hit? TV pictures show him on the ground under Bertel."

"No, he wasn't. There were two shots, almost simultaneous. Has Henry called in?"

"No, he was supposed to be at the Swart building to keep Henson away from Terbose. Anyway, we've got to get you away from this mess. Meet me back at the hotel room."

When Henry arrived at the restaurant, he ran into a very suspicious group. He flashed his badge at the maitre d' and demanded to know what had happened. The story he got dropped his heart into his stomach and raised his blood pressure. "You mean he just went down the elevator?"

"Not two minutes ago. He said he was police, but I don't think so."

"Is the man on the roof dead?"

"I think so. He hasn't moved."

Henry went to the window and confirmed the diagnosis. There was a lot of blood on the coping and a hole in the back of Terbose's head. "There are other police on the way. Make sure they get all the details. I am going after the killer."

When Henry reached the lobby there were only police there. He described Henson to their sergeant. He knew they must find him soon. If that bastard got any head start, he'd be gone. *They'll soon figure out that it was Henson who probably saved the president if I don't get him right away.* He sent the cops to search the building, went outside, and phoned his boss.

Den Kamp was livid when he heard Henry's story. He ordered his lieutenant to join Marion, Neiderhof, and himself for a council of war.

* * *

It took little time for Bertel to organize a panic trip back to Tempe Airport and a flight back to Pretoria. The city Mercedes, with its driver slowly coming out of shock, was commandeered for the task. As the stress from the last few moments began to wear off, the president began to think. "My God, Crane. I guess you were right. The crowd seemed so receptive. Where did the assassin come from?"

"My gut feeling is that den Kamp assigned the assassination to that army lieutenant who killed the major at our training base. It wouldn't surprise me if Neiderhof was involved as well." He quickly described his two meetings with den Kamp, the unlikely story about Neiderhof's injury, and his having called in support from a friend in Zimbabwe.

"We must find this man and reward him."

"No, Nelson, I don't think so. First of all, we don't know who took the shot. It could be I was wrong to call in help and the man sent in was the one who tried to kill you."

"Does that seem likely?"

"No, but we can't take a chance right now. I don't want it coming out that someone in the party called in an assassin. We must not be seen to be resorting to violence. You and I are finished with the old days, even if some people are not."

"You're right. We should stay out of it. Let the man get away. Perhaps you should tell den Kamp about your suspicions. Have him let the man get away."

"It might be a good way to draw out den Kamp. If he proceeds with trying to capture him, I'll know he was the one who plotted against you."

"You're not sure it's den Kamp, are you?"

"I'm not sure I can prove it is." He picked up and opened his cell phone.

17

David stayed on top of the elevator for what he thought must be three hours. It was pitch black, he was tired, hungry, and thirsty, but at least he had a chance to rest. He had done what he could to make himself safe from the pursuit that was going on in the building. Hopefully the enemy would soon give up and begin to look elsewhere. As he clung to consciousness on top of the car, his mind drifted back to the distant past. The top of the elevator could have been his special hideout by the Scioto River, where, as a young boy, he would cower in fear of his grandfather.

It was spring, school had finished for the year, and the thought of being at home each day had been tearing at him. He had loved the closeness he would have with Grandma during the day. She would read with him, and he would show her how much he had learned at school. She would let him go on long walks, though her heart was not strong enough to accompany him. She had made him feel loved.

Then suppertime would arrive. Grandpa would descend from his Cadillac into the warm kitchen with the coldness of the spring wind into their happiness. He would demand to know what accomplishments his young charge had achieved that day and railed on about his sloth when he was told David had only been reading about Anne of Green Gables and walking by the river. After supper, Grandpa's harshness would drive David outside, where he could escape to his hideaway. When Grandpa found him, he would be lashed with the belt, shut in for a week, and denied his favorite books. These were the punishments that made him determined to ultimately escape.

Escape, as he now had to do. The forces looking for him would extract an even greater toll on him if they found him—likely his life. In some ways, he could thank the old bastard for being so tough. At least he'd learned the dangers of being found.

* * *

Den Kamp, Neiderhof, Jackman, and Aflect had just finished their second double Glenlivet when den Kamp's cell phone rang.

A polite voice on the other end asked if this was the head of SAPS. When den Kamp replied in the affirmative, he was asked to call the minister on his cellular immediately.

"Yes, Bertel here," the minister responded from his chair in the manager's office at Tempe Airport where he, the president, and six bodyguards were waiting for the *Falcon* to be prepared for flight.

"Den Kamp returning your call, minister."

"Have you heard what happened here?"

"Yes, sir. I caught it on local TV."

"Local TV! Where are you?"

"There was a news flash on the News Channel here in my office. I always turn the set on in my office during special events." He must be more careful. He was in enough trouble without telling Bertel he'd been in Bloemfontein all day.

"Get in touch with Neiderhof. Find out who fired the shot. I heard someone killed the assassin after he got the shot off."

It must have been just as he was getting it off for Terbose to miss, Den Kamp thought. There is no way Terbose would miss a free shot. "I'll call Neiderhof. Was he not with you at the ceremonies?"

"Yes, but he disappeared. Vanished. I talked to his captain at the station before we left and he hasn't heard from him either. I want a full report on my desk by Monday morning. Get on it right now." Bertel slammed his phone shut. "I'm pretty sure den Kamp's involved in this, Nelson. I'll have Arnold Graham carry out a complete investigation."

"Remember, friend, I do not wish to undo all the goodwill that the people of Bloemfontein have shown for our cause because of some disgruntled police officer. But perhaps it is best to get it out in the open."

* * *

"Well, Neiderhof, you and I have some work to do, so get a story ready by Monday," den Kamp advised as he snapped his phone shut. "Put someone in charge here and come back with me right now. It's going to be a long weekend. I'm not looking forward to this meeting with the minister. I'm damn sure now he knows what happened. We'll all be in trouble if we can't come up with a good explanation."

"What do you want us to do?" Henry asked.

"You and Marion convince the locals that it is important we catch the man who killed Terbose. Get out a story that Henson was the assassin and planted the evidence on Terbose as he tried to stop him. Don't, for heaven's sake, use either name, though. We need to limit Terbose's name in the news as much as possible. If Henson gets out of the city, we'll have a terrible time finding him again. I can use my influence to keep the airport police on the lookout, but if he leaves by car, train or bus…"

"We're on it. How do we contact you?"

"Cell phone. I don't know where Neiderhof and I will be. If things get nasty, we'll all retreat to my condo in Durban. We can figure out how to get out of the country from there."

"Where is your condo?"

"Marion knows."

I'll bet she does, Henry muttered under his breath as the three left.

* * *

There were three elevators in the Swart building. Periodically, one of the other two would swoosh past, disturbing David's reverie.

He heard many voices, scraps of conversations, some of which made him chuckle. Some rides made him almost dizzy. First up, then down, then pause for a moment, then back up or down some more. He had neither thought what it would be like to ride on the top of an elevator in a busy building, let alone experienced the feeling. During one of his rides he overheard a young policeman ask his partner, "Why in God's name are we searching for a man who saved the president's life?"

"Maybe he's the one who tried to kill the president and then shot the guy on the roof."

"Doesn't make sense. The guy on the roof had the Sako."

"Yeah, but that could have been planted."

David knew he couldn't afford to turn himself in. Dominance might be able to convince the people of that second explanation.

During another ride, a man who sounded like a senior officer remarked to a junior, "I had no idea there were so many offices in this bloody building. How many public servants do we need, anyway?"

"There are quite a lot, aren't there, sir," came the discrete reply.

"Who's co-coordinating this search, corporal?"

"I don't know, sir. I think it's the local police."

"Do you know how many floors are left to be searched?"

"I think we've done them all."

"Who the hell are we looking for? They were probably working together. The body on the roof looked like the assassin to me."

"A cop from Pretoria seemed to think the assassin is still at large and set up the man on the roof."

"I'm going to check in with HQ when we get down."

"Yes, sir."

When the elevator remained stationary for a full half hour and David heard no more conversations, he decided it was safe to leave his perch. No one searched the top of the elevators. If they had, he was ready to take out whoever stuck his head up through the top of the car, or even jump to another car as it passed him. He didn't have to. If someone in Intelligence were the enemy, they would surely know enough to look for a trained agent on top of an elevator.

He rode down to the basement and found a side door marked "Emergency exit only—Opening will set off alarm." He got up on his toes and examined the sensor switch that would activate the alarm and found it would not be easy to bypass. He wondered if the front door was locked or guarded. If it were locked nobody could get to the restaurant. The thought of the restaurant made him realize he had not eaten anything that day since the muffin and coffee. He pushed open the stairwell door to the lobby a crack. There was no one at the front desk.

As he came out of the building onto Eerste Street, all was quiet. David looked over at the stadium a block away. He would dearly like to know what happened to the president. David hoped he hadn't been hit. He had always admired Mandela and his courage to endure so many years in prison and come out strong enough to become president of his country. He sure as hell didn't deserve to be shot.

David crossed the street and park, back to the university's hospital where he had left his Rover. The street was deserted—no soldiers, no cops, nobody. It appeared that the search for him was over. The day's excitement was gone, and people had taken the afternoon off to be with their families and keep track of events on TV. He wondered if anyone was still looking for him.

* * *

"Well, sergeant, I don't care what you think." Henry was getting mad at the desk sergeant. He could not convince him to send out a large number of his men to hunt down Henson. "You can get confirmation from your boss. I have a number where he can be reached."

"But my captain says the man who shot the mayor is dead. Why would we look for someone who prevented him from killing our president?"

"Mr. Neiderhof and I both think that the man on the roof was set up by someone else. Don't you care about catching the guy who humiliated Webb?"

"How do we know it wasn't the man on the roof who did that?"

"I'm going to see your captain. I have my orders."

"Yes, sir."

Henry grabbed the phone off the sergeant's desk. "What's his number?" When he located the captain, he made arrangements for himself and Marion, who was outside the station in their car, to meet at Captain Maarten's house. It was after supper when they arrived at the moderate, middle-class bungalow in the Wilgehof district.

Maarten was a bitter man. He knew he was the best policeman in the city, yet one of his lieutenants had been promoted over him as chief of police by Eugene den Kamp. His wife had died three years ago, and he spent most of his spare time jousting with J&B Scotch. For the past six months, the scotch had been winning. He knew Henry but not Marion.

"Come in, come in," he almost stammered, opening the front door and his mouth wide as he spotted the two on his porch. "Let's have a drink before you tell me what's up."

He's already drunk, Marion thought as she hung her coat on the alligator stand in the front hall. "Nice to meet you, Captain."

"Wilhelm, call me Wilhelm, and you must be Marion. Den Kamp's told me much about you." He went and got them a couple of glasses of cheap Merlot while Henry and Marion seated themselves in his unkempt living room.

When he sat in his recliner across from Marion, she crossed and uncrossed her legs a couple of times and said, "Wilhelm, we were speaking with your boss..."

"Yeah, what did you think of him?"

"Well, you and he seem to be doing a wonderful job of keeping the city clean and safe."

"I'd do a better job than him."

Marion slowly crossed her legs again, giving Wilhelm a good view of her inner thigh. "I'm sure you would. The assassination would have never happened if you were in charge, I'm sure."

"Assassination?…Oh yes."

Henry jumped in. "Wilhelm, the man that was killed was a good friend of ours. We would like to find his killer, but your shift sergeant won't help us."

"Yes," Marion added, giving Wilhelm a seductive glance. "I wonder if you could call him and ask him to cooperate."

"I certainly will. Just finish your wine—I'll get you some more after I call."

It only took a couple of minutes for them to extricate themselves from the clutches of the drunken captain and return to the station.

When they arrived, Sergeant Brill was packing up and getting ready to head home. He had hoped that the visit he was now getting from the couple from Pretoria wouldn't have happened till the next day. "So, what do you two want?"

Henry was ready to tear a strip off the sergeant, but Marion waived his off. "Sergeant Brill—Paul, isn't it?"

"Yes, Marion."

These guys are too easy, she thought. "Paul, Mr. den Kamp is really insistent that we catch the man who killed the guy on the roof. Do you think we could get you to set up some roadblocks, especially on the way out to the Cape? We think he'll be headed that way if he's still hiding in the city."

"Why do you want him so badly?"

"I know most people think he killed the assassin and consider him a hero."

"I'm one of them."

186

"Well, we're not and neither is den Kamp. We think he took the shot, then planted the rifle on the other guy. Don't you think a little cooperation would help your career?"

Brill thought for a moment. *What would it cost me to get some night-shift guys to set up some barriers?* "Jesus, Marion, you're probably right." *I better humor her. She could do me a lot of harm,* he thought.

Henry added, "She is right. We'll just get out of your way and let you get to work."

Son of a bitch, I guess it's going to be a long night, Paul thought as he watched them hurry out of the station.

* * *

The streets were quiet as David made his way back to the hospital where he had left the Rover. Apparently the hospital had a "no overnight parking" policy. There were two tickets on the windshield. He thanked God they didn't have a towing policy.

"But, sir, you stayed overnight," the young black garage attendant said accusingly.

"Yes, I'm sorry. My brother is very sick and we were worried he wouldn't make it. I'll pay the full two-day charge." David's Afrikaans was not very good, but the one-hundred-rand note seemed to convince the attendant that overnight parking was not a great sin.

"You should come back tomorrow and settle those tickets with administration."

"I certainly will."

He was not out of the woods yet. As he approached the on-ramp to the N1, David noticed a couple of police barricades being unloaded from the back of a city truck by two officers. He'd better avoid that highway on his way to Cape Town. He got off at the first exit. As he drove, he went over the reasons for his having chosen Cape Town, rather than Johannesburg, for his escape from the country: it was unexpected, away from the central government agencies of whom he was wary, and mainly, a large center with lots of places to hide.

Even the back roads in the central part of the country were well maintained. Staying on the road was not his problem—staying awake was. The tensor bandage of tiredness was slowly tightening around his eyes. Hunger and thirst could be ignored; the piercing of his consciousness by the wolves of sleep could not. He forced his mind back to his youth once again. Even after thirty years, emotions surrounding Sam Reasons were still strong enough to keep him awake.

Grandpa Reasons had been extremely interested in Buckeye football. Although he had never played, Sam secretly watched practices as a student, and, after graduation, never missed a home game. One of the few good memories of Grandpa came when David was ten. It was a cold, blustery November afternoon. David and his Grandpa were in the back seat of the DeVille on their way to Ann Arbor, Michigan, and the annual game between the Wolverines and the Buckeyes.

"This year, David, we have a stronger team than they do, and should be rated number one."

"What does that mean, Grandpa?"

"That's the rating that the press give to the tier one teams in the country."

David had no idea what "tier one" meant. "And aren't we number one?"

"No, the bloody press seems to think that UCLA, out in California, has a better team. You watch us show them this afternoon. Bob White is the best running back in the league. He'll kill them."

David had never heard him so excited. "It's fun going to the game with you, Grandpa. I like it." It was a strange feeling for David.

"Let me tell you a bit about the game. Our chief rival has always been Michigan. They've been beating us for a long time. This year, though, Woody Hayes—that's our coach—has built a strong running game. We only lost once, to Michigan State. They've lost twice. So I think we're better." Grandpa explained to him all about football on the three-hour ride from Dublin to Ann Arbor.

The game itself interested David little. He only noticed the vicious hitting as each team tried to overcome the other. He remembered hitting a classmate named Greg at school for picking on the girls and how that had stopped him from harassing them. But that cold afternoon, sitting beside Grandpa with a blanket over their knees, he learned that sometimes hitting just produced more hitting. The crowd around them, including Grandpa, roared and screamed, even swore at the other team or one of their fans. This had to be more than just a game. When he played games with Jimmy Butts, they sometimes got hurt wrestling one another, but they never really tried to hurt each other. He remembered all the times he would have loved to hurt Grandpa. Life on North High Street was not a game.

True to Grandpa's prediction, Bob White provided all the offensive power the Buckeyes needed. James Pace for Michigan gained more yards, but the Buckeyes overcame a four-point half-time deficit to go on for the win. "Look, David," Grandpa said after the game was over. "See how the Ohio students are trying to tear down the goal post. That's a football tradition."

"Why do they do that? Don't they need them for the next game?"

"Oh, they just build them again. You have to understand tradition. It feels good to get rid of your energy by tearing something down after you've been sitting all through the game. I used to help tear them down when I was a student."

"The goal posts aren't coming down, Grandpa."

"No, they aren't. It looks like they've made them of steel this time. Going to spoil all the kids' fun. Let's go home."

They were safely within the big black car on the way down I-90 before Sam spoke. "Well, David, how do you like football?"

"I didn't like how they hurt each other. Did they have to do that? I saw three guys carried off the field."

"To win, young man, you often have to hurt somebody. You want to be a winner, don't you?"

"I guess so." He really didn't want to win if he had to hurt people. He would rather stop people from hurting other people just as he would like to stop his grandpa from hurting him.

Such remembrances kept David awake while he waited for his escape to the Cape.

18

Den Kamp and Neiderhof had just returned from Bloemfontein by air charter. Den Kamp was sitting quietly in his office, door closed, trying to force out into the open the outline of a plausible story for his minister. It was a daunting task. If he pinned his hopes on making Henson the villain and Henson escaped, then how did he explain Terbose on the roof? It was unlikely that Bertel would believe he was trying to protect the president—not when Bertel knew about Terbose killing the major. If they caught Henson and beat a confession out of him before turning him over to Dieter, it would make the story more believable. If he laid the blame on Terbose, he would have to take the charge of his incompetence. He was also worried that Betel would slap a complicity label on him, but he could probably slough that off onto the police in Bloemfontein. Another way to get out of it might be to make up a story that Henson and Terbose were working together and Henson didn't want to leave anyone around to talk.

That might be an even better story, but it still wouldn't stop Bertel's branding him as incompetent.

For the first time in his life, den Kamp had allowed a man to dominate him, turn his every action to ridicule, and make him despondent and vulnerable. It was Dieter Volmar, not Minister Bertel, who made him feel this way. He actually felt like a failure. He wondered if it was worthwhile to continue with Dominance. He considered calling Henry and Marion back and just letting Henson go.

This feeling had strayed into his consciousness several times since he had watched Dieter's Challenger taxi away from the Tempe business terminal. He thought of Dieter—tall, blond, and handsome, draped in a gray silk suit that must have cost three thousand rand. Even his aircraft looked smarter than all the others at the airport, dressed in the maroon and gray livery of Renaissance Enterprises. Dieter's harangue about maintaining control of operations and only bringing competent people into the organization kept pressing out the thoughts needed to make up a reasonable explanation for his actions over the past few days.

"That bastard is unreasonable," he said, banging his fist down on the mahogany desk so hard that the antique quartz pen and inkstand threatened to jump off.

"Who are you talking about? Den Kamp or the minister?" Neiderhof had been in the washroom for quite some time, and den Kamp had been so engrossed in his troubles that he had forgotten him.

"Dieter. He's spent years trying to get Henson. Now he's upset that we couldn't get him on the first try."

"I think you need a drink, boss. Dieter's not the problem, Bertel is. We need a good story for him."

"I suppose. A drink would be good. There's some Glenlivet in that cabinet over by the door."

Neiderhof got up painfully and poured them both a half tumbler. "What happened to the man who promised me millions in the organization once we got into real action?"

"You're right. It would be nice to have my own jet, and I don't see any way of getting it unless I stick with Dieter. We've failed to get Mandela. Terbose may have been a bit loose, but he was a Broeder and we lost him. It looks like finding Henson may be the only way to get back into Dieter's good books."

"We can still get him. I doubt his first move is to leave the country. All the airports are already on the lookout for him."

"I suppose. Henry and Marion seem more interested in each other than getting Henson. They've already missed him at Jo'burg airport, Klerksdorp, and now Bloemfontein."

"Don't be too hard on them, boss. They've been at headquarters for too long. I'll bet they'll be the ones who find Henson."

Almost on cue, den Kamp's cell phone chirped. It was Henry advising that Henson had been spotted heading west on the N1, the Cape being his likely destination, and now he and Marion were headed that way.

"Maybe you're right, Neiderhof," said den Kamp. "They're on their way to the Cape right now."

"It might be good if they had some help. Mark Bledsoe's an old hand. Have you asked him about Dominance?"

"Last May I approached him. He was pretty cool about it."

"Maybe you should call and ask him to help find Henson. He doesn't need to know the name or why we're looking for him. Then you can forget about the bastard and get on with our story for Bertel."

* * *

Mark Bledsoe, head of the Cape Town police, had been worried that den Kamp's approach last spring might merely be a loyalty test. He had worked under den Kamp when the latter had his present job. He knew den Kamp to be ruthless and ambitious to a fault. Mark had a strong ambition, too, but he was not a political animal. He did not want to become involved in any activity that would jeopardize his retirement prospects. He was at the top rank in Cape Town and knew a further promotion would mean a move to Pretoria or Johannesburg, an event he was not sure he could convince his wife to agree with.

Mark was seated comfortably on his maroon padded swivel chair in his plain but functional office in the corner of the top floor of the police building on Buitenkant Street. It was a Friday afternoon, nearly four thirty, and he was looking forward to a quiet weekend with his family. A trip had been planned, including a picnic lunch to the always beautiful Table Mountain with its view of the whole city, its harbor, and, if the day was clear, the Cape of Good Hope. After the initial frenzy of messages about the president's near assassination and the death of the shooter, things had settled down. He had not heard from den Kamp, though he expected to. His briefing came from Jon Mjaren, who considered the man who took out Terbose to be a hero. Jon seemed a bit hesitant about whether or not he should be found and congratulated, although he did not say why.

Den Kamp called just as Mark was putting his jacket on to leave. "Mark, Eugene here. Can you talk?" den Kamp began without fanfare or small talk, which surprised Mark. The two of them had known each other for years.

"Certainly, Gene." Mark got up, stretched the phone cord to the limit, and kicked his door closed.

"I need you to look out for someone. Someone very dangerous and treacherous."

"I presume we are talking of the killer of the shooter on the roof. By the way, the reports from Mjaren were a bit vague. Was Terbose the assassin, or did somebody set him up?"

"An outsider—we think it was an American agent—set him up. We have not been able to locate the infiltrator. We came close when we closed all the routes out of Bloemfontein, but I'm afraid many of our fellow officers did not carry out the task with any enthusiasm. In fact, a few see Hen—him as a hero."

"How do you know his name? I thought you had never found him."

"I have my sources. Somehow he eluded our net, and now we think he's on the way to the Cape."

"Is he still being pursued officially? They consider him a hero here, too. I guess you were out of the office when Jon Mjaren called me."

"I was busy with other things. Anyway, I want this guy caught. We can't have foreigners running around doing our job for us, even if some people do think he's a hero."

Mark had been a Broeder years ago and a strong supporter of Verwoerd, but he had seen the writing on the wall. It was fine to hope for a return to white rule, but he did not want to buck the present system to achieve that goal. His career demanded he accept his new role as protector of the ANC as the legitimate government, just as he had protected the old apartheid regimes of the National Party. "Why do you think this guy's in Cape Town?"

"Damn it, Mark. We've looked everywhere else." He told Mark about the local police establishing road blocks on all major routes leaving the city, of Henry and Marion searching all of Bloemfontein's hotels, and learning that a white Land Rover, moving at a suspiciously cautious speed, was heading for the N1 just as barriers were being set up. "I'm pretty sure he's on his way to your side of the country." He did not want him to be aware of Henry and Marion's incompetence, so he did not tell Mark about all the times they missed their quarry.

"Don't worry, Gene. If he shows up in my town, we'll find him."

"Henry Jackman and Marion Aflect will be joining you on Monday." Den Kamp wanted to give them the weekend in Cape Town to find Henson. "I probably should have left this 'til Monday and not upset your weekend. I just thought you might put out the word before you go home tonight. I can call Marion and Henry back if you find him."

"Is that bloody necessary? Why do you think I need help to find one man? I know Jackman and Aflect are good, but I don't need them interfering in my backyard."

"No, no, Mark. They won't interfere and, as I said, you will probably find him over the weekend."

"Make sure they know who's in charge before they arrive."

"Of course. I've already done that. Have a good weekend."

"I'll call when I find him. By the way, do you know what he looks like?"

"Just generally. About one point eight meters tall, stocky, about eighty-two kilos. Unfortunately, he's prone to wearing disguises, so what he looked like in Bloemfontein probably won't help."

"We'll find him."

* * *

David had arrived in the beautiful legislative capital of South Africa early Saturday morning. It was a six-hundred-mile drive from Bloemfontein to Cape Town, and he had been forced to use back roads. He was dead tired. A short nap in the parking lot of a truck stop in the desert near Aberdeen had done little to refresh him. A huge steak dinner with all the trimmings at the truck stop diner had helped. He had driven trusting only his instincts and the memory of the road map he had studied back in Dublin. He dared not ask for directions. He did not know who was involved in Dominance. Someone was still after him. David was completely on his own. He was used to that, but it forced him into a kind of paranoia at times. He had completed his mission. Now he just needed to get out alive.

It had been a strange mission. He had stopped the assassination. According to news flashes that came over the car radio, the mystery man who had saved the president was quite a hero, yet the police were still after him. The scraps of conversations he heard on the top of the elevator, the setting up of roadblocks, and the siren that roared by on the main highway just as he had left it, proved that. He wished that he and Grant had set up a contact. They had probably identified the Rover by now, so he did not want to drive the Rover right into Cape Town. About ten miles east of the airport, in the faint pre-dawn light, he found an abandoned barn and ditched it there. As he had done in Klerksdorp and Bloemfontein, he walked with the graying of the morning sky behind him toward the gradually yellowing tops of Devil's Peak and Table Mountain in the distance. Exhausted, he dragged himself through the maze of ramps and roads, finally arriving at a row of sleeping cabs at the Cape Town's airport's Arrivals level. It was far too early for much air traffic, but cabbies were ready for any overnight flights.

David tapped on the window of the first cab in line. The cabby's smile convinced David he was not a threat. "Could you take me to a nice downtown hotel?"

If the cabby thought there was anything strange about a tired-looking man without luggage, who clearly had not arrived by air, asking for a ride from the airport, he gave no sign. "Yes, sir, the Graeme Hotel right down by the stadium is the best we have—at least in my opinion."

"Are there any closer to the waterfront?"

"Yes, there's a huge one, The Breakwater Lodge, right near the water."

"Well, let's go there." David felt the best way to stay away from whoever it was that was after him would be among the crowds he heard flocked to the Victoria and Albert Waterfront, the center of Cape Town's tourist district.

"What kind of an accent is that, sir?"

"English. I'm from Birmingham. Ever heard of it?"

"No, sir."

They passed beautiful countryside on the way downtown. Two golf courses, well watered and extremely lush, lay on either side of the main road just past a spaghetti-like interchange. The Table and Devil's peaks rose majestically through the morning mist. "Isn't that a hotel over by the golf course?"

"Yes, sir, that's the City Lodge."

Whenever possible, David booked rooms in two hotels if he had to stay in one place for two or three days. It was a safety precaution, and if the enemy ever found one, they generally stopped looking. *Maybe I should book here*, he thought, *then head downtown and stay at the Breakwater*. Besides, if this cabby is asked where he dropped me, he'll lead the police here. "I changed my mind. Can you get off the road and get me to that hotel?"

"No problem, sir." They left the main road at the next interchange and headed back to the hotel that adjoined the Mobray golf course.

David checked into the City Lodge as James Kildare. He felt it was safe to haul out his old identity papers, at least for the time being. Police in Cape Town should not be aware of the VP from Bethlehem Steel. He went up to his room and tried to make himself a bit more presentable, but still a scruffy looking professor. Then he grabbed another cab to his more permanent accommodations down by the waterfront.

The second driver was a bit more talkative. He recognized David's British accent right away. They had a pleasant trip.

During the ride, David had a chance to admire the layout and architecture of the second largest city in South Africa. "You live in a beautiful city, young man."

"Yes, sir. I guess I am lucky. The pay's not so good, though, unless you have a government job or work in the factories."

"Still not fair to blacks, then?"

"No, sir, but we're getting better. Say, did you hear about the assassination attempt in Bloemfontein?"

"Yes, I heard it on the airplane coming in last night."

"I wonder who saved Mandela. He's done a lot for the country already."

"Do you mean Mandela or the man who saved him?"

"Both, I guess." The cabby laughed at the correction of his word choice.

* * *

Henry and Marion arrived in Cape Town on the first commuter flight of the day. They rented a Mercedes from Hertz at the airport and began their trip into town along the same route David had taken three hours earlier. They had both been to the Cape many times and were not awed by its scenery. Henry was anxious to find a hotel and some rest. He was also interested in getting Marion's attentions away from their boss and back on to him. Henson was his third priority.

They checked into separate rooms at the Metropole, an old, quaint hotel in the heart of downtown. Henry alerted den Kamp of their arrival and learned that the police in Cape Town would also be out looking for Henson.

"What do we do when we find him?"

"Take him to our safe house outside Delft."

"What if the police find him?"

"Call me. I will get Bledsoe to turn him over to us. Henry, it's up to you and Marion to keep up the side. We failed in Bloemfontein. You two have failed too often. It is no way to run an organization. The only way to get back into gear is to get Henson's head on a platter for Volmar."

"We'll find him." Somehow, talking to Eugene motivated Henry up to an intense level of desire to succeed in this mission. "Has the minister shown up yet?"

"No. Neiderhof and I are still working on the story for him."

"Would you tell me what it is? It might be good if we were all on the same wavelength."

"I'll give you the gist of it when we finish it tomorrow. You find Henson."

"Yes, sir." He hung up and called Marion's room.

A sleepy voice answered. It temporarily dissolved Henry's resolve to find Henson.

* * *

Room 220 in the huge breakwater Hotel overlooked the inner quadrangle garden. On his way to his room, Hans Geldhart spent some time checking the hotel and its exits for possible escape routes. The complex was actually three large buildings joined by an underground garage. The spaces between the buildings were too wide to consider jumping from roof to roof. The garage seemed to offer the best escape route.

Twenty minutes after Hans Geldhart had checked in, a clean, well-dressed man approached the desk. He had a specific request. "I would like to have a room overlooking the inner courtyard."

"But the rooms on the front overlook the beautiful waterfront, sir."

Interesting, David thought. *The clerk didn't assign the waterfront side to my alter ego.* "Yes, I know, but I want quiet and the inner room seems to be more secluded."

"That's no problem. Room 316 is available."

"Do you have anything at a lower level? I need quiet to do some work and have found that noisy parties sometimes happen on the higher floors."

"Certainly, sir. I quite understand." The clerk thought David must have a screw loose. Everyone wanted the upper floors. "Let me see…there's room 127. It's right at the back corner of this building, though."

"Excellent."

"Right, Mr. Kildare. And how will you be paying?"

"Oh, sorry, cash."

"There will be a deposit then, sir. Five hundred rand."

David counted the money out of his belt. He wondered if the clerk might make a connection between two men checking in within an hour of one another, both paying cash.

"Here's the key. Oh, by the way, sir, here's a brochure of all the services we provide in the hotel. I hope you enjoy your stay."

David desperately needed sleep. His body was rebelling against the onslaught of pressure and long hours to which it had been subjected over the past three days. Still, he needed to take some precautions before he slept. As Kildare turned to head to his room, he literally ran into a small black man with a big smile. Willy Umbasi apologized profusely as he helped

David recover his balance and his dropped case. The first thought to go through David's mind was that the encounter was not accidental. Perhaps Willy was police and had frisked him. The two spoke for several moments in the lobby. David thought it might draw more attention to himself if he brushed off this friendly worker than if he just remained in the lobby talking to him.

David found a kind of openness in the man. He was friendly and seemed helpful. Most importantly, he appeared to pose no threat. Later, the clerk at the desk confirmed that Willy was indeed an employee of the hotel.

Willy enjoyed listening to David's American accent and told him so. He guessed David was from the north, and David advised he was here on holiday from New York. When their chat ended, David headed to the elevators and Willy to the door.

As he walked home, Willy felt certain that David was in trouble. His having to know where each of his contacts stood before he opened up to them had given him the ability to read their fear. Perhaps Colonel Bledsoe would like to know about this stranger. It might be worth some money. Before he called, though, he decided to learn more about James Kildare. Perhaps his troubles were not with the police.

David headed for Geldhart's room. He had decided it was safer to use this room, as Kildare's name had appeared on various forms from Johannesburg to the Cape. On the way, he took a swing by Kildare's room and installed a couple of hair-thin paper strips in the door. When he arrived at room 220, he collapsed, face down on the checked coverlet, not even bothering to undress. For no apparent reason, however, sleep would not come. When the forces arrayed against him seemed so strong that he felt helpless to fight them, his mind should have shut down the destructive images that haunted it. Instead, the bed made him remember a time when bed had not been such a safe place. It had been easy for his grandfather to find him there.

Appearances had been terribly important to Sam Reasons. One evening, when the Reasons were entertaining the mayor of Columbus and his wife, David had snuck out of bed, run down the stairs, and interrupted their polite, after-dinner conversation in the living room. "Gramma, I forgot to tell you this afternoon, but I lost my ball down a hole in the back field," David started excitedly. "I think a big squirrel lives down there."

"David, squirrels do not live in the ground. They live in the trees. Marie, please return David to his room. I will deal with him later."

"Oh, Sam," Mary Enright, the mayor's wife, intervened. "He's just excited about seeing the animals. Tell me, David, did you see any chipmunks too?"

"Yes, and the B'nard's cat..."

"That's B-E-R-N-H-A-R-D, David. You must learn to speak properly. Now go to your room."

"Yes, Grampa." David slunk back up the stairs. He knew what was coming and thought of opening his bedroom window, jumping down onto the veranda roof, and leaving home for good.

Later that evening, when the guests had gone, the elder Reasons administered a sound whipping with his thick, brown leather belt.

David slept deeply for ten hours. He awoke with a start in the blackness of the Cape Town night. Was there a noise in the hall? What had wakened him? Then he realized the length of time he had been asleep. He put his head down once more and dozed for a short time again, waking when Sunday morning's rays caressed the pastel pillows on his bed.

19

Willy Umbasi liked to consider himself a black patriot. He had left his home in Soweto Township in 1976 at the age of fifteen after his mother and father had been killed by ANC guerrillas. Not being politically mature at the time, he failed to make the connection between his parents' occupation—part-time farmers and full-time, paid police informants—and their assassination by black guerrillas. The lesson he learned was that the supporters of the African National Congress were savages who had killed his parents, and the white police who found the culprits and put them in jail were his protectors.

As soon as he was able, he moved to Cape Town and discovered that young black men, willing to work hard, were in demand as waiters and busboys. He found himself a job at the Breakwater Hotel. Willy was friendly and outgoing by nature. He formed short-term but trusting attachments with many of the patrons of the Breakwater's main restaurant, Stonebreakers. One of them was then Lieutenant Bledsoe.

Bledsoe found a way to use Willy's personal qualities. Like most policemen in a coercive, terrorist state, Bledsoe was able to recognize weakness in his enemies and turn it to his advantage. He convinced Willy that the ANC were just as savage in Cape Town as they were in Johannesburg, and it would be of great service to the police if Willy infiltrated their organization. He promptly and cheerfully took up his parents' occupation.

Willy was not entirely motivated by patriotic considerations. It was profitable to play both sides of the street, feeding information gleaned from patrons to the police and vice versa. His busboy job at Breakwaters paid only 250 rand per month, but it put him in a position to meet many clandestine visitors—particularly Americans who had no love for the ANC—willing to pay for his services as an information officer in the local underground. After a few errors, Willy learned what questions to ask to determine the visitors' intensions and whether or not they would be of interest to Bledsoe. The police were also fairly generous when Willy could supply them with information concerning particular visitors, such as the man he had run into in the lobby. At age thirty-five, Willy had a nest egg of some 25,000 rand with which he planned to buy a comfortable house in one of the northern suburbs in the very near future. Willy had never bothered to make the connection between the BOSS and the "white oppressor." Attitudes he took up in childhood provided a blindfold on reality, particularly when it was not in his economic interests to question those attitudes.

On Sunday, Willy showed up for work at eight as usual. He found David alone at breakfast in Stonebreakers and joined him.

"Good morning, sir. Another hot and muggy day, I think."

"Yes, your weather here is not like back home. We have winter up north."

"I wonder if I might be of assistance to you as a visitor to our city? You seem to be here all alone."

"Yes, I am just here for another day or so, after a holiday in Kruger National Park."

"Perhaps I could tell you about a few of the bright spots to visit over the next day or so. Sort of give you a good feel for the city."

Willy knew that this stranger had no intention of visiting any bright spots. He saw David's eyes wander out to the lobby at frequent intervals and knew he was assessing each passerby. He told David about the Castle, Koopmans-de Wet Museum, and the Kirsten Bosch Gardens, wished him well, promised he would be available any time to provide guided services, and then left. It was time to call Bledsoe.

He seems like such a nice young man, David thought as he sipped his espresso. He wished he could trust him completely. They might have become friends. But trusting anyone in the country, which still held the forces of Dominance and racism, wasn't possible. Tiredness, bone wearying exhaustion, and stress had an amazing effect on David's psyche. A good night's sleep had not completely removed the cobwebs that the spiders of fear and exertion had woven into his subconscious over the past four days, but it made him much more aware of the danger of allowing Willy further inroads into his confidence. He ordered and drank another espresso, paid the check, and returned to his room.

On his way, he passed Kildare's door and two hair-thin strips of paper lying on the patterned carpet. Instantly David knew who had betrayed him. He headed down the back stairs to the parking garage. It had only been ten minutes from the time Willy left the restaurant until he got to Kildare's room. It was unlikely anyone else would have found him so quickly without Willy's help.

David had with him the Smith & Wesson and money belt with papers and cash. He had no clothes other than the sharp Kildare suit he now sported. As he raced into the parking garage, he wondered why the police or Dominance agents went to Kildare's room instead of the dining room. It was probably to protect Willy.

The garage was a sea of cars. It seemed almost everyone staying at the Breakwater drove a BMW or Mercedes. In case he needed to make a quick exit, David jimmied the door of a BMW 735i and pulled out the ignition for hot wiring.

He moved across the aisle to a point where the slope of the entrance ramp provided a triangular shaped niche into which he could crawl. He pulled a couple of large metal garbage cans in with him and hid behind them, hoping anyone looking in the garage would start with the cars. He hunkered down to wait for the inevitable.

Five minutes later, a uniformed constable opened the door of the garage and started down the aisle straight in front of him. Now he would see if his theory about where they would look was correct. David tightened his grip on the Smith & Wesson.

The constable was thorough. He went right to the far end of the garage under the south building and then came back along the far two lines of cars that were hidden from David's view. He heard the boots on the concrete—pace and stop, pace and stop, pace and stop—and listened as the sound began dying away to his right. When he heard the steps no more, David made the assumption that the constable was now under the north building and slipped out the exit door.

The brilliance of the noon sun hit him like a sledge. The weather was clear and hot. Good weather for hunting, he mused, much like it was in Bloemfontein. Kildare's sharp suit and two-day-old shirt were no match for the devastating sun. It seared through him.

As he casually strolled down Potswood, past the Somerset Hospital and onto the Victoria and Albert Waterfront, he expected each moment to hear that dreaded call from behind him. None came. It seemed the constable was still busy checking cars. It was a great relief when he was able to merge himself with the busy, happy crowds that strolled, shopped, lunched, and generally enjoyed the beautiful surroundings of Cape Town's modern waterfront.

The first thing David needed was a different appearance. Shops along the quays provided Dockers, a T-shirt with a picture of the waterfront, canvas deck shoes, hair dye, and toiletries. A public washroom was the best he could do to transform himself into a blond waterfront denizen who somewhat resembled Hans Geldhart.

Now it was time to phone Grant. David knew he'd be worried sick. He assembled a mass of coins in various souvenir and variety shops and headed for a pay phone outside Pinns Jewelers.

David did not know how much electronic monitoring Dominance could handle, and he wasn't taking any chances. The NSA had no trouble picking out trans-Atlantic calls. It was early Monday in Washington when the phone at Fieldstone Enterprises rang, and Grant answered on the first ring. David thought Grant might've been sleeping in the office as he gave him his report.

Grant's reply was brief and euphoric. "I'm glad the package arrived safely. When can we expect the bill?"

"It will take a couple of days to test the item. Tuesday they should be ready to submit an invoice. The competition must be a bit out of sorts."

"I've heard nothing from them." Technically that was true. Grant had heard nothing from Dominance. He had heard a great deal about the success of David's mission and had spent the weekend denying any CIA involvement to the press, the CIA director, and even the Secretary of State—personally. "Would it help if I sent some technical support to assist with the testing?"

"If I don't call by tomorrow night, you may assume some help is needed. Good-bye, Arthur." David severed the connection.

* * *

The hot Sunday weather seemed just about right for Marion and Henry. It was amazing how heat seemed to increase their sexual appetites.

Several times during the day they returned from fruitless searches of the streets, bars, hotels, and shops to fall together into their unmade bed with an urgency, which, if given to their search, might have already netted them Gregory Henson.

When they were lying exhausted on the damp and crumpled sheets and trying to think whether it might be better to give up the search and concentrate on each other, Henry pulled himself from his stupor and remarked, "You know, Marion. There are still a couple of hotels out toward the airport we haven't searched. We've assumed he would stay downtown. We need to get that bastard before Bledsoe does."

"He wouldn't stay out by the airport; he knows that's the first place we'll look. I've got an idea. Why not let Bledsoe do the dirty work? He's got more resources than we have. Why don't we go try to find Henson's Land Rover?"

"Won't it be at the place he's staying?"

"Henry, you're not thinking. Has Henson ever led us to where he was staying by leaving his car there?"

"No, you're right. What's your plan?"

"We'll go out to the countryside and ask some local farmers if they've seen the car. It's quite distinctive."

"And what if it's wrecked?"

"If it's wrecked, we join Bledsoe in the search."

"That's good thinking, Marion. We can get some explosives and rig it if it isn't. We'll talk about it in the morning. Let's get some sleep."

"Tired, huh." Marion was beaming with the compliment but realized she really must let her partner get some rest.

"Exhausted."

20

David began his run down Strand Street as soon as he heard, "Halt!"

His mind had been casting about all afternoon for a way to get out of the country. If the police got to his hotel that quickly, they would have the airport, train, and bus depots covered. It looked like he'd have to get back to the Rover and drive out but didn't want to do that in daylight. Taking a taxi back to the barn would put the police on his trail right away. He just hoped they didn't find him before dark. The plan almost worked. Darkness was approaching when he heard the challenge.

Just as he felt the man was getting close enough to take a shot, two pillars topped by carved lionesses, which guarded Cape Town's castle entrance, appeared on his right. He could see there was some decent cover in the park behind the gate. Apparently his pursuer had the same thought.

Glancing back, David noticed a sharp movement across his trail. The officer was ready to risk exposure to a counterattack to prevent him from entering the grounds. He would need a second or to two stop, aim, and fire. David raced through the gates and veered right behind the pillar. A shot rang off the stone, right next to where his backside had been a second earlier.

The policeman raced quickly into the grounds, hoping to nab his quarry before he hid himself in the many hedges and thick thorn bushes. As he ran through the park entrance, he was greeted by a savage blow to the gut, delivered by the foot of his intended victim. Before the man could restart his breathing, David was into the hedges that fronted the ancient stone walls of the fortress.

The night was deadly quiet, belying the pace and ferocity of the chase that had taken place under its stifling stillness. When he could breathe again, the constable decided that it would be better to call in backup before continuing the search for his vicious enemy. In ten minutes, three constables and Colonel Bledsoe had arrived at the castle gate.

"Target moves...like the bloody wind, and took...me out with one blow. I'm...sure he's still...on the grounds," the constable reported to his superior.

Loyal Willy had advised Bledsoe a half-hour ago that he had spotted Mr. Kildare heading downtown. Bledsoe had decided, in view of den Kamp's interest, to take a personal hand in David's capture.

David soon heard voices approaching his hiding place. For the next fearful minutes he practically forced his body into the loamy ground. His heart jumped into his throat. As he lay there David was reminded of a time when he was only ten years old. He had been hiding in the packed earth under the front porch stairs, scared to death that Sam Reasons would find out that he only got a C in history on his Christmas report card. To escape this fear, he withdrew into himself. He painted pictures in his mind of life as it would be when he grew up.

David was concerned that he was living his whole life in a negative way—continually fleeing tyranny. Here he was again, cringing in the shadows of Cape Town's ancient castle.

But it wasn't all negative. Someone had to make sure that Mandela's assassin was stopped so that the president could continue the fight against racism. That action was positive. Did he really have to kill the assassin and disable the policeman who just tried to shoot him? Was killing the only way to stop oppressors? Sometimes, yes. They would have killed or disabled him. The rule of law was fine, but sometimes it was another law that applied in a country like this where at least some of the police still supported lawlessness. In South Africa, the winds of apartheid were no longer a raging storm, but the racist attitudes of his current enemies certainly gusted strongly against those who would foil their evil plans.

The search by Bledsoe's constables eddied around him. His pursuers knew of his ability to protect himself with violent action. The policemen, while willing to poke about in the thorny branches that were near the paths, were not ready to risk an encounter with the menace deeper in the foliage.

The damage done to his constable took the edge off Bledsoe's enthusiasm as well. He felt that Kildare was probably still hiding somewhere in the park but did not want to risk any further damage to his men. The ANC were now the ruling political party. He and almost all of his fellow officers supported them. His boss in Pretoria seemed to be an exception. The positive attitudes of other countries toward the new government had left him with less motivation and ruthlessness in hunting down this enemy who had eliminated a Broeder. What kept up any motivation at all was his feeling that, perhaps some time in future, a strong leader like Botha or Verwoerd would replace the present black regime and reinstate the old order. Years ago, he would have called out half the force to arrest the assassin of Terbose, and not given up until he found him. Now it seemed more important to ensure the safety of his men and himself until he reached retirement, or until apartheid was revived. He called off the search after ten minutes, telling his officers that Kildare must have left the grounds.

When David emerged from hiding, he realized he needed to rest. At forty-four, one good night's sleep was not enough to undo the damage inflicted on his body by the previous three days of stress and action. He needed to regain more energy before he could escape this unfriendly city.

The night was hot and damp. The castle ramparts, built by the Dutch in 1666 as a fortification against Spanish invaders, stood out starkly against the December sky. As breaks in the clouds periodically uncovered the face of the moon, David had the impression that guards determined to protect the old racist regime were mounted along the parapets.

For a time he considered obtaining his rest right in the castle park's undergrowth. At his age, he risked, at the very least, an aching back and muscles. Also, sleeping in the undergrowth meant returning to his hotel without having changed his disguise, and in daylight. He would only be able to return to the City Lodge, and that was at least three miles away. He decided it was better to get there now when it was still dark. He dragged himself and his bag of clothing and makeup out from under the bushes.

The way back could be alive with cops. Also, after being questioned by the police, cab drivers tended to remember fares and where they delivered them. After a tour around the castle to make sure that his pursuers had given up the search, he began a circuitous route back to his suburban hotel on foot.

As he snuck along, he wondered how they had picked up his trail when he went back downtown from the waterfront. It seemed as though they were waiting. It was not far from the hotel to the waterfront. He had to pass within a block of the Breakwater. Willy could have spotted him. It was time to do something about Willy. David cursed himself for even considering that someone in this country could be a friend. He should have known better than to trust him. He wondered what made him do it. Perhaps it was the continual stress of being on his own in a foreign, and sometimes vicious, environment. David went to a phone booth at the corner of Hatfield and Orange, looked up Willy's number, and dialed.

The insistent ringing of the phone wakened Willy at 12:20 a.m. He had been having a dream of life in the years to come, without the need to be continually on the lookout for new information and clients, and having to be careful about what he said to everyone. The phone seemed to mark an awakening to a brighter future. David's voice surprised him. He thought that his elusive friend would have left the country or been arrested by Bledsoe by now.

"Willy, I need you to do me a favor," he heard as he became more alert. "I have a meeting tomorrow morning at the airport and need my stuff from my room at the Breakwater."

"Do I need to guess why you can't get it yourself tonight, or are you going to tell me?" Willy was now more awake and trying to figure out what was going on. Either Kildare was hooked up with a lady, or Bledsoe was hot on his tail.

"You won't guess who I met in the bar at the Metropole tonight."

"No, but I can guess why you need me to get your stuff. Where should I send it?" Willy asked.

"Just have it sent to the SAA counter at the airport by noon tomorrow." David hung up. He didn't need any more questions.

Willy sighed and went back to sleep. He was not finished with Mr. Kildare.

The patchy cloud cover had become nearly full. The streets were thinly traveled. After calling Willy, David shuffled along through back alleys and side streets for about two hours, several times stepping into doorways or behind garages or hedges to avoid police patrols. The sweat and grime of tramping the streets the entire day made him look more like a wasted party animal than a professor, but the last thing he needed was to be pulled aside for loitering and questioned. It was a long, tiring trip to the City Lodge, and it was nearly 3:00 a.m. before he got there. Alertness waned. He thought only of rest.

The City Lodge was one of those new South African hotels, built in the late 1980s and catering to the new, rich black South African and foreign tourist. The real draw was the golf club. Since Willy did not know of his room there, he doubted Bledsoe would have men waiting for him.

The employee's entrance in back of the kitchen, which was fortunately vacant at that time in the morning, allowed him to slip into the lobby without going through the front entrance. When he first registered there, he hadn't noticed the beautiful decor. The walls were done in light beige linen finished wallpaper that must have cost a fortune. Period armchairs and chaises were strategically scattered to provide guests with some privacy amid the bustle of the normally busy space. In two Queen Anne chairs situated in a small alcove, he saw the suits waiting. David felt awfully exposed. The police eyed him and would certainly recognize him if he attracted their attention by exiting too quickly. Apparently they did not notice that he had come in from the kitchen area behind the front desk.

Automatic response kicked in. David held up his bag of clothing and makeup to the clerk on duty and declared in a loud voice, "I need these cleaned and back in my room by four this afternoon." The suits looked over but did not make a move toward him.

David then took a quiet stroll to the elevators, went up one floor, ran back down the emergency exit by the kitchen, and vanished into the cloudy night. He hoped his body could keep him moving until he retraced the early Saturday morning taxi ride back to the airport, found his Rover out on the Stellenbosch Road, and got out of the country.

After the first two miles his legs and mind began to cramp up. He was near the terminal building and desperately wished he could risk heading in and getting a cup of coffee. Nothing was open in the built-up areas surrounding the airport, just as nothing had been open at the Mowbray golf club. He still had ten more miles to get to his car.

Just as the sky began to gray ahead of him, the fog in his mind began to lift. The city streets in suburban Belhar afforded him some protection from police and Dominance agents who would no doubt be looking for him either in town or on main roads. The increasing light seemed to dispel some of his fatigue.

Most of the people in South Africa would be pleased with what he'd done. He wondered who in hell had the power to turn out police forces in both Bloemfontein and Cape Town to find him. It had to be someone in headquarters—either police or security. It could be the Intelligence service, but he didn't think so. It was probably police who were after him, and they rarely danced to the tune of the Intelligence drummer. He and Grant were right. Dominance wielded some pretty potent power in this country.

As David passed the airport, he noted two police cars headed through the gate on Quarry Road. His car would have to wait. He slid painfully under a lush aloe hedge beside the road. There were no houses around. If he was going to drive to Namibia, he'd better get some sleep. It was nearly noon. If he stayed under the hedge awhile, perhaps the police would give up the search and go somewhere else.

David began to think back. Funny how protected he could feel, hiding in an aloe hedge, outdoors. It should have made him feel exposed— police cars at the airport, no papers, no luggage—just a car in a barn ten miles away, a money belt with a lot of cash, an old Smith & Wesson, and his own wits and experience. All the stress, danger, and lack of sleep had finally given him an, "Oh, well," attitude.

His internal clock wakened him two hours later. It was time to head to the barn and his Rover. He rubbed his eyes and painfully pulled himself out from under the bushes into the searing sunshine.

21

On Monday morning, Henry and Marion spent a short time in Colonel Bledsoe's office. Bledsoe briefed them on how they had found Kildare at the Breakwater on Sunday morning and how he had eluded them after injuring one of his constables. Marion almost blurted out a den Kamp diatribe on inefficiency and corrected Bledsoe about the name of their quarry but was able to catch herself in time. She told Bledsoe they would not consider interfering in his search. Henry briefed Bledsoe on the plan to find and wire Henson's car and asked for some Semtex or other explosives and a few electronic components. Mark agreed wholeheartedly. It would keep them out of his hair while he tried to find Kildare.

As the pair began their search, they discovered that there were a few farmers who were sympathetic to the cause of catching the man who had assassinated Broeder Terbose. Apartheid was formally dead, the laws had been changed, but in Cape Town, as in the Transvaal, some men's hearts still yearned for the past.

While searching, Henry and Marion began to call at the various farmhouses around the city, they got their share of, "Why, do you want to give him a medal?" Many farmers thought the Englishman, praised so highly by the media, to be a hero. They also found some who lived with the assumption that the white man was innately superior to the black, and offered to help.

By noon Henry was getting tired, hungry, and horny. "Jesus, Marion. How many farms are there out here anyway?"

Marion sensed they were on the right track. "Let's just check out a few more places. That run down place looks deserted."

They thought they should check for habitation before searching. "Who wants to know?" was the surly reply to their question about the possibility of a vehicle being stored in the farmer's barn. He appeared as old and run down as his property and didn't take to strangers asking questions. Marion noticed a nasty blunderbuss of a shotgun stowed on a rack in the kitchen.

"We're police and are trying to find the man who killed a Broeder in Bloemfontein."

"What makes you think he's here?"

"We know he came to the Cape in a white Land Rover. Have you seen it?"

"What's it worth to you?"

For twenty rand, Marion and Henry received the news they'd been waiting for.

Henry went back to the Mercedes and hauled out the satchel containing the explosives, wiring, and tools from the trunk. He was anxious to show off the knowledge he had gained as an eliminator of ANC terrorists. He started by removing the camshaft cover of the Rover and stuffing the Semtex under it.

"Why are you doing that?" she asked on cue.

"He'll look under the hood before he starts the thing. This way he won't see the explosives." The wires were set so that the first revolution of the shaft would push them together, short out the circuit, and set off the Semtex. Henry then ran the thin wires down the back of the engine and through the firewall with the ignition wires, covering them with grease. His final task was connecting them through the ignition switch.

"But won't he look under the hood and see our finger marks in the dirt?"

"We clean everything off, then put the dirt back."

As they were walking back to their car, Henry's cell phone buzzed. It was den Kamp. "Henry, report. Have you got Henson?"

"We will have solved our problem when Henson tries to start his car. We found and wired it."

"It would be better if we caught him alive. Now Dieter won't have the joy of disposing of him himself. At least we'll be rid of him. What are you going to do now?"

He wondered if his boss would ever say anything good about him. His flat reply was, "Head back to town. Check with the police to see if they've had any luck."

"Keep me informed. Is Marion with you? I'd like to speak to her."

"Yes, here she is."

"Yes, Gene, I'm pretty sure...No, not a sign. I think we were looking in the wrong place...He knows...What do you mean by that? How can I, and work with him to find Henson? We'll get him." She snapped the phone shut.

"Hey, don't break the thing. He's wondering what we're up to?"

"Yeah, but he doesn't know anything."

They went back to the farmhouse, advised the old codger not to go joy riding in the Rover or tip off anyone poking around it, and headed back to the hotel at a speed that could earn them a hefty fine.

* * *

Upon arrival at the farm, David paused in a forested area near the gate that protected a winding drive up to a rundown, grimy gray farmhouse, a dilapidated barn, and two collapsing outbuildings. There appeared to be no tracks leading through the gate other than the familiar deep-ribbed ones of the Land Rover. Several crackles were organizing their evening's itinerary, but there were no signs of human stirring in the area. The farmhouse still looked deserted. If anyone lived there, he had no intention of telling them he'd come back for his car.

He quietly approached the barn. The budding hedges and small shrubs provided good cover. He paused often to listen for any possible intrusion. Nothing moved.

He opened the barn door a crack and slipped in, noting that the Land Rover appeared normal and untouched. An outside inspection of the vehicle revealed no finger marks in the three-day accumulation of dust.

Before getting in the Rover, he reasoned that a couple hours sleep would be in order. He was still dead tired. The rest in the hedge had restored his brain function, but the ache behind his eyes was growing and his senses felt dull. Adrenaline got him this far, but he needed more sleep before he started the long drive out of the country. As it did in the aloe earlier that day, his mind began to work on escape and evasion and how it had worked out the first time he had been tracked.

By 1982, David had been under contract with Grant for nearly a year. He had learned tradecraft during several weekends they spent at Virginia Beach, pretending to be on vacation. He thought he was ready to be sent on a proper mission.

David lived in a three-bedroom side-split on Maple Street in the west end of Fairfax, Virginia. He received minimum contract payments and expenses from Grant's operating budget, but his grandfather's estate allowed him to furnish his home elegantly. There was a pool in the backyard, a backyard that was decorated on summer weekends by some of the fine-looking single women who greatly outnumbered the unattached men in that government bedroom town.

Grant decided before David was even hired that they would never be seen together near Washington. No one even knew he and Grant were associated. He worked out of one of the spare bedrooms when he was not out traveling on some routine delivery mission to Montreal, Canada, studying some new language at the Berlitz School in New York, or researching a terrorist organization such as the Red Brigades in Rome.

"How many more messages do I have to take to the RCMP or French Sureté? What's in them anyway?" David asked Grant during a meeting at an expensive restaurant in Phoenix. David never called the office unless he was on a mission which Grant was handling personally, and Grant never called David.

"You don't need to know what's in the messages. I don't." Grant handed him a business-sized white envelope, which David put in his suit pocket. "This is your fourth trip. There have been no problems on the other three, have there?"

"Now that you ask, on the last Montreal trip, I thought someone might have followed me from the Dorval train station to the drop in the park at 32nd Avenue in Lachine."

"I don't remember your telling me that when you got back."

"It didn't seem important enough. It's only in thinking back that I remember a gray Escort that seemed to follow my cab right to the park. It didn't stop, though, so I thought it was probably just a coincidence."

"Very few coincidences in this game. You should have reported it. I know they got the message through routine confirmation, so no harm appears to have been done. You enjoying the work?"

"Seems awfully routine. Are you sure we're doing any good?"

"Sometimes you just have to keep on keeping on. We try to stay compartmentalized, so I can't really tell you the reasons for your trips and all the study, but yeah, it's important. Do you feel ready for a bigger mission?"

It seemed to David like this bigger mission was just another ordinary drop to the RCMP in Montreal. He did not know it was a test. He was determined, however, to find out if he was being followed. Instead of taking a cab from the railway station, he called Avis and had a K-car delivered. As he started around the Dorval circle, he spotted the same gray Escort that he had wondered about on the previous trip pulling out of the bus parking lot into file behind him.

David took off. He had been in Montreal in cabs twice before and knew how to navigate the circle. He cut over sharply while accelerating into the inside lane as if he were going to continue around the circle and head back to the airport or up Cote-de Liesse Road. At the last moment, he cut back across three lanes and headed down Dorval Avenue. He could hardly believe that not one person honked. If he had done that in Washington, there would have been a ten-car pileup. *I guess I lost them, though.* As he turned right on Lakeshore, his rearview mirror told him the Escort was still a hundred yards back.

His instructions were quite clear when this happened—abort the mission and return to Fairfax without delivering the package to the dead letter drop, but David was curious as to who was interested in what he was doing.

He got on Dorval Avenue via back streets and headed toward the VIA station. Just before entering the circle, he pulled abruptly into an Esso garage across from the Dorval Gardens shopping center. There was no place for his escort to park on the road, so it passed the station and stopped in the lumberyard lot just around the corner.

David left the K-car beside the maintenance bays, jumped the fence behind the garage, and crept around the back end of the lumberyard to get a better look at who was in the Ford. A thin-faced man in a black fedora sat in the passenger seat looking back toward the Esso station. The driver, florid faced with a heavy mustache, was scanning the area and spotted David with his head stuck around the corner of the building. He nudged the passenger, and the two jumped out and headed toward the quickly disappearing form of the new recruit who had just blown his mission.

They soon gave up the foot chase. David may have been a bit remiss in his application of trade practice, but he was in shape. By the time he had reached Lakeshore Road and slipped into the Dorval Tavern, the two were three blocks behind. They returned to their car to watch for the return of their quarry until they saw the K-car being removed from the garage by an Avis employee.

David returned to Baltimore via chartered aircraft.

The next day's debrief in Philadelphia was not unpleasant—just a bit embarrassing. The blown mission and failure to follow instructions delayed his being given any real intelligence work for six more months.

David finally drifted off in the musty barn. He awoke precisely two hours later. He had developed that sense of time over a series of adventures. He would no longer have been alive had his subconscious not learned to wake him when necessary.

The most vivid memory was his visit to Afghanistan in the winter of 1989. His assignment was to warn the rebels in the mountains near Herat of an impending Russian advance into this far western province. The Afghans had secretly requested the CIA to act as an outside contact for the provision of arms and intelligence about Russian activities within their country. After a particularly close brush with authorities in Kabul who were sympathetic to the Russian cause, very similar to the bristles he now felt from the South African police, he was forced to use a native disguise and go underground. Eventually, he was able to secure himself in an arms shipment being sent west by rail, due to arrive in Herat at noon on January 18.

He had to stay awake most of the two-day journey and shift his position often to avoid the constant searches of the cargo. By the morning of the eighteenth, however, he had to sleep, just as he did now, but needed to awaken an hour before arrival in order to move into the hills before the train neared the Russian encampment east of Herat. He awoke exactly one hour later, and, after rolling down a steep embankment away from the slow-moving train, looked up to see guards lifting the tarpaulin which, three minutes earlier, had hidden not only four half-tracks and a million mortar rounds, but also the person who was soon to report that fact to the rebels.

It was time to get on the road and out of South Africa. He quickly went over the Rover once more, slipped in, and inserted the key. As he turned the key through the accessory catch, the motor cranked to an abrupt halt and then the panel lights went out. *Dead battery. Shit.* David popped the hood and jumped out of the Rover. The battery was still attached; nothing looked out of place. David knew he had to find another way out of this place. Slinking back through the small opening of the barn door, David had a premonition things just weren't right. As he took his second step out of the partially open barn door, the explosion knocked him flat and covered him with dust, straw, barn boards, and blackness.

* * *

Grant Weldman was worried. Forest had requested his services only a month before, and he had to send David into South Africa without a properly prepared internal contact. He thought it would be possible to run David himself, but there had been no contact since David had called him from the pay phone on Sunday morning. It was now late Monday in South Africa, and no call.

Obviously, the mission itself had been a success; the *Washington Post* front page blared the news that President Mandela had been saved from assassination by an unknown benefactor, thought to be British. Grant knew that vehement denial of any CIA involvement was the best way to ensure the press assumed that they were involved, thus turning attention away from the ANC. Frank Black, the *Post* reporter covering the case, took the bait. When he read the article, Grant was relieved. There was no mention of ANC participation.

To help the international press come to the same conclusion, he made a call to Bill Saunders in Frankfurt, checking that he had returned safely and also making sure he called the German newspapers to deny CIA involvement. The *Frankenpost* had been happy to report that inside information from an informed source indicated that the CIA, not the British, was involved once again in South African politics. Other European papers picked up the call. It took only about two hours after The *Frankenpost* hit the street for the phone calls from State to the CIA to start lighting up the circuits. Accusations and denials flowed back and forth. It provided an excellent smoke screen to cover the ANC.

Grant was feeling quite pleased with himself when he got the summons from Edwards. He knew he was in trouble when Edwards's secretary showed him into the office. She normally just pointed out the door. Something big was up. The director of operations was also there. He and Edwards had obviously been having words. They both stood in the middle of the room, fists clenched.

"What the hell do you mean, leaking a story to the press that we were involved in this South African thing?" The anger previously directed toward Edwards had found a new outlet.

"First of all, sir, I did not leak any story to the press." That was technically true. He had asked Saunders to give the *Frankenpost* the story. "I merely responded to Black at the *Post*, denying our involvement."

"What about the European story?" Edwards wanted to know.

"What about it?"

"Did you leak that?"

"Certainly not. I have a friend over there who had some peripheral involvement in the operation. Maybe he got carried away when things turned out so well."

"Who is it?"

"I'd rather not say."

By this point the director had calmed down a bit. He realized Grant was not about to break trust with any of his operatives. "Now Grant. We're all friends here…I can probably have State find out who let out the story. In fact, I'd love to drop it back on them. They've been after my ass all day."

"I still can't tell you, sir. Security, you know. Why are the two of you upset? The operation was a success."

"You know damn well why, Weldman." Edwards was not so forgiving.

"Image is still important, I guess." Two sets of eyebrows went up. He wondered if one or both of these gentlemen might have a bit of knowledge about Dominance.

"I want a full report on this debacle on my desk by Friday."

"Right. Can I go now? My agent still isn't out of danger." Both sets of eyebrows went up once again.

"And who might that be?" the director wanted to know.

"I'd rather not say, sir."

"Oh, for Christ sake, get out, Weldman!" Edwards shouted.

Sorting this out with his boss was going to be difficult. As Grant walked back to his office, he asked himself, *I wonder what would have happened if Mandela had been assassinated. Probably nothing. These guys wouldn't be interested. Just another killing of a black African leader.*

Later that afternoon, most of the staff from the Pickle Factory had packed up. All day, between calls from State and Edwards, he had to figure out how to get David out. He did not want to undo all his good cover work by having Forest call Crane Bertel but saw no choice. He picked up the phone.

22

At about the same time as David was flattened by the exploding Rover, Mark Bledsoe received a strange phone call from the constable he had assigned to the Breakwater Inn.

"What do you mean, 'is Kildare black'?"

"Well, sir, this little black man set off the alarm we installed on the room registered to Kildare. Told me he had a call from Kildare to get some of his stuff from his room and take it to the airport."

Bledsoe was worried that Willy's cover might be blown. "No, constable, Kildare is not black."

"What should I do with this guy?"

"Bring him down to my office. I want to personally question him, so don't just drop him off at the desk."

"Right, sir. On my way. By the way, should I come back and leave the alarms on?"

"No, just come in. Kildare won't go back there now."

* * *

David woke up in a dimly lit bed-sitting room with an acoustic white tile ceiling and drab walls. His head felt like someone had driven nails into his sinus cavities. When he tried to move his arm to check for blood, he found it bound to the steel frame of the bed. As his mind slowly began to function and refocus, he realized that the safest thing would be to appear to be unconscious until he could determine where he was and who was holding him. No telling what they'd do to him if they thought he wasn't. He closed his eyes again. He was sure it wasn't the local police. They would have him in a guarded hospital room with barred windows, and this room bore no resemblance to a medical facility. It must be Dominance. He hoped they'd give him a chance to identify them.

A few minutes later, he heard the door open and a feminine voice tell him, and whoever else was listening, that the patient was still out. He heard no reply. When the door closed, he decided to check on the strength of the tie-downs on his arms and legs. They were firm but not immoveable, so he was sure that he could wriggle free once he knew how much time he had. Waiting for the next room check was the best he could do to estimate the time he had to get out of his bonds and out of the room. In the interim, he craned his sore head around in an attempt to discover both his clothes and an escape route. The former were neatly folded on a chair beside a window, which appeared to be the best possibility of the latter.

It was very much darker, and about an hour later, when he heard the door open again. This time a male voice demanded that the woman make sure he was still out. She grabbed David by the hair and pulled vigorously. The test almost brought tears to his eyes. She left and he went to work on his bonds.

After fifteen agonizing minutes, which hurt his head more than his arm, he had removed his right arm from the leather strap. It took another quarter of an hour to remove the other straps, slip out of the bed and into his clothes, and tiptoe over to the window. Lifting the blind slightly revealed that he was on the second floor, there were no obvious guards outside the house, and a Mercedes had been conveniently left on the driveway to help him escape. *Too easy*, he thought.

Toward the rear of the house, across about twenty yards of lawn, lay a thick cedar hedge. Beyond that, in the dim light of a partly clouded half-moon, appeared to be a vineyard. The leaves of the grapevines were thick and lush and would provide ample cover if he could reach them. More important, the quick view out the crack in the blinds showed a veranda roof below the window, so that his decent would be silent, and a lot easier on his concussion. He searched the horizon for clues as to where he was but could only tell that it was dark. Escape first, orientation second, seemed to be the best plan. He didn't even know what day it was. He slowly raised the blind and the window and slipped out onto the veranda's roof.

* * *

The call to Dieter from den Kamp that morning had come with welcome news. Dieters's concerns moved to how to get Henson out—out of his life for good, out of Dominance's way. Henson was being held in a police safe house near the airport, and he had just had his secretary make the call to Frankfurt to get the Challenger gassed and ready. It was going to be a fine day.

* * *

David leaned over the edge of the roof to ensure he wouldn't come down right outside an occupied room. No lights showed from the windows that gave onto the veranda. He lowered himself on the edge of the eaves trough and dropped the final six feet to the soft grass. The impact made his head feel like it had split open, but the dizziness lasted only a few seconds.

About halfway to the row of cedars, the alarm was raised, and David sprinted. He heard the *crack, crack,* and felt the rounds whiz dangerously close to his already ringing ears as he dove through the hedge. Once in the vineyard he felt relatively safe—able to move quickly, hunched over between the rows, remaining invisible to anyone more than ten yards away and not in his row. He heard sounds of pursuit, so he kept dodging between rows until he arrived at an almost impassable vine-clogged hedgerow at the edge of the field. There he pried himself a small entrance, hid, and waited to see if his pursuer had the nerve to penetrate the blind. He did. The field sloped upward slightly from the hedge to the house so that the head of his adversary was vaguely outlined against the slate gray sky.

Henry moved cautiously toward a point in the hedge about five meters from David's hiding place and began to shake the bushes in an attempt to flush out his quarry. "I got you, you bastard," hissed his assailant as he moved steadily closer. David slipped deeper into the shadows.

After he passed, David made his move. He slid on his belly toward the edge of the thicket, leapt to his feet, and took Henry out with an open-handed chop to the neck. Henry's Beretta fell to the ground. David swooped up the weapon, pummeled Henry in the face with the pistol, and hurried away, leaving Henry—whom he did not recognize from their previous encounter in Bloemfontein—alive but temporarily unfit for duty.

* * *

"My phone is secure," opened Grant once he had reached Forest Burton in Zimbabwe on the third try. "Your service is not much improved since we last spoke three months ago."

Forest put down the phone without responding. He hoped whoever had been listening on his line would not recognize Grant's voice. He had noticed some unwanted attention from what he thought were South African security agents over the past two days. Two sturdily built blond men in light-colored safari suits had followed him into Fullerton's Haberdashery yesterday, and he had heard several strange clicks on the phone line. He was sure all of this was somehow connected to his having called on Grant to help stop the Mandela assassination.

He pulled aside the fawn-colored living room drapes a fraction of an inch and saw the agents waiting patiently in their light blue Volvo 850 opposite his neighbor's house. In order to call Grant without their interfering, he would have to get out of the house without being noticed.

Something in Grant's voice had alerted him to the fact that there was a problem in South Africa. He decided that the best place to make the call would be the apartment of his friend Susan, a lady unknown to the South African police.

After retrieving a forged passport, driver's license, and credit cards in the name of Trent Williams from his desk drawer in the study and collecting a light jacket, dark glasses, and hat, Forest slipped out the window of the guest room at the rear of his house, slid down the roof of the kitchen, and left his property over a rear fence into a narrow alley. In this high-end neighborhood, collections and deliveries at front doors were not acceptable. He noticed no telltale movements in the shrubbery that disguised the messiness of the alley, no sudden withdrawal of shadows into garage doorways, and no unfamiliar parked cars. It appeared that the agents were content to keep an eye on the house, to let him know he was under observation.

Forest walked two blocks to the nearest main street and called Susan's work from a pay phone. He was surprised to learn she had gone home just after lunch, but no one at work seemed to know why. He completed his journey to her home on foot. Susan buzzed him in as soon as she recognized his voice.

After climbing the three flights of stairs, he immediately noticed the look of fear and panic on Susan's face. "Forest, someone called me at work today and warned me not to get in touch with you. Why are you here?" After Forest had calmed her somewhat, she told him the details of the call: tone, accent, threatening words.

Although she had helped Forest with many routine assignments over the past six years, she never realized that there was a possibility of danger looming over their activities. "I came straight home after I got the call. Couldn't work, I was so scared."

"I'm sorry, Sue. I had no idea you were in danger. In fact, you probably aren't in danger. These people only want to keep an eye on us. Two of them are over near my place but haven't done anything to me. Even so, we should probably get out in the country to a safe place."

"For heaven's sake, Forest. Where could I go that's safer than here? Couldn't these people follow me if I left? Tell me what we're up against."

"First we better get out of here. I have to make a phone call." He grabbed Susan's arm before she had a chance to object, and led her down the back stairs and to the train station, three blocks away.

While seated on one of the well-worn pine benches, Forest told Susan the history and status of the situation in South Africa. Susan was very sympathetic to David Reasons, or as Forest knew him, Gregory Henson. He left her as a lookout and went to call Grant.

When Forest finally got through to him, Grant was a bit surprised at the length of time it had taken before his call was returned, and this had increased his concern for David's safety. The tension obviously showed in his less than cheerful opening, "I thought you weren't going to call back."

"Sorry, but our friends have been really close," said Forrest. "You remember my associate?"

"The one who did the excellent assessment of the failed delivery to Khadafi?"

"Yes, well, they seem to be onto him too, and I hadn't even told him about this business deal."

"It sounds like it's time to take positive action. I'm very sure our client is in trouble, and don't know if it's the police, or someone else who's involved. It fits with your confusion about who was aware of the relationship with your associate." *Good thinking, Forest,* thought Grant, *not letting whoever might be listening to this call know that your associate is female.*

"How can I help?"

"How soon can you get there?" asked Grant.

"Can you help us out with some transportation, info as to our client's location, and a travel stipend?"

"Of course. Go to Cape Town. I expected to hear from our client as soon as he arrived, but haven't yet." He did not want to tip off a listener to the fact that he had heard from David.

"We'll move fast."

"I'll have money waiting for you by 10:00 a.m. tomorrow at the Stanbic bank, in the name of…?"

"Do you remember my last job for you?"

"Yes."

"The man we were investigating had a protector."

"Right," Grant replied. His prodigious memory produced the name Trent Williams. "You better make your own travel arrangements, though. I'll make sure there's enough money to cover them. Call me with a report every second day starting day after tomorrow at 10:00 a.m. your time."

Forest knew it would be difficult lying low in South Africa. Although he hadn't been there for ten years, there were certain to be a lot of people who remembered them. In signing off, he merely said, "Don't worry, we'll get him out somehow." He damned well didn't yet know how.

"Good luck to you and your associate," were Grant's final words. He was glad to have someone familiar with the territory on the mission but wished there had been time for some proper planning. He hoped they weren't jumping into the same fire as David.

Susan had been watching all the entrances to the station while Forest was on the phone. She reported that there were no unlikely arrivals whose purpose was other than rail travel.

"Susan, are you willing to go back into South Africa with me tomorrow?" Forest asked.

"God, Forest, you know how I hate that place. Why?"

"Gregory Henson's in trouble. Grant Weldman, his handler—that's who I was talking to—hasn't heard from him and has asked me to try to get him out. I'm so well known in Cape Town that I thought you could be a big help by diverting the police."

Helping anyone to get away from the police was appealing to Susan, in part because it was BOSS who had murdered her husband, and the thought of returning to her unsafe apartment were enough to convince her to help. "I will as long as we don't go near Soweto," was her tense reply.

"Thank God, Sue. I thought I would have to go there and worry about you here. At least we'll be in it together. Now we have to keep moving to avoid whoever it is that's after us until we can pick up the money tomorrow and get out of here. I'm pretty sure they'll have realized I'm not home by now."

They rented a car, made a quick stop at Sue's apartment to get her papers, headed out to the countryside, and stayed overnight in separate rooms at a pension.

23

As David moved cautiously through the open countryside toward an ever-lightening eastern sky, he began to notice familiar landmarks. He passed an opening in a broken down, vine-covered fence and thought he recognized what was left of the old barn which had nearly finished his life. Farmers rise early, and he had to slink into copses and behind fences as he saw lights turn on, heard tractor motors begin to rattle, and dogs begin to bark.

At least his early morning stroll helped withdraw the nails that had been piercing his head for the last few hours. He was even able to think a bit more clearly as he gradually shook off the adrenaline rush that accompanied dangerous combat, and he began to look rationally at his situation.

He wondered if Dominance was some group other than the police. The police didn't use Berettas, but that might not mean much. The guy at the bus depot in Klerksdorp was in plain clothes. Maybe he preferred a Beretta to the normal Smith & Wesson. Perhaps it was Intelligence that took him to a safe house. He didn't think the police used safe houses. If they took him to a safe house, though, he wondered why? Was someone else trying to find him, or were they trying to keep him away from the police? There were still too many variables and not enough information to find an answer.

After two hours, David reached a farmhouse that looked deserted. He did not realize he had walked in a circle and was right back where he started, except he was approaching the farm from the east instead of the west—from the direction he had originally come from when he hid the Rover there. He finally caught on when he spotted a few boards and burnt hay sticking up in the field between him and the house. It seemed to be deserted when he hid the Rover in the barn, so it probably was now. If someone was there, they would probably have had the Rover removed. The farmer might have been planning to steal it until the Dominance people came along and wired it. *Anyway, the last place they'll look is in the same place they found me before.*

He watched the back door from behind some eucalyptus for about half an hour. When he found no sign of a farmer, or any other activity, he slipped up to the weathered gray door, tried the latch, and found it locked—not a good sign. He did not wish to alert a possible occupant by breaking the door down, so he moved cautiously around the concrete perimeter of the basement until he found a dust-covered window that had been left open.

The old, musty basement was filled with cobwebs—a good sign. The creaky cellar stairs led him to a basement door that suddenly opened and revealed the twin barrels of a menacing, ancient twelve-gauge shotgun. The tall white farmer who wielded it looked as old and menacing as the weapon. Before David had a chance to move, the rough old codger had slapped him on the temple with the barrels of the gun. He awoke in the middle of the dirty wooden kitchen floor, tied to a chair with butchers twine, and a dirty tea towel stuffed in his mouth, secured there with duct tape. His head returned to its previous painful condition.

* * *

Forest and Susan had no time to stop at a hotel, shower, and prepare to find and rescue David. They had flown into Windhoek, Namibia, and from there, flown into Cape Town. They discovered Cape Town International crawling with police and customs agents who were checking the papers of everyone who was either leaving the Cape or arriving from a destination outside the country.

"Thank God these policemen weren't on the force when I was here," Forest remarked to Susan as they stepped up to the Immigration counter. The Trent William fakes and Susan's regular papers seemed to satisfy the agents, although their names were taken down, and he doubted it would take the police long to make the connections. They got right to the Hertz counter and rented a beige Nissan Pathfinder.

While Forest went to the men's room, Susan took the risk of asking one of the policemen the reason for all the security. The young officer, stricken by Susan's beauty, was happy to report a few details of the Bloemfontein events and their search for the killer of Terbose. Not much to go on. He would not say in which direction the search lay, except that they thought their quarry was near the airport. He wanted to impress Susan with his inside knowledge. However, it did not take long for his sergeant to drag him away to check other passengers. Many old policemen did still not accept fraternization.

Forest watched the last part of the exchange from the shelter of the washroom doorway. He saw the lustful glance of the young constable and the vaguely familiar face of the sergeant. He had to delay his return to the impatiently waiting Susan until both policemen moved back into Arrivals to check another group of passengers from Johannesburg.

Susan was seething by the time he arrived. "Jesus, Forest. That took a long time. Why did you just leave me standing here?"

"I thought I recognized the sergeant. Anyway, how could you take such a chance? Now that young constable will remember us."

"He was going to remember us anyway. I'm sure he thought nothing of me asking him what was going on."

"I hope so." Forest's protective instincts were in full flight.

"So, do we take his word for it and look around the airport?"

"Too much area. We need to talk to someone we can trust, someone who'll give us more details."

"Do you really think the police will tell us anything, Forest?"

"Not the police," was Forest's reply. "There are a lot of people around who will be thankful Henson took out the assassin and will be happy to help us. We just have to find one and convince him or her of our sincerity."

"Now that you mention it, I think there is someone. One of the Jo'burg officers who investigated Clayton's murder in 1985 would be retired from the force by now," Susan said. "I think he came to Cape Town. The raid took his wife as well as Clay. He might help us." A tear ran down her cheek.

"I don't suppose you remember his address." She did not see Forest's smile or pick up his humor, being too engrossed in her own sad memories.

"Jesus, Forest. That was in 1985, and I haven't heard from him since…" she snapped out before she realized he was trying to cheer her up, and smiled. "His name was Eldon Freeman; at least I remember that."

It didn't take them long to find Eldon. He lived in a small apartment on Lowry Road, overlooking Trafalgar Park in downtown Cape Town. The reunion with Susan was sad and poignant, but the retelling of the sorrows of the past seemed to be cathartic for both of them. Soon they were talking, with hope in their voices, of the wonderful future the country could look forward to now that apartheid was history.

* * *

Eldon turned out to have a wealth of information. He had followed the news of the unsuccessful assassination attempt on radio and TV for the past two days, and thought there might have been some connection between their agent and a mysterious explosion at a farm about five kilometers east of the airport. It seemed to Forest a good place to start. He knew a bit about how Henson operated from past discussions with Grant, knew he would lie low, if possible, until the search had passed him. It was likely that he was still in the area. He certainly had not left by airplane. Forest declined Eldon's offer to use his apartment as a base of operations, concerned that they might place him in too much danger. They struck out for the farm, east of the city.

They had purchased a pair of binoculars in Harare to authenticate their cover as bird watchers on a holiday in the Cape, and these allowed Forest to study the ruined barn from behind the same copse David had used two days earlier. There was no evidence of police or agricultural activity. Many vehicles had recently used the drive, but none were in view, and the barn was in no condition to hide anything. The house looked deserted. They walked quietly past it to the flattened barn.

They, like the police, sifted through the wreckage of the barn and the Land Rover. "Thank heavens there's no evidence anyone was killed in the explosion," Susan remarked. They found nothing, however, which would indicate a direction that David had taken.

"It looks like we are just going to have to canvass the occupants of the local farms. I don't see any easy way. Henson does tend not to leave a trail, but maybe he's still on the loose."

"It will be very dangerous for you, Forest. One of these farmers could remember you from your days with the BOSS."

"Yes, but you might have noticed that this whole thing is getting dangerous. I owe a great debt to Grant Weldman. He helped me get safely out of Cape Town years ago and has been my main client ever since. I'll risk a lot to help get Henson out of South Africa. I only know Henson through Grant. I don't even know his real name. I bet Grant's the only one who does."

"That's pretty far-fetched. He must have friends and relatives who know who he is."

"Sure, but people he works for, except Grant, don't know who he is."

"Somebody in the CIA must know."

"Nobody but Grant. He doesn't really work for them. Funny way to put it, I guess, but you could call him a private anti-terrorist—emphasis on the private. I think Grant hires him on contract. Remember, never mention the name Gregory Henson to anyone but me. Not even Eldon. Speaking of Eldon, I wish you would go back to his apartment and wait for me. This explosion and the condition of the Rover makes me realize how really dangerous the people who did this are."

"Not on your life. I'm coming with you. Eldon's memories and my own got to me. I really want to become involved now."

Throughout the day they went from farm to farm in the area. Although the farmers had not been particularly cooperative, their story about searching for a bird watching friend who tended to become disoriented when first visiting a new area had seemed to allay any suspicions thus far. No one appeared to have seen Henson, but by process of elimination they gradually reduced the number of possible hiding places. To make sure they did not miss a hidden Gregory at any of the farms, they were sure to make a loud announcement of their names and the purpose of their search, knowing that Gregory would be able to detect a rescue attempt. It was tedious work, and by ten in the evening both of them were exhausted from both the strain and the long fear-filled hours. They secreted the SUV in a small thicket, tilted back its reclining seats, and slept in the cool night air.

Early the next morning, they had a revelation. "You know we never searched at the farm where the wreckage was," Susan said as they drove down the lane past it on their way to catch some of the farms where they got no response the previous day.

"Jesus, you're right. It would be the last place the police would look for him. Let's try it." They boldly strode up and banged on the weathered door.

The dirty old gray farmer was most uncooperative. Forest was pretty sure that the man knew something, so he decided to change the occupation of the object of their search from bird watcher, which would not get the old man's attention, to dangerous criminal. The strategy worked but almost backfired when the farmer produced his shotgun from behind the door and warned them off.

Forest's nervous system went on automatic. Before the ancient could get the gun pointed, Forest had it out of his hands. It took Susan about two minutes to find Henson gagged and bound to a chair in the kitchen.

"Grant sent us."

"I figured I would be handed over to the enemy any minute." David's voice was quiet and shallow.

They replaced Henson with the farmer on the chair and the three of them left.

* * *

It was still dark when Marion set out to find Henry. After hearing the shots, she assumed that he was close by and would soon bring their captive back to the house, or return to gather the appropriate tools to bury him. A few hours later he had still not come back and she started to worry.

Maybe Henson got away and Henry took off after him. Maybe Henson took out Henry. She called den Kamp in Pretoria and informed him of her missing captive and compatriot. Den Kamp was none too pleased.

"Find them." Den Kamp preached, "Report back to me just after first light."

Funny, Marion thought, *Eugene must be onto something. He hardly got mad at all. I thought he would tear a real strip off me.*

The abating darkness of the warm December morning made the search pretty simple. Ten minutes after she left the house, she found the still unconscious Henry at the bottom of the vineyard bleeding from his brow. A firm shaking revived him, and the two returned unsteadily to the house.

Henry made the report to Pretoria. Den Kamp told Henry in no uncertain terms that it would mean a return to routine police duties and a demotion if they failed to recapture or kill the elusive assassin. He also told him to be on the lookout for Forest Burton and his female assistant. Marion's contact in Harare had called and told den Kamp they were missing and presumed to be on the way to the Cape.

The now contrite pair returned to the police headquarters building on Buitenkant Street in Cape Town. Although the locals resented the official interference, they were friendly with the agents themselves. Henry was well known and much respected in Cape Town. Marion's beauty dropped jaws.

The main subject of discussion around the office was of the Bloemfontein affair and the hunt for the assassin. The police were split about twenty percent against and eighty percent for Kildare. Even by talking to the ones who wanted the killer caught, Henry and Marion could find out little in the way of concrete information concerning his whereabouts. There was speculation that he had already left the country, or returned to Johannesburg. It seemed the locals had as much trouble as they did.

By about noon, all hell had broken loose. One very irate Boer farmer had called in to tell the police that three strangers had bound and gagged him earlier that morning. It took all the patience Henry and Marion could muster not to leave the building in unseemly haste with two uniformed local police.

The last time they did the opposite of the police, they were rewarded with the capture of an unconscious David. Since the police were on their way once again to find David near the airport, they decided it would be more fruitful to look for the two accomplices, who must have left some trail in the city.

The search for the rest of the day netted them nothing.

24

Susan drove on back roads heading north, Forest kept a lookout for police, and David slept in the back of the SUV. They were all tired, but David's injuries and fatigue made him a rather shaky pilot or navigator.

They had left the farm at around a quarter past eight. The climbing early summer sun had split a cloudless azure sky and created a beautiful backdrop for the rugged landscape they were passing. But now that the sun had risen, the possibility of giving a suspicious police car the slip became slim. Their best hope was to be in an unexpected area when the old farmer raised the alarm. Susan drove through dry gulches and over rocky desert plains until noon, when they decided to head back to the coast and stop for lunch in the port city of Saldanha, well north of the Cape. Stopping at a lone restaurant or inn out in the countryside would leave them dreadfully exposed. Forest felt it would be much better to get their lunch in a fair-sized town.

The three hours of sleep renewed David, and they were able to get down to some serious planning over a substantial lunch of beef stew, home-baked crusty rolls, and chef salad at the café in the Saldanha Bay Protea Hotel. None of them had eaten for about eighteen hours, which made the high quality hotel food taste even more delicious.

The first thing they decided was that it would not be safe to retain the Pathfinder for longer than the rest of the day. Even though Forest had paid cash for its rental, the police would soon have his description to show the rental agencies.

"I think it would be a good plan to drive the rest of the day and stop near a town where we could reasonably expect to find a replacement car," David suggested. "Then we could hide the SUV, use it as a hotel for part of the night, and go into the town on foot in the dark to pilfer new transportation."

Forest knew there were lots of ravines in the area north of the wine district and very little population. "We could put the van into a ravine where it probably wouldn't be found for a week."

"Once our descriptions are out, the police will be looking for us wherever we go," David said. "There will be very few places we can be safe."

"Jesus!" exclaimed Susan. "You guys have been at this violent business for years. I've only been involved for two days, and even *I* know it's not safe." They all laughed. The tenseness of the flight and their fear of capture needed to be relieved.

"Would you do something differently, Forest?" David asked.

"I like the idea of changing cars every day, but it might be safer to get some camping equipment and sleep some distance from the car. It's the car that will be spotted first."

"I like the camping idea." David knew enough about leadership to bring the others into the making of plans.

"I'm not much help with that one," Susan explained. "I've never been in this part of the country."

"It seems to me the police will look for us to get to the nearest airport and leave by plane," Forest reasoned. "There are small ones at Carnarvon, about five hundred kilometers to the east, and at Springbok, four hundred klicks north. Our best bet would probably be to go northeast between them toward Langebergen. If we need an alternate route out at that point, a boat down the Orange River could get us into Namibia." His years chasing ANC rebels throughout the country had left him in good stead.

"God, Forest, you have some memory. I was thinking, though, don't the South Africans still control Namibia?" David wondered.

"Not anymore. Sam Nujoma got rid of most of the politicians and bureaucrats who were under Pretoria's influence."

David liked the idea of Namibia. "My original alternate plan included a flight from Cape Town to Windhoek, and then on to London. Since we can't fly there, we better get the camping stuff and get out of this damn country."

Saldanha had many shops near the hotel where David could purchase both the elements of his new birdwatcher disguise and the camping equipment. Soon the three of them, camping gear stored in the rear, were driving through the rough, deserted countryside toward Loriesfontein, where they planned to ditch the SUV and spend the first night. This time, David drove and Sue and Forest slept.

As the day passed, the low-lying coastal lushness gave way to the Kalahari-type veld of central Cape Province. Toward dusk, David spotted a narrow, rutted, overgrown track moving off into the scrub toward the purpling mountains to the east. At about the same time, a police car came around the bend ahead of them, sirens blazing and lights scattering the lengthening evening shadows. There was no time to turn around and escape discovery by pulling into the brush just past the shoulder, or duck down the original path David had selected for hiding the vehicle. The police car flashed by, obviously on another call. But the officer had gotten a good look at the northbound SUV. David watched the cop in his rearview mirror. Before reaching the turn, his brake lights had come on. David accelerated at the same moment, and they rounded the next bend before the policeman had executed his turn. These maneuvers wakened Forest and Susan.

Now it was a race to the nearest cover. David would have wished for a more responsive vehicle, but he kept the speed well up in the bend, barely missing the gravel, and a certain rollover into the bush. Before they spotted the police car rounding the bend, they found another path leading toward the ridgeline of an escarpment. David flung the car into it. He knew they had no chance of outrunning the cop on the paved surface, but perhaps this little used track was sufficiently rough that the high road clearance of the Pathfinder would give them an advantage.

The ride was terrible. Several times the three of them were slammed sideways as the tires jammed in rocks. But they kept moving. The dust they were raising would allow the policeman to follow until the dark of night that was fast approaching.

They kept to the path for several minutes, stopped, and got out. They could still hear the roar of the heavy engine in the police car, but it was not close.

"We are going to ditch the car anyway," Forest suggested. "Let's do it now and put some distance between us and the cop."

David agreed. "I'm sure he'll get help before trying to follow us into the brush."

They took the gear and the belongings they had from the SUV, strapped them on their backs in the shoulder packs that Susan and Forest had purchased before leaving Harare, and struck off into the brush. They heard the police car stop at the SUV after they had gone a half-kilometer or so.

The country through which they traveled was rugged. Wildflowers, for which the area was famous, bloomed in great abundance. They could soon feel the evening desert chill descending on them as they trudged toward Loriesfontein. Once it became fully dark, a dull, first quarter moon provided some light to guide them through the sparse undergrowth. They needed to get near civilization before stopping. The local police would be on the lookout for them by now and soon would be scouring the area. They also needed to use the darkness to obtain a replacement car.

Forest was quite sure that Loriesfontein was only three or four kilometers away from where they had left the van. Twenty minutes later he was proved correct, as they topped a ridge and saw the lights of the small farming community spread out before them.

Once again, the bird watching binoculars came in handy. Even in the gloom they were able to make out the town's main features. It was well spread out, like many other desert towns, and had numerous small pockets of housing broken up with a golf course, rugby fields, parks, and even tennis courts. Each of the pockets was elongated as they clung to the three roads that passed through the area. This meant that quietly starting up a vehicle in the darkness would not likely be noticed by neighbors and would probably not be discovered until morning. David had the Beretta he had taken from Henry but hoped he would not have to draw more attention to them by having to use it.

"I think we should stop and try to get some sleep," David said. "We'll need to post a watch, though. I'll let you two sleep for about two hours. Then I'll get you up, Forest. It's now ten, and we should go get some transportation by about four. That leaves us two hours each of guard duty."

Halfway through David's shift, there was a rustling in the bush about ten meters away from the quickly assembled tent which now held Susan and Forest. David moved to intercept the intruder, his Beretta drawn.

It was pitch black, the thin moon completely covered by dense cumulus. As David moved the bushes aside just at the edge of the tent, the outline of the policeman hurled itself into the shelter. He shouted, "Freeze," pointing his revolver and flashlight at Sue and Forest. They blinked to full wakefulness. David opened the tent flap behind him and hissed a warning to drop his weapon. The young officer was apparently only used to dealing with minor criminals. He turned on David and was about to squeeze off a shot from his Smith & Wesson when the round from David's Beretta tore it from his hand. The constable howled in pain and terror and dropped to his knees, just as David's hand chopped down hard on his exposed neck. He hit the hard ground face down and unconscious.

"Jesus, Gregory, did you have to hurt him that bad?" Susan was not used to having to quickly render a deadly opponent immobile or to David's lightning reflexes. "I hope you haven't killed him."

"He's not dead, Susan, but I can't be taken prisoner in this country. If I have to hurt or even kill someone who is threatening us, so be it."

"Well, I'm not sure I want to be part of it," was the tearful reply. "I can't imagine ever being able to hurt someone that badly."

Forest had never seen David in action. He was awed by the speed and power of the American. In the past, he had been violent, if necessary, himself. He felt the need to somehow show his determination, strength, and courage to counteract the impact that David's quick handling of the policeman had made on Susan.

"I'm a bit out of shape for that kind of action, but I remember many times as a BOSS policeman chasing enemies of the state back in the eighties. See this scar." He pointed to a nasty welt down the right side of his neck, extending from earlobe to shirt collar. "In 1983 I had the privilege of fighting the man who hired us. Crane Bertel used a kitchen knife to free himself from my grip."

It had been so long since Forest had been involved with violence that he sympathized with Susan's revulsion over David's felling of the young policeman. Forest realized certain men were able to handle violence better than others. Such men often evoked strong feelings in women. He was concerned that Susan's outburst could be a signal of a budding emotional attraction to their strong, determined companion.

"Unless that young officer was a complete fool, we can expect company very shortly." David was anxious to get into action again. These moments of high tension were bringing out another strong feeling—a desire for the woman who had risked so much to save him, was so repulsed by his violence, but, somehow, also attracted by it.

They disassembled camp quickly and made straight for the town. During the hike into Loriesfontein, they agreed to a change in plan. It was obvious that their route out of South Africa to the northeast would be far too treacherous. Local police forces would have been alerted. They decided the best way to escape would be to return to the South and lie low until the police were less pressured to find them. Finding a vehicle, breaking in, and hot-wiring it proved no difficulty for David and Forest, and they were soon on their way back to Saldanha in a five-year-old Opel Rekord wagon.

The return to the coast was uneventful. Before they reached the seaside, and just as dawn was beginning to break, they discovered a deserted, and apparently abandoned, boat launch ramp near the ocean highway. David suggested this might be a good place to ditch the Opel, which had raised no interest during the early morning return trip. Forest and Susan agreed, and after their belongings had been removed, Forest drove the car down the ramp at some speed and leapt out before the car hit the water. They anxiously watched the car disappear. When there was no trace of the car or its bubbles, the trio started the pleasant, overland, three-mile trek back into Saldanha under a warming and cloudless sky.

"You missed your call to Grant!" exclaimed Forest. "Weren't you supposed to call every second day at ten o'clock?"

David was well aware that Grant would be concerned, and realized that the stop in Saldanha should be a good place to make the call. "Don't worry. He knows the kind of stress we're under. Besides, it's only eleven-thirty."

No one showed the slightest interest in them as they calmly walked up to a small isolated motel called the Sea Breeze on the outskirts of the town, registered in three rooms, and found a phone booth in the Shell station across the street. David placed the call to Grant at 12:05.

As soon as Fieldstone responded, Grant cautioned David. "I have the president in my office with me."

"Good morning, sir. Isn't it a bit early for you to be up?" David was very curious as to why the Head of the CTC would be in Grant's office at six o' clock a.m.

"You've created quite a stir in the head office," was the cool rejoinder. "I don't recall ever having to answer so many questions about a late delivery before." Grant had obviously briefed Edwards on the communication strategy they used.

Grant interrupted. He thought further talk would damage an already fragile security. "We're certainly glad to hear the parcel finally arrived safely. It did arrive safely?"

"Yes."

"I'm afraid we can't do much officially to help you smooth the feathers of our client, though. They resent they had to go over your head to straighten out the problem." For this David read Dominance was furious that he had killed the assassin instead of the assassin killing Mandela.

"I'm also well aware of that. No matter what I do, I can't seem to make them happy. Even their agent is in the act." David was not about to remark on the presence of Forest and Susan in the country, as he was unsure how much Grant wanted Edwards to know. "It looks like I will be here until the customer is happy. I hope I can straighten things out in the next couple of days, then come home."

Edwards intervened. "You've done a good job. Good luck. Sorry I can't pull any strings to help, but this one seems to have everyone in a lather. As you know, I never get involved unless the problem gets outside the normal delay." From this, David understood that Edwards was being chastised for getting the CIA involved in black ops. He heard the chief's footsteps receding, "...and you still won't tell me who he is, will you, Arthur?"

David heard the soft click, which meant he was no longer on speaker. "Are you in trouble over this?" he asked his handler.

"Yeah, but not as much as you are, buddy. Let me worry about the boss. Just give me a call every second day. How about four o' clock p.m. your time, though. I need the sleep."

"All right, my friend. Don't worry. We'll keep them happy."

"By the way, were the papers I sent helpful?"

"You'll never know. I would still be explaining the original delays if not for them. The client now understands the reasons for the first holdup. Now I have to explain the second."

David was concerned about the possibility that one or more of them would get caught and have to be left behind. Now that they had freed him, he wished there was some way to get them safely back to Harare, but he couldn't think of one. He did not mention this to Grant.

"Talk to you on the twenty-third," was Grant's sign-off.

The three bird watchers spent the evening at the motel. No sign of pursuit showed up. Apparently the authorities were looking to the northeast as they had hoped.

25

"Forty-two here," was the imperious response Den Kamp got when the call from the Black Forest came through on his private line. "Why did you call my office and stop me coming down there to eliminate Henson?" Dieter was actually airborne when den Kamp had called his office to inform him that there was no need for the leader of Dominance to make the trip.

"He escaped from the safe house. Two agents were sent in to extract him when we had him dead to rights," den Kamp lied. "The trio is now missing."

"You have failed so many times. Do you not have the resources to find him?"

"I need no help."

"We need a success to show to the group, Forty-seven. There will be defections at the meeting in Rio if there is nothing to show from your operation. We must be getting stronger, not weaker."

"We will find them. I will let you know immediately," muttered den Kamp.

"Do not fail again," was the reply from Germany.

* * *

Mark Bledsoe was confused. It was the end of the day and he sat quietly in his office. The Cape Town police had covered every square inch of the town. His officers had spread the word to other forces in the surrounding countryside. The infiltrators had been reported near Loriesfontein last night. Two of his best detectives had flown to that outpost early this morning and, about 11:00 a.m., found only an irate store clerk who's Opel was missing. They searched from the air all the byways in the area including the Orange River, right up to the Namibian border. It was 8:00 p.m., and they had found nothing. He knew that in cases of well-trained agents, if you lost the trail, it was very difficult to pick up again. He wondered why the young police officer hadn't called in back up before making his move. Bledsoe scowled as he recalled that in July of 1971, as a young constable, he had moved by himself on an ANC cell in Cape Town. He had wound up in the hospital too, with a fractured arm and blurred vision that lasted for a week. It was time to go home now. He was getting a splitting headache.

* * *

After a pleasant supper at a wonderful waterfront restaurant called the Wharf, Forest decided to head for their hotel bar and catch the rugby match between the Bloemfontein Cheetahs and the Springboks on TV. David and Susan went back to their rooms.

David couldn't sleep. He wondered if Susan felt the same as he did, or had years of loneliness dulled his senses? Was it really attraction to him she was showing?

When he could wait no longer, he got up, dressed in sweats, and went down the hallway.

He knocked and the door opened immediately. Susan stood with the bathroom light behind her, covered only by a mauve nightgown she had bought in the hotel's gift shop. Her erect nipples seemed to burn through the silk. They embraced, mouths hungry for each other. David felt the heat of Susan's body through both their clothing. It had been so long. He wanted to tear her gown and have her standing in front of the unlocked door. Instead he pulled away. "I want you so much. I didn't know…"

Susan hugged David's shoulders, lifting herself off the carpet and wrapping both her long legs around his waist, her breasts brushing his face. Her heat rushed to his core, and David sank to the floor. Susan pressed him back against the foot of the bed and untied his sweat pants as he raised the film of her gown over her head, taking her breasts in his hands. His lips tenderly pinched her nipples. Susan's strong hands dropped the gray sweat pants under his butt, and she guided him inside her.

It seemed like no time had passed when they both climaxed. They stayed wrapped together for several minutes before David could talk. "Susan…"

"Shhh, David. Don't talk. Don't even think. Just feel me close, as close as we can get."

An hour later, it was a much longer trip for David back to his own room.

* * *

Tuesday morning started like any other for Mark Bledsoe. He slumped sleepily behind his desk, thinking they we're spinning their wheels,

261

trying to find this elusive Kildare. He considered calling den Kamp and telling him to look for his own intruder, but instinct made it hard for him to let go. This guy had injured one of his men, killed a Broeder, and put a constable from Loriesfontein in the hospital. Maybe they should have one more try and then call it quits.

Just then, he heard Marion and Henry come in and start talking to his secretary. "Would you two mind stepping into my office for a moment?"

"Certainly," was Henry's response. "We would like to talk to you about joining forces to capture the enemy agents."

"Now wouldn't that be nice. What have you two found out? You've been tramping all over my territory here without even letting me know where you are or what you're doing."

"We're in the dark as much as you are," Henry said when he and Marion were uncomfortably seated opposite Bledsoe.

"Well, I guess Pretoria is taking more interest in this case than just keeping up on its status. What does den Kamp think?"

"Well, sir, den Kamp is anxious that this case be resolved quickly, and he thinks we've screwed it up pretty badly," Henry advised.

"Okay, I agree, but you haven't been alone. My people have lost them too."

The ensuing discussion shed little light for both parties. Henry knew he could do better by cooperating with Bledsoe but loathed to reveal that they had already captured Henson, failed to report this fact to their Cape Town colleague, and then let him escape. They did clear the air and agree to report to one another in future. Both sides were mystified as to how three foreigners could completely vanish with so many police looking for them.

Henry and Marion started off to try to regain the scent.

"Well, Marion, life should be a bit easier now that we have Bledsoe on our side."

"You think so?" was the sarcastic reply. "He would be with Dominance if he were really on our side. I don't agree with den Kamp calling him in. Too many of us are working on this." Marion had an intuitive feeling that the whole case should have been dropped once Henson slipped away from them at Bloemfontein. Neither of them was aware that the whole purpose now was to strengthen the group through the avoidance of failure—to show some success and competence. She felt they were only involved in revenge.

"Let's not go into that. You know how den Kamp is. If you don't follow orders without question, you're out. All we know is that we have been directed to find the three agents and either eliminate or capture them."

"Okay, then. Where do we start?" was the surly reply.

"Well, obviously they left the Cape, at least for a while. They were spotted heading for the Namibian border near Loriesfontein. The locals seemed to think that they might try to leave by river, but the helicopters couldn't find a trace of them. The last time the cops looked near the airport, Henson went in the opposite direction. Perhaps the three of them are doing that again. We should see if there is an obvious place they might return to in Cape Town."

As the two set out into the bright, clear December morning from police headquarters on Buitenkant Street, Marion mused, "I wonder if we should head for the castle. We need to do some thinking, and that'll be a quiet place."

When they were seated on a bench, quite near the place where David had escaped from the police three days ago, Henry began. "I think you should go through all the hotels and any other spot where the two from Zimbabwe might be."

"Are we back in Klerksdorp? Wasn't that my job then?"

"Yeah, and you found his hotel then, remember?"

"Okay, where do you look?"

"I think I'll go through the police files. Try to find some association with the past. Remember Burton was with the BOSS back in '85, and he might have worked through some friend or other."

"What about the woman? I asked at the desk this morning and nobody seems to have heard of her."

"Well, we know she works with Burton in Harare. The name Susan Bernard hasn't rung a bell with any of the police in Pretoria either. I called last night when you went out for some air."

"Why didn't you tell me?"

"You looked so good when you came back in."

"Okay, so maybe you can find something in the files on her as well as Burton."

Within eighteen hours, the duo had arrived at the bachelor apartment of Eldon Freeman on Lowry Road.

* * *

Forest, Susan, and David were having breakfast at the motel's restaurant. Forest sensed what had happened between Susan and David the previous evening, and he felt a pang of jealousy. Anxious to get them apart, he started to plot their return to the Cape and subsequent flight to freedom. "I have an idea, folks," he suggested. "Let's get back to Cape Town by boat."

David had not considered that possibility. Before finally falling asleep after the emotional surge had abated, he had considered escape possibilities. Automobile, train, aircraft, and Shank's mare had crossed David's mind—ship had not. "Let's think about that for a while," he said.

264

David knew his covers of VP of Sales and itinerant professor were blown. The names Trent Williams and Susan Bernard would also be well known to police and whoever else was looking for them in Cape Town. "I wonder if we can really afford to go to Cape Town without new passports," he mused out loud. "We won't get on a flight with the ones we have. They'll light up the computers like a shuttle launch pad at night, even if there are no agents looking for us at the airport."

"You get to call Grant tonight," Susan remarked. "Perhaps he can get us new papers."

"I'm sure he can," David replied. "But I'm not sure I want to wait the four or five days it will take them to get here."

"What do you suggest, Gregory?" Forest was anxious to leave and knew that taking road transport out of the country would be almost as dangerous as air because of the time they would be exposed to detection.

"Well, Forest, your boat idea is looking pretty good. It could get us to Cape Town, but then if the police catch wind of our plan, we won't be able to get out of Cape Town."

"But why not get on a boat to Europe or South America from here? I saw lots of them in the harbor," Susan said.

"Yes, and did you see the number of Naval vessels? This is the biggest South African Navy port, isn't it Forest?"

"Yes, and the trip from here to the Cape goes through some of the roughest waters in the world. If we can get there by car, we might ship out of the Cape on a freighter. The dock area is really a yuppie paradise, and there would be plenty of chance to blend in with the tourists there. Here we'd stand out like sore thumbs."

"That could take a month. I have a job to go back to in Harare," Susan complained. "Besides, you can't take a boat to Harare. There's no water."

Forest laughed. "It may be a month before it's safe to go back."

"Should I give my boss a call?"

"You're sure he's not involved in this, are you?" Forest replied.

"We don't know that, Forest," said David. He didn't want Susan frightened. "You can check that out when you get back before letting Sue back into her apartment. Someone tipped off the police, or whoever it was, to your connection with Forest. The plan would be to get the three of us to an African port by boat, then fly you and Forest to Harare."

"Well, we go out either by road, air, or sea, and it looks like the last may be the safest," Forest offered. "I can't imagine spending two or three days on the road with every cop in Cape Province looking for us, and also don't fancy sitting around for a week waiting for new passports."

"Seaports are a lot less controlled than airports," David said. He was now seeing the functionality of the waterborne alternative. "I'm sure we'll find a skipper to bribe into taking us on without asking too many questions."

By ten o'clock, they were ready to leave. Forest rented a nondescript minivan, and they packed and hit the road. A brief stop at a south end shopping center produced the necessary purchases for new identities.

The cool, sunny day sported a few ominous cumulus clouds over the mountains to the east. Under David's expert direction, each took turns in the partial privacy of the back of the van going through the metamorphosis to new identities. Susan emerged as a portly schoolteacher, thanks to some strategically placed foam and an oversized, matronly dress, Forest as a construction worker, and David as a gentleman farmer, in town for a holiday. By the time they reached the Cape in mid-afternoon, rain had started in earnest.

David wanted to move as soon as possible. Every minute counted in this town that was an ever-present danger. "Do you know how we can find out what ships are in port and when they're leaving, Forest?"

"Well, they might have moved it, but the port manager's office used to be in the Lourens Muller building near Table Bay. It would probably be the best place to pick up shipping intelligence."

"It would be best if we weren't seen around the docks until it is time to leave," suggested Susan.

"Damn good idea," said David. He was happy that Susan was thinking as part of the team. He was concerned that their encounter the previous night and the violence near Loriesfontein had somehow pushed her away from the action they now needed to take.

"Maybe we could make some calls from your friend's apartment, Sue," Forest suggested.

"I didn't know you had a friend here in Cape Town. I thought you were from Soweto." David was worried about anyone knowing they were back. He had been compromised too many times.

"Oh, Eldon's all right, Gregory. He's the policeman who investigated my husband's murder back in 1985. Now he's retired and living in a small apartment on Lowry Road."

"Remember, that's close to the police station, though," Forest interjected.

"Will he be able to update us on the situation?" David asked.

"If it weren't for him, we never would have found you," Forest stated. "He told us of the barn exploding."

"Seems like a good risk to find him." David hoped the cops wouldn't be looking for them two blocks from the station.

They parked the car in a public lot on Somerset Road and took two taxis to Lowry, David in one and Sue and Forest in the other. The rain had hardly abated, and the drivers did not seem particularly interested in out-of-towners. They arrived within a minute of each other.

When Sue pressed the bell to Eldon's apartment, the "Who is it?" that came out of the speaker, after a full minute's delay, did not sound like Eldon.

"We're friends of Eldon. Who are you?" Sue blurted out before David could stop her.

They heard the speaker say, "His landlord," as David dragged them out of the building.

26

"You will tell me where they are. Tell me now. I'll keep beating you 'til you do." Henry was holding onto Eldon's wrists with his right hand and pummeling the right side of his face and skull with the barrel of his Beretta. There was blood everywhere, enough blood to make Marion feel sick. She did nothing to stop the awful attack—just stood there, her mouth open and her hands clenched.

"I will never betray them. I want the police."

"We are the police." Another savage blow nearly ripped off his ear. Eldon passed out.

"Henry, you can't just beat people to get information. We don't even know if he's had contact with them."

"The little bastard knows where they are."

"Maybe he doesn't." Ever since that call to den Kamp on their first day in Cape Town, Henry had acted like a madman. He had wired the car to kill Henson. After they found out Henson had been at the Breakwater, he wanted to rig the door with explosives instead of just an alarm. Luckily for Willy, she'd convinced him it might kill a maid instead of Henson. She came over close to Henry and spoke softly to calm him. "Please stop before you kill him."

"I want to get Henson."

"So do I, but do we have to do all this killing? What if Bledsoe finds out?"

"Den Kamp can worry about Bledsoe. Look. He's coming to. Where are those agents hiding? Now! I want to know now!"

"I don't know." Freeman was gulping for air. His eyes were completely swollen shut, his voice only a whisper.

"Yes, you do," was followed by another blow to Eldon's temple with the Beretta. This time, it killed him.

"What the fuck, Henry? Now what?"

The doorbell rang.

"Jesus, do I answer, or just let it ring?" Henry shouted.

"It might be just the people we're looking for," Marion answered. "I'll answer it."

"Henry, you go down the back stairs fast, and I'll go down the front. We'll try to trap them in the lobby."

By the time he reached the street, Henry saw the three racing through the pouring rain into Trafalgar Park in the direction of the Castle. It took him only twenty seconds to find Marion and take off in pursuit.

* * *

"I want you two to hide in the castle grounds while I go and find out what happened at your friend's apartment." David did not want the two of them exposed to the dangers he was sure awaited them there, not realizing that those dangers had followed them to the park.

"Eldon was a special person," Susan intervened. "If something's happened to him, I want to find out who did it."

They were hiding in the shrubbery inside the main entrance on the opposite side of the castle from where David had been chased three days ago. The rain was so hard that the normal flow of tourists into the most remarkable of Cape Town's attractions had dried up. They were alone and it was quiet, except for the splatting sound of the downpour striking the pavement.

They soon heard two sets of feet sloshing along the sidewalk. David knew it was time to take a stand. "Forest, take my weapon and remove the first person to step through the arch. I will make sure the second one doesn't back him up."

"But, Gregory…"

"We don't have time to argue, Forest," David hissed as he threw the Beretta to him and went back out through the gate and behind a privet bush beside the sentry box, pulling Susan with him.

A minute later Henry edged nervously through the arch, Beretta held high and ready to shoot at the first thing that moved. He was faced with an earnest Forest and a loaded 9mm pointed straight at his forehead. Three paces behind, Marion crumpled as she was raising her drawn weapon—her right knee having lost its ability to support any load due to a shattering blow from the arch of David's foot.

The shock of changing from pursuer to the pursued caused Henry to pause. Forest fired before Henry had a chance to aim his weapon. A reflex shot left Henry's Beretta and slammed harmlessly into the stone of the arch. A small circle of blood pooled just above the bridge of his nose as he slowly crumpled to the sidewalk.

David grabbed Marion and clamped his hand securely over her mouth. "Jon, go out on the street and find us a cab. I want to have a word with our captive."

"Don't hurt her too much, Gregory," Susan implored.

"I have no intention of hurting her. All right, lady. No yelling, or you wind up just like your friend over there." David removed his hand. "Who is after us beside you and that stiff over there?"

Not a sound. Somehow she knew enough not to speak. It would identify her as the person who held him captive at the farmhouse. Better to keep him in the dark.

"We better get out of here quickly. There'll be someone who heard that shot. Let's get this corpse into the bushes and go." David ripped both sleeves off Marion's soggy green jacket, bound her hands behind her with one and her ankles together with the other. The best he could do to stop her from shouting was jam his handkerchief into her mouth. Then he and Susan dragged both of them into the bushes. Each of them now had a weapon.

"Allison, you go get another cab for our trip to the airport. We need to split—"

"But, Gregory—"

"No buts. Do it now. We don't want to be caught all together." Susan left to join Forest. She began to get the picture. Gregory was trying to protect both their identities and destination. She rushed out to the Strand.

David kicked Marion square in the jaw to knock her unconscious, then followed the pair out to the waiting taxi.

The one-hundred-rand note David handed the driver got them rapidly out of the area and back to their car. It was David's hope that a further one hundred rand would ensure his silence, but he doubted it. Perhaps it would at least stop him from raising an alarm.

"We only have a few minutes before the alarm goes up," David advised as they climbed back into their van. "First things, first. This van may be compromised. We better get another."

"What about Eldon? Can we go check on him?"

"I don't think that's wise. The two who chased us probably called in back up before they left his apartment. We need to find a safe place to hide. God knows where that is." Once they were relatively safe, there would be time to think about Susan's friend.

They ditched the car in the parking lot at the City Lodge. David had done the unexpected so many times, he hoped the enemy would not suspect that he would go back to where he had almost been caught. Finding the car there would make sense and lend some credence to what David hoped would be the woman's story that they had headed for the airport. To reinforce that subterfuge, the three went to the cabstand in front of the hotel and took a taxi there.

David knew the police would be all over the building. He also knew they would be looking in the Departures area. "Cabby, would you please drop us at Arrivals? There is someone we must meet."

"No problem, sir. You three are pretty wet. There is a good place to dry off there."

"Allison, did you tell the company to send our luggage to the airport?"

"Yes. They said the clerks at the SAA counter would tell us where it was."

Forest felt a twinge as he realized he had added little to this mission since being hurt by the deepening relationship between Sue and David. "Was it SAA or Lufthansa, Allison?"

"I don't think Lufthansa flies in here today." David was pleased with their little game. The cabby would not be able to remember if they were going out or coming in and whether it was SAA or Lufthansa they used.

When the cab that had brought them pulled away, they moved to the head of the outgoing line and grabbed the first one for the return trip into town. There was no time to dry off. They dared not go into the terminal building. It was Forest who first thought of a way out of their dilemma.

They were revved up. The action at the castle had heightened their thoughts and their nerves. "I guess that will teach us to try to walk from Departures to Arrivals," he laughed. "Now we're soaked, proper."

"Why didn't you just go through the terminal building?" the confused cabby asked. "There's a passage, you know."

"No, we didn't. It would probably help if we learned Afrikaans. Then we wouldn't get dropped off at the wrong spot. I thought *Uitgang* meant we were foreigners coming in."

The cabby laughed. "Do you want to go back and pick up your bags?"

"No, we had the SAA agent send them to our hotel." Forest was still thinking.

"Okay, which hotel?"

"He said the Graeme down by the waterfront was one of the best."

"It sure is. Pricey, though."

"Hanged the expense," David chimed in. "We're on holidays."

In thirty minutes they were checking into the luxurious hotel with a good view of the waterfront from its upper floors, and all the amenities except one they could possibly need for the next few days. The missing amenity was safety. There was no way of telling when the cops would turn their search back to the waterfront.

As they waited in the check-in line, they all agreed to book only one room. David still had a passport for Hans Geldhart, and he used that and a thousand rand deposit to book a suite on the top floor. The social arrangements were going to be a bit difficult, but using Trent Williams and Susan's identities would probably prove fatal. It had now been four days since David had used Geldhart's name. Hotel desks that been told to watch for it had hopefully forgotten by now. No bells rang as they took the ancient lift up to the third floor and tiredly plunked themselves down on the soft sofa and two arm chairs in the beautifully decorated sitting room.

* * *

Marion limped to police headquarters, which was only a couple of blocks from the castle. She was a sad sight by the time she got two constables to help her up to Bledsoe's office—hair flat against her face and back, both sleeves ripped off her expensive Dior jacket, and hardly able to stand.

"What happened to you?" Bledsoe asked as he jumped out of his chair and helped her to a soft chair beside a coffee table in the corner of the office. "Where's Henry?"

"Henry and I were heading towards the castle when we spotted three individuals that met the description." Marion left out the death of the retired police officer. "As we pursued them into the castle property…"

"Get her a blanket and some warm tea," Bledsoe barked to a subordinate.

Marion told Bledsoe of Henry's murder, her wounding, and the escape of the three agents toward the airport. After a quick call to Dispatch to send a crew to the homicide site in Castle Park, Bledsoe called for a car and they drove out to the airport.

Once again, the trail got very cold. After four hours of waiting, they eventually realized they'd been had, gave up, and returned downtown to the morgue to identify Henry's body. In the interest of keeping their quarry off guard, Marion convinced Bledsoe to keep Henry's death out of the press for as long as possible. She hadn't gotten up the nerve yet to mention Eldon's killing.

As she went back to the Metropole in a taxi, she wondered if she should just tell Bledsoe the whole story and get it over with. She felt pretty sure they would not catch Henson now. *But it was not Henson who killed my Henry.* She started to get mad. *It must have been that guy Burton who used to be BOSS. Maybe we can still get him. If Henson's smart, he'll dump Burton and the girl and get out on his own. Maybe then we can catch the bastard who killed Henry.* "God," she mumbled. "I didn't realize how much I cared about him."

"Pardon, ma'am?" the driver asked. Marion didn't realize she had spoken aloud.

When she got back to the hotel, she called den Kamp. "Gene, it's Henry...Henry's dead."

She had practically summoned him to Cape Town.

* * *

"We're still having problems with the client." The rain had stopped, David had found a phone booth at the waterfront where he had hidden before, and was making his 4:00 p.m. check-in on the twenty-second. "There are definitely two groups involved now. The client's purchasing people are not the problem. We think two outsiders deliberately tried to stop the shipment. I'm told they were not Cape Town natives. I caught one trying to forge papers."

"I've heard nothing from the client for the last two days. You must be doing something right. But if you embarrassed a company man, we will no doubt hear something before long."

"It looks like I'll have to stay for a few more days. Can you get in touch with their president?"

"Don't call in again unless you have something I should know."

"Hope to have everything fixed in two days." David broke the connection and returned to their hotel in plain view of several dockworkers, none of whom seemed to have the slightest interest in him.

When he got back, they all sat about glumly. The recently renovated hotel was certainly made to order for a return to their passion, but Forest stayed in the room all the time, and both David and Susan were too preoccupied with plans to abscond.

Susan tried to reach Eldon on the pay phone in Chariots Café a couple of times each day, with no success. Once, a stranger answered, but Susan hung up immediately. They did not dare use the room phone. They used room service for all their meals.

Other calls were made to the Port Manager's office from various spots around the docks. It took one full day to determine that the freighter Kujawy, presently tied up at berth three on the shore side of Duncan Docks, was leaving with general cargo for Rotterdam on the twenty-fourth. The freighter had a shipment of parts for the Fiat truck assembly plant at Apapa, Nigeria, and would arrive in Lagos on the twenty-sixth.

It was a simple task for David, posing as a tourist on a run through the seedier side of the waterfront, to meet the Polish captain on board his vessel. The crew took only a passing interest in the natty Englishman who asked to meet with Captain Negorny. The promise of twenty thousand rand, about three year's pay, was enough to convince him to take on three passengers without papers before sailing on the twenty-fourth.

They now had a full day to kill. Susan was most concerned about Eldon and continually pestered David to find out what happened to him. There was nothing in the papers about his, or any other, unexplained death, and David was sure that the police were using a ruse to try to draw them out. It could have been that Eldon was still alive and they had not found the body in the castle park, but he doubted both suppositions. He finally, reluctantly agreed to accompany Susan to Eldon's apartment immediately before departure. Her gratitude was obvious as she jumped into his arms and hugged him. Forest was not impressed.

Police activity did die down. They went out only once on the twenty-third, but when they did, they encountered no evidence that they were being sought. No patrol cars drove slowly through the Eastern Mole, Table Bay, or out onto the sea wall. No constables checked out rooms at the hotel.

27

It was Thursday night, almost a week after the assassination attempt. Bertel had summoned den Kamp three times since Monday morning. At the first meeting, den Kamp had merely explained that he was still in the dark about events in Bloemfontein because he had not been there and was waiting for a report from his chief of police. At the second, he admitted that Terbose was the assassin and could not understand why Neiderhof had failed to apprehend him before the attempt. He failed to show up at the third and was now in his office with Neiderhof awaiting a further summons.

"Neiderhof, I really can't think of anything that's going to keep the bastard off my back. We can't say Terbose wasn't involved. How can you be an innocent bystander, framed by Henson if you're up on the roof of the building? Even if he believes Terbose was framed, it still doesn't get us off the hook. I can deny knowing about it at all, but from the way the minister has been talking, he knows there's some connection. He just can't prove it."

"Can we somehow blame Intelligence?"

"I don't think so." He went on to tell his co-conspirator about the lunch meeting with Arnold Graham some months ago. "You give me an idea, though. Maybe we should start thinking like Intelligence people. Start sowing seeds of half-truths."

"What do you mean?"

"Well, let's say I leave a message at Bertel's office this afternoon, after he's gone home, telling him I'm sick and tired of not getting answers and am personally going underground to find out what really happened. Then I can take off, shut down my cellular, maybe even take on a disguise like Henson, and go to the Cape to find him myself."

"Excuse me, but doesn't that leave me holding the bag? When Bertel can't get hold of you, he's going to call me."

"Why don't you just disappear? That dipso captain of yours wouldn't be able to find you if you were in his living room in his suit. You know, it might be a good idea if you went to my condo in Durban. You could start working on travel arrangements to get the three of us out of the country while I'm in Cape Town. If Marion and I can't find Henson in a couple of days, we'll join you and all take off together. I'm sure I can get Dieter to take care of us in Germany, at least 'til we get our feet back on the ground."

"Have you checked with him?"

"Now, why in hell would I do that? Admit failure? I'm not going to call on Dieter unless it's completely hopeless."

As den Kamp began to scurry around packing clothing and small valuables in a suitcase, Neiderhof began to think that failure was imminent.

At noon on the twenty-third, den Kamp joined Marion in her room at the Metropole. Although Marion's knee hurt like hell, it did not stop her from participating in the game she loved best. She still had den Kamp under her spell.

After they roused themselves from the particularly warm session, den Kamp pulled on his clothes, turned to the still recumbent Marion, and asked her, "Are there any leads?"

"Just that I overheard Henson say they were going to leave me in bushes at the castle, then head to the airport."

"You don't believe that, do you?"

"Not now. Bledsoe and I went to the airport and looked for them for four hours. They are either out of the country or hiding in the city somewhere."

"What about Bledsoe? Is he still helping us?"

"I'm not sure. I think he admired Henry, although he was a bit pissed off when he found out about the Eldon killing. I told him it was an accident. Eldon was old and wouldn't tell us where his friends were. Henry just got mad and hit him a bit too hard."

"Hasn't Bledsoe found a trace of them either? He should have been able to. Maybe he isn't really committed."

"He pulled off two of the four undercovers he had assigned to the search. He found their van and kept checking departures at the airport. He probably thinks they left the country."

"More effort might have produced somebody who drove them after they dumped the car."

South Africa's nascent Dominance organization was getting a bit slim. Den Kamp was not understanding in the least of the failure of Henry and Marion, though his sex life would take a turn for the worse if he began berating her for it. There were no options now. He had to help Marion and make peace with Bledsoe. He would have called off the whole thing if it had not been for that call from Dieter, that constant pull of wealth and fame with which the German teased him. Things were bad in South Africa. He might not escape jail if Bertel really pushed it. His only real future lay with Dominance. "It looks like we better get moving. I have a feeling that Henson and the other two are still around."

Marion was sent back to Eldon's apartment to wait after a lavish supper at the Metropole.

* * *

On the twenty-fourth at two in the morning, it was time for the three to plan their final moves. They left the lights off, heightening the nearly unbearable tension.

"Let's go over the essentials once more," David started. "Susan and I will walk to Eldon's apartment at 4:00 a.m. Interrupt me if you see something wrong. At the same time, you walk to Grosvenor and rent us another car at the railway station. Better not use Trent Williams again." They needed the car in case something went wrong with their use of the freighter.

"But the only other name I can use is my own. Won't that be just as dangerous?"

David rifled through his money belt. He pulled out an international driver's license in the name of James Kildare. "Here, try this one. They won't check the picture. The police know about this guy, but keep your thumb over the picture and talk with an American accent. The agent won't give a damn. Flash lots of cash. Do you have enough?"

"About five hundred rand, but I should probably have at least a thousand."

David produced the money. "Try to give part of that back. I may need it if the captain tries to increase the cost of our trip."

"And I pick you two up in front of the Nico Malan Theater on Oswald as soon as I can get there."

"Yes, and we head immediately for Berth 3 at the docks where the Kujawy is tied up."

"Sue and I stay in the car while you go on board to set up the trip with Negorny," Forest concluded.

For the next hour they all waited, absorbed in their own thoughts.

Even in the predawn darkness under the yellowish glow of the sodium arc streetlights, David recognized the stakeout. "It looks like too much of a risk to pay a visit to the apartment. That lookout has probably spotted us by now. I wish I could see who it is. I know how much you cared about Freeman. When you get back to Harare, have Forest find out what happened to him." As he said this, he pulled Susan back around the corner they had just rounded.

"I understand," Susan said tearfully. "It's just that he was such a nice man, and if he's dead like you think, I hate to see his killer go unpunished."

"Don't worry about that, Sue," David stated. "His killer is either dead or injured."

They reached the theater and the new Opel sedan Forest had rented. Just as they were getting in, the steel gray Mercedes that had been parked in front of the apartment came slowly around the corner behind them.

Forest was an excellent driver, but the Opel had a problem putting any distance between them and the more powerful Mercedes. They were also worried about the regular police. They could not afford to be stopped.

"Stop around the next corner. We have to forget the car. We'll split up and head for the docks on foot," David directed. They were only four or five blocks from the waterfront.

Forest did not question David's order. He made the turn, leapt out, and headed straight for the harbor.

"Susan, stay right here in the shadow of that building entrance," David ordered. "We need to split up so we aren't both caught." She moved away quickly, just as the Mercedes turned the corner. David headed toward the car, his Beretta drawn.

Marion stopped. She could not effectively drive and shoot. She jumped out, staying in the cover of the open door. David did not have a shot. Before he could find cover, she fired.

The stab of pain in his left thigh brought David to a sudden halt. Marion stood up from behind the door and re-aimed at his forehead. He thought he was finished when another explosion rang out much closer to his ear. As he fell to his knees, thinking he was done for by the second shot, he looked up to see the woman who had captured him and nearly stopped them at the castle crumple to the road under the car door. Susan had nailed her in the chest with a shot from the Beretta that David had taken from Henry's corpse.

Susan was next to David, and he could hear her soft cries. She reached for his handkerchief, tore a large hole in his trousers, and began stanching the flow of blood. In a minute or so, David realized that he could stand, and they made their way unsteadily back to the car. There was no way he could walk to the docks.

It was amazing that the two shots in the early morning had not attracted some police attention. Perhaps it was the frequency of shooting that occurred in Cape Town every night, particularly by the newly formed vigilante groups that seemed to be carrying justice to a new level. No police cars arrived before they were able to slip away in the Opel.

Morning was finally exposing itself behind a cloud-laden sky as Susan slid the car through the unguarded gates at the docks. They drove past the slumbering ship that would hopefully take them safely out of the country. Forest waved from his hiding place behind some oil barrels near the fence and Susan helped David hobble over. It was now 5:40 a.m.

"Jesus, Gregory, what happened to you?"

"Well, there's good news and bad news. The bad news is that woman who was chasing us caught me on my way to the docks…"

"That's not the way I saw it," Susan interrupted. "You were trying to get caught to keep the heat off us, when that bitch shot you."

"No, no. We needed to separate," David continued. "The good news is that Susan took out the lady who wounded me."

"Are you going to be able to see the captain, David?" Forest asked. "It's almost time."

"Looks like you will have to do it, Forest. I'm going to need help just to get to the ship, and I'd rather he saw me after he agreed to take us." There were already stirring on ship's decks, which were barely visible in the light from the dull sky. "Here's the twenty-nine thousand rand I have for him. Try to save some of it, though. He'll probably take us for twenty."

Captain Negorny was somewhat suspicious of Forest, obviously not the person with whom he had made the deal. He countered Forest's offer of twenty thousand with twenty-five thousand. Forest accepted. Soon the three of them were tucked away in the visitor quarters located two decks below the bridge, on the starboard side.

David's wound proved easy to handle for the ship's cook, who also acted as doctor, nurse, and general administrator. The bullet had passed through cleanly, and some antibiotic cream, a clean dressing, and a couple of painkillers soon had him resting comfortably.

The *Kujawy* cleared the harbor at exactly 6:27 a.m., just as den Kamp set out to find Marion, who had failed to return for her regular morning pleasures after a long night on stakeout. There was no sign of her at Eldon's apartment. He did hear sirens from the north and wondered if that had something to do with Marion's disappearance, went back to his hotel, and got the message from Bledsoe.

"You're up early this morning, Bledsoe. Did you find our killer?"

"No, but we found Marion. She's pretty bad, Eugene."

"My God, what happened? Where is she?"

"They got her to The Somerset hospital down by the waterfront. Apparently she has a bullet lodged close to her heart."

"She's alive, though?"

"I think so."

"Did whoever shoot her get away?"

"Yes. My desk didn't hear about it until six forty-five. There was a lot of blood on the road and the sidewalk. Looks like she might have hit one or two of them before she was shot."

"But there's no sign of them?"

"No. I had my men scour the area to no avail. The killer or killers just vanished. Probably went to the airport, but my man there says he's seen nothing."

When Eugene heard this, he knew in a flash what had happened. "Mark, did any ships sail this morning? I'll bet they went out by cruise ship or freighter. I'm off to the hospital now."

"I'll check." He hung up. *Den Kamp is probably right*, he said to himself. "Get me the port manager," he yelled to his desk sergeant.

By the time Bledsoe got to the docks, all he found was a vacant berth three and traces of blood on the cope wall.

By 3:00 p.m., den Kamp was in Durban calling Dieter Volmar.

"What do you mean the package is lost?" Dieter couldn't believe it. "Why are you calling on an open line?"

"I'm not at home. The three left by ship this morning. No one thought of that." The pretense of a successful operation was gone.

"You had your agents plus those of the customer looking for them. What are you covering up?"

"They were very clever, and I think they must have disguised themselves," said den Kamp defensively.

"So I guess your agents weren't clever enough, Forty-seven. You should take better care in selecting them."

"I may still be able to get him. I suspect he is on the way to Rotterdam."

"Perhaps we can get our Dutch friends to intercept him when he reaches Holland. We will have to look into better training for your agents. We must be more sophisticated than the competition."

"There may be a way to get it before it reaches Holland," den Kamp volunteered. "The ship they took has a stop in Lagos before it leaves Africa. I could probably get there. Try to convince the police to arrest them. My minister is going to make it too hot for me to stay here when he finds out what happened, and he will find out soon."

"Why wouldn't your minister be happy? His friend is safe and sound."

"Some errors were made. He thinks I was involved in the plot. I don't think he bought my story."

"Well, if you think you have some chance of getting them in Nigeria, do it." Dieter was still anxious that some positive outcome resulted from the mess.

"I will try," said den Kamp.

"Try? Forty-seven, we don't need any more 'tries.' Either do it, or bloody well forget it."

"I'll go to Lagos tomorrow. If they get off the ship, we will take them. We have no particular influence in Nigeria, so getting on the ship could prove difficult."

"You had better take them out, not take them. I don't see how you can arrest them in Lagos." Dieter was wearying of the detail and anxious to get on with plans for a stronger organization. "Let me know how you do."

* * *

The *Kujawy* docked at Apapa's longest quay at 10:00 a.m. on the twenty-sixth. As David, Forest, and Susan strode down the gangplank, Susan suddenly crumpled, three shots rang out, and David and Forest flattened themselves against the deck of the boarding ramp. After ten seconds there were no more shots, and the two of them moved toward Susan.

David reached her first, pressed his fingers to her carotid, and found no pulse. Anger—deep, strong, virulent anger—rose like bile in his whole being. He had found a warm, sensual, woman who had found a way to touch him, and now, in a breath, she was gone. As he regained his speech, he turned to his companion, fire in his eyes. "Whoever did this is dead. Find out who." With that, David raced back on board. Forest and the crew looked after Susan's body.

The crew and captain of the *Kujawy* were very discrete about the number of passengers they had boarded and the number being disembarked at Lagos. The police performed a perfunctory search of the ship and questioned Forest, or Trent Williams, for about twelve hours, but could not shake his story. They finally determined that the shots came from an old warehouse across from the quays at Apapa, and must have been fired by some crazy. Three spent 9mm casings and some scuffs in the gravel told the story.

* * *

Albert van Royen, secretary to Prime Minister Enders, was happy to assist the head of Dominance. After all, it would be simple. The man was on a ship to Rotterdam. He could easily arrange to have this Henson taken off and brought to an untimely end before he had a chance to leave for the States. Two phone calls from one with so much influence were all it took to set it up.

* * *

The voyage to Rotterdam would last three days. It took David only an hour, alone in his cabin, to realize that it would be foolish for him to complete it. Their enemy knew the *Kujawy*'s itinerary and would no doubt have a welcoming party ready for him in Holland. How to get off was the problem.

Captain Negorny was helpful. He really had not expected to get twenty-five thousand rand just to transport two to Lagos and one to Rotterdam. After the shooting in Lagos, he was not really looking forward to explaining David's presence to officials in Holland.

Their solution was simple. The voyage to Rotterdam could bring them within a mile or so of the English coast as they left the channel for the North Sea. David offered two thousand rand for a ride in a power launch to the port of Dover.

After the arrangements were made, David returned to his cabin. The rest of the voyage he spent mourning Susan. If anything, his deep craving for revenge increased as he brooded.

He returned home on the thirtieth, completely wrung out and flat. He doubted he would ever meet anyone like Susan again. Even the release from tension failed to give him any solace.

With all the publicity, David felt it would be impossible for Henson to completely escape the conversion back to Reasons if he merely followed a normal route back to Dublin. From the National Airport in Baltimore, he phoned Fieldstone Enterprises. "The testing is complete. I will meet you in Tucson, Arizona, seven days after I began the delivery." By their code, he knew Grant would understand that he meant Knoxville, Tennessee, and seventeen days. "I will leave instructions for you at the desk."

Grant and David met at the Knuckles sports bar at Knoxville's elegant Hyatt Regency on the thirty-first. Over wings and chips, they began to piece together what they had learned from the mission. The main questions were, who was the leak in security in CTC, and who was running Dominance? There were not many answers.

"Okay, David, let's go at this another way. I knew you were going to South Africa. So did Edwards and the director—and I think Curstan over at the FBI had a hint. Anyone else you know of?"

"I didn't tell anybody. I guess Elinor knew I was out of the country. I take my dog over for her to mind when I leave, but I didn't tell her I was going to South Africa. Just that I'd be out of town for a week or so."

"We're not going to find out, are we?"

"I don't think so. In South Africa, it was definitely the police who were involved in trying to get me. I could tell by their tactics it wasn't Intelligence."

"So, I guess we learned something. It was terrible losing that lady from Harare."

David could scarcely speak. "I'll get the bastard who killed her, Grant. I don't know how, but I'll get him."

"I'm sorry, David. I didn't know."

* * *

Dieter understood den Kamp's failure. In ten years he had not been able to trap the wily Henson. When den Kamp called, he was ready to forgive him. "Yes, you can come to Germany. I'll have a job for you in my company. What about your boss? Isn't he going to come after you?"

"I've left the chief of police from Bloemfontein to take the blame. Hopefully the minister will accept him as the villain. If not, let him try to find me. Marion and I will be there in a few days. It'll be three days before she gets out of hospital. We have to cover our tracks here too. I realize we underestimated Henson. I was foolish to plot the assassination with only three in my crew."

"Yes, we must get stronger before we take on any further tasks. I just received word from Holland that Henson was not on the freighter. Twenty-five had the captain sweated a bit and found out he got off in England. I want you to bring a full report to the conference in Rio. It was a dismal failure, Forty-seven. How will we be ready for Spain?"

"Spain, sir? Have you got an operation planned for Spain?"

"Yes, we'll talk about it when you get here."

* * *

Bertel had no knowledge of den Kamp's hideaway. He had heard about Henry Jackman's death and Marion Aflect's injuries, but had no idea of the whereabouts of den Kamp and Aflect. He wondered why his calls to his chief of security went unanswered. Even Jon Mjaren, who Bertel questioned several times, had no idea where he was. Bertel had thought to call a full-scale intelligence investigation into the assassination attempt and den Kamp's disappearance. He couldn't leave that job to the police because, as den Kamp had shown, he couldn't trust them, but ultimately, he decided to let sleeping dogs lie. It might take Truth and Reconciliation back several steps if he began to prosecute broeders for crimes he couldn't prove they committed. The only one who felt his wrath was Piet Neiderhof. It took only a month for him to appoint a new chief and get on with the process of trying to make his country safe for all its people.

* * *

When Eugene took Marion to his condo in Durban after a six-day stay in the Frere hospital in Cape Town, she showed little interest in pursuing a career in either policing or Dominance. The bullet from Susan's gun had been removed and the slight nick the bullet left in her aorta repaired, but the strength of spirit she had gained through both her sexual domination of the many men in her life and the confidence in her ability as a police officer had waned to the point that all she wanted to do was sleep. She was not even interested in having den Kamp in her bed.

Den Kamp was getting worried that Bertel might launch a massive search for them and desperately wanted to get them to Germany. At noon one day, after they had been in Durban for a week, he crept into the master bedroom where Marion slept and gently shook her awake. As soon as she seemed to be paying attention he said, "You know, Marion dear, I fear if we stay here much longer, the minister is going to find us and prosecute."

"What can we do? I don't feel like traveling anywhere. I'm so tired. Where would we go?"

"Dieter has offered us jobs in his development company in Germany."

"Germany? That's a long way away."

"I know, dear, but it's not safe to stay here. Perhaps if I got you to Harare you would be out of Bertel's clutches. I could go on to Germany to work with Dieter, and you could join us when you feel better."

"But, I'd be alone."

Den Kamp was beginning to tire of her whining. "Yes, but that's better than being in jail."

"Jail? Why would I go to jail?"

"The minister doesn't take kindly to people who try to assassinate his beloved president. We would go to jail if he catches us."

"I guess I have to go, but I want to be with you."

"You will. I'll make the arrangements to get us to Germany. I'm sure the airlines have a way to transport invalids."

"Invalids! I'm not an invalid."

He resisted the obvious. "Yes, you are. Go back to sleep, dear. I'll get to work on our trip."

* * *

When den Kamp and Albrecht arrived in Germany a week later, Dieter had a limo waiting for them in Stuttgart. It took them to a furnished two-bedroom apartment in a new condo building on Schlosstrasse, not far from the Renaissance Developments building. Dieter had taken out a mortgage on the condo and wanted den Kamp to assume it as soon as he was able. Den Kamp's gratitude was so great that he took it over right away.

The first time Dieter and Marion met at Dieter's mansion on Leopoldstrasse was quite an occasion for the three of them. Even though she was still weak, she remembered Dieter's wealth and power and was much impressed by his size and bearing. His face held a certain sensual openness which drew her to him immediately. Neither her reaction nor Dieter's obvious lust went unnoticed by den Kamp. He realized that he would be giving up more than his country to get away from the long arms of Crane Bertel. After several bottles of fine Rieslings from Dieter's favorite Eckberg winery, they sat down to a fairly simple meal of schnitzel, potatoes, and salad. After dinner, some fine Auslese wine, and Courvoisier, they arranged the first meeting of the new Dominance Headquarters staff to be held at Dieter's Renaissance office on Monday morning.

By Monday, Marion felt better. She had spent a glorious Saturday night in Dieter's bed and was prepared to continue with the process of world domination. Den Kamp had been out to a local bar, watching a football match between Stuttgart and Munich on Saturday night and, while he failed to notice Marion's exit to Dieter's bed, he did hear her return. At the meeting, he and Dieter sparred warily at first, but den Kamp soon realized that Dieter's coolness towards him stemmed from his failure to remove Mandela at Bloemfontein. Theirs would not be an easy collaboration.

Dominance headquarters staff then got down to business—the terrorist takeover of Spain.

About the Author

John Whitaker was born in India to medical missionaries. They left and moved to St. Catharines, Ontario when John was only six-months-old. He graduated from the Royal Military College and the University of Toronto with a degree in Mechanical Engineering and spent a first career in the military. He retired from the RCAF as a Major to a second career at Spar Aerospace and a third with the Canadian Coast Guard in Toronto and Sarnia where he headed the Marine Navigation Services Division. After fully retiring, he and his wife trailered through most of North America while John wrote much of the Dominance series.

He and Lynda now reside in Toronto.